WAY OF THE

SHANON SINN

Enjoy!

Shanon Sinn

iUniverse, Inc.
Bloomington

Way of the Wraith

Copyright © 2011 by Shanon Sinn

All rights reserved. No part of this book may be used or reproduced by any means, graphic, electronic, or mechanical, including photocopying, recording, taping or by any information storage retrieval system without the written permission of the publisher except in the case of brief quotations embodied in critical articles and reviews.

iUniverse books may be ordered through booksellers or by contacting:

iUniverse
1663 Liberty Drive
Bloomington, IN 47403
www.iuniverse.com
1-800-Authors (1-800-288-4677)

Because of the dynamic nature of the Internet, any web addresses or links contained in this book may have changed since publication and may no longer be valid. The views expressed in this work are solely those of the author and do not necessarily reflect the views of the publisher, and the publisher hereby disclaims any responsibility for them.

Any people depicted in stock imagery provided by Thinkstock are models, and such images are being used for illustrative purposes only.

Certain stock imagery © Thinkstock.

ISBN: 978-1-4620-1526-9 (sc)
ISBN: 978-1-4620-1527-6 (hc)
ISBN: 978-1-4620-1530-6 (e)

Library of Congress Control Number: 2011907505

Printed in the United States of America

iUniverse rev. date: 07/20/2011

To my sister Sunni, who encouraged me to share the tale I thought I never would.

If you stand straight, do not fear a crooked shadow.

—Chinese proverb

1

A freeze ripped through him and choked him. He could no longer breathe. Icy frosts of a thousand bitter hells clung to him. The chill of an arctic funeral pyre. Black glacial rivers poured into his heart and exploded out through his spine.

Somewhere far away the gunshots and explosions seemed unhurried and as warm as mother's milk. He longed already for the pain of a few moments ago, a pain that he had wished then would simply end. That physical searing would seem like such a minor inconvenience now.

He heard his voice, a whimper really, in the distance. It did not sound like it should be his voice but somehow he knew that it was. He had no control, as if there was some disconnect. He could not alter these sounds, but he could hear clearly what was said.

"So cold ... I love her, promise ... tell her ... So very cold ... My mom ..."

There was a cough, a moment of silence and then a sniffle. He heard the crying now. He felt no shame. There was only fear.

He spoke aloud, but his fellow soldiers did not seem to hear him as they fired their weapons at the enemy. He thought that perhaps they did not even know that he had ceased to fight.

He was vaguely aware, though, that he should be ashamed of his lack of composure. It was a spectacle in the face of the inevitable. His actions contradicted everything that he had believed to be true in his life. His vocalizations on the subject matter of God and the afterlife for so many years seemed so hypocritical and ego-based. There had been no surprises here. *Death comes at the end of every road*, he had always said.

He had known on some level all along that this would happen here, in this very desert and on this very spot. This morning he had known deep down that it would be today. He had felt so strongly that he would never see them again when he had said good-bye. He was so afraid, though, so very afraid. And cold, too. Damn, he was cold.

There was a path before him, a warmth of sorts that seemed composed of light. Even from this distance, he could feel the cold being erased from him by this soft yet all-encompassing warmth; he had a vague feeling of being picked up and becoming weightless. Womanly creatures with wings of the softest touch served bottomless cups of honey mead. The scent of jasmine, thick and sweet, clung to them.

Forgotten friendships beckoned to him, and relatives were excited to hold him. His memory started to ebb. Upon hearing a whisper of his name, he knew a chair in the great hall awaited him. He started to move towards the light that pierced so fiercely and lovingly through his darkness.

So cold. He could see his breath and could smell a thousand banquets and the perfumes of a hundred priceless concubines. He could feel the anticipation of the warriors who wished nothing more than to share the tales of battle and valour. He heard the calling of his childhood dog, the most faithful companion of his life, barking with sheer joy at his inevitable arrival. He wondered if Steve was there as well.

There was someone else ... or something, rather. A presence so familiar and grand as to bring tears to the brims of his eyes. One moment she seemed somehow a mother, then a lover. Then there was a different sense, a different being ... a brother and a father and somehow, now, even a son. No, that was wrong. Not a different entity—the same. It was familiar. He knew this one somehow. The mere suggestion of a reunion drove an ethereal, electrical part of him wild.

He instinctively moved towards the warm light. He felt peaceful and calm—emotions he had never felt so completely ran deep through to his very core. He felt the cold peeling away from him like a dirty garment, tattered and worn, crumbling beneath a warm, tropical waterfall. He felt forgiven and accepted, tolerated and loved.

He felt peace.

He would not, could not, look back. Moving with a floating grace, he glided towards the stairway perfect and proud, ancient and inviting. A sigh left him as he surrendered.

"No!" A booming voice from behind him roared. "Fight it!"

A slight curiosity stalled him for the fraction of a moment. Something crashed up ahead of him. His head turned, and he felt the cold wash over him once more.

Behind him was the most chaotic scene imaginable: a nightmare holiday from the minds of serial killers painted with darkness, violence, disease and pestilence.

Who had spoken?

He felt the way to the light close behind him and started to panic as the warmth suddenly faded away.

He was falling, and in falling he found that his feet touched solid ground. He turned quickly and started to bang on a large stone set of towering doors fitted for a castle. He knew that they had not been there before, and maybe did not truly exist there now, and if he blinked even the sight of them would no longer exist.

The pathway that was once kind had abandoned him and left him. Nothing beautiful remained in the place where bliss had lived. This way was closed to him forever, and he knew it. Tears of despair crashed out of his eye sockets and ran down his face. His fists pounded against the doors.

A screaming wailing howl, so inhuman as to paralyze him to the bones, broke into his manic state. He spun back around in terror as fog descended everywhere.

He saw the battle now through newborn eyes. Explosions rocked the hilltops in the darkness, but still they came. They were suicidal riflemen from scores of Muslim nations. Darkness fell heavy around his dead countrymen. Even with the might of the military's colossal bombardment, the battle seemed far from won. Artillery raked the hills, and the carrier's canons strafed the enemy without mercy.

The initial improvised explosive device, called IEDs, had crippled the convoy, and an attack now took place that he would never have believed possible if he was not a spectator. It was the Battle of Mogadishu, the Tet Offensive, Blitzkrieg, and the Alamo all upon the same canvas before him. People would die, and individual acts of valour and cowardice would decide the fate of the day. The end seemed incredibly uncertain.

This was different than the war of cat and mouse that he had been fighting for his whole tour of duty. This was not the months and years of small firefights and secretly hidden IEDs. Whole tours would go by with a dozen Canadian soldiers killed. Huge operations often yielded only suspected dead insurgents as the enemy dragged off its fallen. This was an engagement the likes of which no one had seen in this country since the initial invasion of 2002. It seemed to defy all logic and intelligence.

For a moment the scene stirred something within him. He reached for his rifle, but it was not there. His tour had its fair share of sketchy and fear-riddled moments, but nothing even remotely compared to this. Before this, a very bad day had been when someone he knew had been killed by an IED during a dismounted patrol. This war had no storming of the beaches of Normandy; it had no Vimy Ridge or Passchendaele; it was no Thermopylae.

He had seen death and had even been responsible for it in his life ... the arm of tragedy here. He had heard the explosions and seen the Russian machine gun fire from tribal insurgents beat at his weary feet. He had seen a suicide once—and the tattered remains of a headless corpse who had prematurely detonated his own instrument of destruction for reasons unknown.

No, this was a new kind of war, and not the Hollywood version of an insurgency that, in reality, took place in shadows and under the cover of darkness, where dawn left no corpses. The battle before him did not seem like it could exist at all, yet it did. He and his companions had been completely taken by surprise by the volume and velocity of an attack that was presumably impossible for the ragtag groups of religious fanatics to orchestrate.

He wore only his tan undershirt and combat pants. On his feet were black boots instead of the usual desert issue he had been wearing earlier. Contrarily, his pants were of the desert pattern and not the green worn back in garrison that would be worn with the black boots. His K-bar knife hung at his belt. He seemed to have no other possessions. He looked then at his hands, and they seemed different somehow: not only were they charred and burnt, but they looked like they belonged to a stranger.

All of these realizations took place in the span of a moment.

The screaming, wailing sound returned and echoed around him, sending a shiver through his frozen reality that was not born from some frigid, unforgiving physical element. He looked at the battle through new eyes, shifting his focus away from the physical as he searched for the source of the sound. He felt them widen in awe as shapes and shadows he had seen, but had seemed to ignore a moment before, began to reveal themselves.

He had not seen, truly seen, moments before these shadowy, whispering creatures in flight who were tearing at one another. Dark shapes clashing desperately all around him in smoky, unformed images. There were Roman-dressed shadow soldiers in a phalanx surrounding his fighting countrymen, especially the dismounts that had exited the carriers after the initial IED strikes. They, the living, were pinned down and were dying.

These Roman shades, these protectors, were locked in position and being forced back by hordes of the most menacing beings imaginable. Towering, red-eyed creatures neither man nor beast seemed to roll out of inky black clouds of darkness.

The Romans displayed no fear but were being torn apart nonetheless.

There seemed to be other allies of his living brothers present as well, but these were few and far between. Barely seen women on flying horses flung arrows from the sky. Giant arcs of fire attempted to dismount and destroy them one by one. Huge, transparent, armoured warriors of gleaming gold light appeared from the mouth of a young soldier who was lying behind his weapon, praying. These beings were torn apart by the rat-headed shadow creatures that leapt upon them.

There seemed to be other allies present that he could sense but not see, as they were buried behind so much chaos and filthy shadow as to almost make them invisible. A C9 gunner, his section mate, kneeled irrationally out in the open, firing fearlessly with a Hollywood, reckless roar coming from his lips. In front of this gunner, barely perceptible, were two tattooed titans with horned helmets and braided beards. One wielded a monstrous axe, and the other had a colossal stone hammer. Together they carved such a path into the advancing hordes of darkness in a berserker rage that he wondered if the machine gunner could be harmed at all. Here and there on the side of his countrymen were beings of all sorts in chalky, braided shadow—dragons and creatures as dark and intimidating looking as the enemies ... but they were far too few.

The screaming, wailing sound ripped through him again. He knew that scream sounded for him. Something was coming—something more menacing than anything that he had witnessed on what he discerned was some madman puppeteer's playground. Something omnipotent wanted him. For some reason he knew this.

He scanned the dark, writhing masses for the source of this newest terror.

It pushed through the hordes, throwing aside anything that blocked its path. The being stood a full half body above the swarming chaos and held aloft a tangled-handled scythe with an impossibly long blade. The weapon was held above a black-cloaked, skeleton-like face. The spectre did not appear to touch the ground but hovered through the battle. Weapons that passed through the dark garment seemed to displace the fabric, which would scatter outwards in shards and return to take the form of a cloak once more. To his horror he realized that this exploding and reforming coat was composed entirely of what looked to be flying insects, all dark in color.

He tried to focus his eyes and see the terror as more than a distant shadow, and he was rewarded somewhat as the being came slightly more into focus.

As the shade threw back its head and shrieked once more, he saw the white of the skull was not what he had supposed, composed of bone, but a writhing mass of maggots feasting upon the face itself—and one another. The eyes, perhaps the most frightening aspect of all, were surprisingly human and bulbous. These whites were blood red, and the pupil was black as hate. A grin that to him was both frightening and homicidally self-amused completed the face.

He threw his hands over his ears and screamed in terror. The foreign shrieking sound had paralyzed him and had frozen his legs to the ground. Never in his wildest nightmares could he have imagined such horror, and yet what frightened him more than the evil appearance and the unholy wail was an innate knowledge that the creature before him was somehow commonplace in this foreign yet familiar landscape.

Skeletal hands pulled back the scythe and started to swing it at an impossible speed. He leaned away, raising his arms in a gesture of self-preservation. A ringing sound exploded around him. The clash made him start and look up quickly.

A shadowy man in a black cloak held a shimmering sword before the scythe. His features were wrapped in shadow, and the cloak hovered madly around him. The unexpected saviour was struggling to hold back the enormous blade, which was being pushed downward.

"The mosque!" It was a strangely familiar voice, the same voice that had called out to him before. Now it was filled with urgency and dread. "Run!"

The harvester of souls hooked around his jagged blade and flicked his wrist, flinging the dark-cloaked man to the side and into the earth like a ragdoll. It was clear that he would not likely be any more help to him in the immediate future.

However, he had known at once of the mosque about which the man had spoken. Another lifetime ago—or what had seemed so long ago but was perhaps only a half hour or less before—he had seen it at the last village.

He started to run.

His legs barely seemed to move. He felt like he was in one of those childhood dreams where he seemed to be running through water. He knew the creature would come for him. He knew the horror would overcome him. He knew that this would happen soon.

He passed into the thickest of the chaos, trying to confuse the beast. It seemed to work to a slight degree; the creature waded into the battle behind him while swinging the bladed weapon wildly.

He stepped over some familiar bodies and stopped short. He saw himself, or what he thought was once himself, but he looked burnt as if by fire. A flash of a thousand half-formed memories entered him, and remorse washed over him. He felt the shame of a thousand selfish deeds, a million lies to himself and others, and a billion self-righteous, ego-based desires. He wanted to stay and stare at himself, or what had been him, but he knew that he could not. He wanted to try to remember what name he had been called before he moved on. There was a hesitation as the tug-of-war struggled between what had been his life and his new sudden need for self-preservation.

A winged warrior woman of brilliant light suddenly appeared beside him. She crouched and cradled out of a nearby body a man he knew he had loved in life. It was the cocky machine gunner who had seemed protected by the two large Viking warriors, who were no longer nearby. She lifted an electric twin image of the deceased from out of the body. She held him as a mother would hold a long lost son, and this somehow broke his heart. He felt so alone and abandoned. The spirit in turn started to wake, as if from a sleep, in the valkyrie's arms. The pair seemed oblivious to his observant existence. He knew that this deceased friend was feeling something akin to the warm light that he had been denied.

His trance was ruptured by the tragedy that befell them next. A wild swing of the harvester's blade meant for him ripped the cradled soul in half. There was a blue flash as the spirit dripped to the ground like melting wax.

For but a moment, there was a sense of surprise from the reaper as he took a step back. He had crossed a line that should not have ever been crossed. The valkyrie's face contorted, and her beauty was replaced by a maw of fangs that screamed for revenge. Her hair was wild golden fire, and her eyes were the red of the storm's ocean dawn. A silver sword of light, almost Japanese in nature, flew from a sheath as she advanced towards the reaper.

He cowered to the ground before the battle. Both entities seemed to be collectors of the dead. He wasn't sure how it worked, who got to collect who and why, but it was obvious that there was no love shared between the two beings and that some sort of a rule had been broken.

She started with a downward stroke that seared the flies it passed through. Her blade left an arc of crimson flame behind it. In a wide overhand swing, the reaper responded with a head-severing blow that could have easily finished his slightly shorter nemesis. She dropped quickly below the weapon and thrust her blade straight out into the upper chest of the demon. As he fell to one knee, he brought the scythe back around and severed the valkyrie from her shoulder to her opposite hip. She crumpled upon the ground and fell to fiery embers.

The reaper leaned forward with his head down, clearly wounded. He supported himself upon the mangled shaft of his weapon, still on one knee. There was a sense that he was regenerating.

The dead soldier, the silent witness to the fight between the great beings, stood and prepared to flee. He was horrified by the chaos that continued around him. Courage from a life once lived seemed like a distant memory, as foreign as an old man's memories of the womb.

Thunder burst through the clouds, and a lightning bolt brought forth rain. He sensed that it would now storm in this new world only and not back in the land of the living. He knew that the realm of sand, and the life-timid, hard-coaxed farmer's fields around him, would remain as dry as dust. He also sensed that the rain was some sort of response to the battle that he had just seen between the two collectors of the dead.

Everything became stranger to him even as the reaper became more and more whole and gained back his strength.

There was no sensing of things and how they worked, but there was an awkward knowing and continued fear that he was in trouble to an even greater degree. Yet before him, still smouldering, was the angel's sword, the weapon of the valkyrie. There was a moment of sheer panic as he realised what he had to do. He leaned forward tentatively, forcing himself to move despite his terror.

The weapon was almost too heavy to lift, but he was able to do so awkwardly and slowly. He spasmodically raised it as high over his head as he could, just as the demon creature looked up at him.

He let the weapon fall, gaining momentum of its own weight, upon the vulnerable harvester of souls who was still kneeling. It cut through the being's neck easily; there wasn't even a whimper as the nightmare creature fell to ashes. Unlike the valkyrie's sword, the scythe left with him very quickly and did not remain upon the field of battle.

He then moved through the fighting masses as quickly as he could while dragging the heavy sword behind him. He needed to go towards the mosque, although he had no idea why, except that he had been told to. He had a sword that did not belong to him. He had killed a being he knew he had no right to kill. He didn't remember who he was and didn't know what type of strange nightmare he had woken up in.

However, he knew innately that he would still be hunted. For what or why, he could not say.

There was another thought in his head as well. It seemed as if it came from a memory a millennium distant. The thought told him that everything was moving as it should. On top of that thought was a need for revenge buried beneath an ocean of fear.

2

He struggled to run, dragging the heavy sword behind him. He could hear the howling of wild, rabid dogs approaching from his rear and from the rocky hills on either side of the darkened road.

With the weapon's weight in hand, he could not run but could only shuffle. He scanned the hills as he moved and saw dozens of fiery sets of eyes.

He was their prey, and they were the hunters.

He was startled for a moment, when out of the darkness ahead of him came the shuffling sound of many feet followed by movement. Roman or Greek soldiers, he was not sure which, rushed past him in formation, presumably heading for the more chaotic scene of the battle. There were maybe a dozen of them, and they jogged past with spears glistening in the night that screamed of discipline, pointing in precise unison to the heavens. Many of them seemed to be wounded, however, and had dents in their armour and shields.

He stepped to the side of the road to let them by. It was an automatic reaction because this was what he would have done in life. As they quickly moved past, an officer banged his arm across his chest and raised it to the sky in a salute towards him. He was too surprised to return the gesture immediately. Before he had a chance to consider asking for help, the soldiers had passed.

The salute confused him. He did not understand the affinity. Maybe they saw in him a fellow soldier who had fought against the sources of darkness as they may have done centuries earlier.

He hobbled quickly, turned a bend in the road and saw the mosque in the distance. The rounded top of the structure stood higher than any of the mud compound walls or grape huts that surrounded it. It seemed to be bathed in a white, peaceful light that softened the landscape around it.

He could hear the many canine paws hitting the ground as he

approached the first building of the village. Squeals of glee issued from some yelping beasts, and guttural and base sounds gurgled from others.

He spun around and awkwardly raised the sword above his head; his heart pounded in terror. He hoped that the creatures would fear this item that he could not truly wield.

Dozens of the beasts began to circle him like sharks. Black-matted hair, thick with maggots and cockroaches, hung in patches across their lanky bodies. Steam rose from their yellow snarling, salivating maws. Eyes of fire brought waves of hopelessness into his very fabric.

He backtracked slowly with the sword above him, letting it drop slightly to keep back one of the braver beasts. The growling intensified as their eagerness almost possessed them. It was then that his eyes fell on what he knew to be the master of these hounds of hell.

On the road it came, pulled at a slow trot: a chariot ... and on it an unholy figure. A pair of white stags yanked awkwardly at the two-wheeled vehicle, though the animals looked to him like twin rats with their pink eyes and puffy faces. What appeared to be blood dripped from their magnificent horns and was splashed across their bodies. When they snorted, yellow and black teeth were exposed from mouths that bit into barbed-wire tethers. Each hoof sent sparks flying into the air as it touched the roadway.

The rider wore a black fur coat that steamed; it looked freshly torn from some hapless animal's flesh. A dull iron helmet with giant ram's horns rested upon his head. His mailed fist held a spear blackened with coagulated blood. He could not see those eyes in the shadows of the helmet, but he could feel the gaze nonetheless. He knew that his destruction was both near and inevitable. He tried not to sob.

He kept backing away quickly as the chariot approached and the dogs continued to circle. He could see the vehicle more clearly now; it was composed entirely of decomposing, severed heads whimpering in pain and in sorrow.

He tried to turn and run. The first dog sprang out quickly and tore into his arm. He screamed in pain and in terror as the teeth scraped against his bone. A burst of energy came into him, and he dropped the hilt of the weapon onto the crown of the animal. It yelped in both surprise and pain and jumped backwards.

Maybe it was his unwillingness to die that made him suddenly feel as if the weapon had grown lighter. He swung a wide arc and managed to catch one of the creatures by surprise in the throat. A black substance that looked to him like oil gushed onto the ground. The dog staggered back and forth like a drunk as it fought the inevitable need to collapse to the ground. The other beasts grew wary. He spun and ran.

He was near the temple now. He dared to think that he just might make it inside. He heard the nearness of the dogs and spun once more as a particularly large mastiff leapt up at him. The charioteer simultaneously threw his spear with unnatural quickness. He knew then that he was finished. There was no way that the spear and the dog could both be avoided.

It happened simultaneously. The dog's open maw smashed into something unseen an inch from his throat. The spear was so close to his right eye that he could not focus upon it for the split moment it took to slam into the same apparent invisible field. A sound like thunder accompanied the impact and sent him sprawling upon his back.

He struggled to gain his feet as quickly as he could, and two more of the leaping creatures bounced away from him, apparently hitting the same barrier. The chariot sped closer and reared up short as the stags' front legs pawed into the air. With a leap the attacker pounced from the vehicle, simultaneously swinging the spear, which had somehow returned to its master's hand. Sparks flew as his spear blade cut into this same field once more.

"He is mine!" the charioteer's voice boomed.

Two magnificent beings stepped from nowhere. They each appeared to be of Middle Eastern descent with noble beards and turbaned heads. Both wore white robes that were wrapped loosely around their bodies, covering them completely except for their large, golden, birdlike wings. They held naked golden scimitars and round shields of the same radiant color. They looked so much alike they could have been twins.

"He is on sacred ground! If you try to enter, you will die!" The first one roared, allowing him to believe that these two were in fact responsible for the protective barrier that had saved him.

"I will wait, then! You cannot hide him forever, fools! He will leave eventually!" The voice boomed like thunder even though the words seemed crackling with tension.

He saw the helmeted charioteer rest, almost humanlike, on the road. He leaned on the spear shaft of the weapon that had returned to his hand, patiently putting all of his weight against the staff.

He could feel the chilling stare from beneath the helmet and knew that those shadowed eyes never left him, nor would they as long as he was exposed out in the open. The dogs, like their living, breathing counterparts would likely have done, sat down to wait.

"So cold," he said with a shiver in his voice to an old, bearded man that approached him inside the plain-carpeted temple.

The brown-skinned old man looked him over as if studying something of great importance and curiosity. His dark eyes suddenly went wide at the sight of the sword, whose tip was unceremoniously buried in the dirt.

"Can you help me?" he asked the man, completely humbled. He knew that he was dealing with elements he could barely fathom, but the man's energy screamed to him of trust. "I am very cold."

"Were you Muslim?" the man asked plainly. He seemed to expect the answer to be no.

"I am not religious at all, sir. I am spiritual. I believe I was … I have always thought that all of the gods were the same being, revealed in different ways to different people."

"Interesting," the man stated. "You are much closer to the truth than you realize, and as far as I am concerned, your answer grants you protection here. It is our belief that if someone asks for help, they should be given it."

A woman wearing a burka, her face completely covered, approached with a bundle in her arms and handed it to the old man. She seemed to have come from nowhere and turned to leave quickly.

There was a brief moment when he almost felt as if their eyes had met through her veil. There had been a buzzing sensation in his head that caused him to lose concentration. He felt his eyes drawn towards her in pity as she rapidly vanished from where she had come.

The silver-haired old man seemed to read his mind. "Women are not less than men, although in many ways the culture in this land seems to contradict this." He paused and looked to where she had disappeared. "She simply believed what she was taught in her life so strongly that she is unable to move on. The locals are aware of her, believe me. Sometimes they can smell her cooking. They know that her presence is good, though, and she is seen as a saint of sorts. They even know who she is—or was."

The old man shook out the bundle the woman had brought and wrapped the newcomer in a black cloak. The soothing effect was immediate; he did not feel as cold. He remembered reading ghost stories as a child that spoke of spirits wrapped in blankets and thought that this could very well be the reason. "What happened to her?" he dared to ask.

"She was raped and killed a few years ago, near where your people are fighting right now. The men who did it are fighters of God, or so they preach. They are still alive and will survive this battle once more. They are protected by very dark forces, I'm afraid."

The old man sighed before continuing. "She was born into this land, this life, for a reason, and she lived here so that her spirit could grow. Now she is trapped here by her own unwillingness to let go. For how long I do not know. Probably she will remember one day and maybe even forgive. Until then, I believe she sees in me a father and lives under my care, as she was an unmarried virgin in life. Now in death she lives in shame. She is safe here, though."

Both men were silent for a time.

"And you? What is your story, old man?"

"Well, my son, first of all I only look like a man because you interpret me as such, just like she does." The host laughed at this, mostly to himself as if there was some joke that was impossible for another to get. But soon he grew serious once more. "I enjoy the innocence of the recently deceased, but you cannot delay here for long. They will cover your every possible escape and could wait for eternity if they chose to. You might never be able to leave, and I sense that you need to keep moving. I have rarely seen a hunter so enraged. I need to ask you some questions, and you need to answer them as quickly and concisely as possible. Can you do this?"

"Yeah, I can." His own voice sounded fragile to him.

"What is your plan? Why are you earthbound, and what is your mission?"

"My plan?"

"Yes, your plan! Listen, I can't help you unless you trust me! Tell me the truth!"

"I don't know! I don't know what's going on or why all of this is happening! I don't even remember my name!" He sighed in frustration.

"Do you have a spirit guide?" The old man asked as his silver eyebrows furrowed over dark eyes.

"I don't know," he answered. "Although there was a man who was trying to protect me from the first hunter. He was thrown far aside. That was before the valkyrie and the reaper fought."

"This was how you got the sword?"

"The reaper killed her, and I picked it up. I managed to kill him with it ... and then I ran here."

"You killed him?" The old man may have not been human, but his face was a mask of utter astonishment.

"I think I did."

"For the love of Allah. This may even be worse than I thought! For some reason you are earthbound, but neither mindless nor lucid. The hunter thinks it has claim to you, or maybe it just wants you because you are unprotected. My friend, you will be hunted for eternity because you have attacked, and maybe destroyed, one of the collectors of souls. On top of all of this, for good or bad, you have a divine being's weapon! I don't even know what the rules regarding that are."

"What should I do?" the soldier asked, starting to panic. Yet a subtle voice in his head calmly whispered to him to stay calm; everything depended upon his survival.

"You must leave now! You can possibly escape through the underworld. All holy places, like mosques and temples, are attached to one another through the cosmic web. This applies to the true holy places only. For earthbound spirits, these worship grounds are islands of safety from the hunters, as are graveyards. This is due to old treaties that usually still stand. You need to go far from here ... and try to remember why you are even here in the first place! You must leave before this ethereal escape is blocked, for that will be the hunter's next step—to cage you in. For now, you will most likely be underestimated, and so it is an ideal time to make good your escape. On your journey I would hide that sword if I could, until you can use it."

"I cannot thank you enough!" Tears welled in the soldier's eyes. "How is it that I can find my way to these pathways between holy places?" he asked desperately.

"You really can't see her, can you?" The old man smiled behind his silver-lined beard.

He clung to the wolf's warm fur as she carried him into the abyss. There was a feeling of weightlessness and of nothingness. He sensed alien and ancient beings observing him from the thick darkness.

The wolf, apparently his spirit animal, seemed to pay the spectators no heed. In fact she seemed to be somewhat excited to be helping him on this journey. She sped onwards on running legs with her tongue flagging from between her smiling teeth. He could barely see her in the thick fog. He could barely see anything.

It seemed very satisfying to him to be this close to the canine. His whole life he had felt an affinity for wolves. Strange how he remembered so little of his life, but he remembered this truth so clearly now.

It came to him. Every Christmas season he had tasked himself to find a calendar of wolves before the new year began. He also had a T-shirt from Golden, British Columbia, with a wolf on it that he almost wore to a fault. Anytime he watched TV and was channel surfing, when he came upon a nature program featuring the mammals, he was hard-pressed to change the channel. That really used to bother her ... *what was her name again?*

He remembered an old movie that had something to do with the author Farley Mowat. It was called *Never Cry Wolf*. He thought it was written about the author's own experiences, but he couldn't remember. The story was about a man who lived in the tundra with wolves and showed how intelligent and non-threatening they really were. He remembered that the man in the movie ate mice to somehow show that the wolves could survive on rodents. Was that movie even real? He seemed to remember the film having a deep impact on him at a very early age.

Nothing had moved his soul like the howl of the wolves. There was a place that he used to go fish and camp before life got so complicated. He used to stare at the northern lights and bask in the soulful ballad of the sacred night. It never mattered to him whether he caught anything or not on those trips; fishing wasn't the real reason he came.

They used to bring beer up to that cabin. One time one of his Sioux buddies, Darwin, brought some weed. He hadn't really smoked it before in his life. The separation from society and the closeness to nature seemed to warrant him partaking in the drug that particular trip, though. He ended up feeling pretty strange that night; he had wandered off and gotten himself completely lost in the woods.

He was so messed up that he had imagined a wolf had found him and led him back to the rocky shore of the lake. He had not been afraid at all. Once he was led back to the shore of the lake, the animal seemed to indicate which direction he needed to travel to return to the cabin. He had started to walk. When he turned back around a few moments later, the wolf was nowhere to be seen. Later his mind had dismissed the drug-induced incident as fantasy. He never mentioned the incident to Darwin or Steve, or to anyone else.

He now pressed himself, blade and all, tight against the wolf's warm body. He felt these memories and more run through him. Tears welled in his eyes, and he clung closer to the animal. He felt so safe, and for the first time not cold at all. The rocking motion of the beast seemed to be hypnotic. A sensation not so different from sleep came over him.

3

He had no idea where he was but sensed that he was alone once more. It was pitch black, and he was cold again despite still wearing the cloak. His body felt inflamed from many wounds that had most likely been sustained at the end of his mortal life. His arm, where the ghostly dog had bitten him, throbbed and burned.

He knew that he was back in the world of pain and nightmares.

The soldier pulled the cloak around him tightly, starting to move slowly as he dragged the heavy sword behind him. The sound of the metal scraping on the stone echoed through the dark, wet corridors that seemed to stretch out in many directions. Mice or rats could be heard squealing in the darkness around him, as could a nearby trickle of water.

He could make out that he was in a large room with dark doorway openings everywhere. He sensed that he was underground and that he was not alone.

There was a brief moment where he was sure that he had heard a bell jingling, but he could not seem to determine from where the noise came.

Every direction he looked in seemed to grow darker than where he was before. Out of the corners of his eyes, he could swear that faint beings of light walked to and froe. When he looked directly at the source, however, there was nothing there.

He heard what sounded like a chain jingling. He paused to listen for a very long moment. Again there was no further noise that could confirm what he thought he had heard.

He awkwardly lifted the sword off of the ground. He didn't want to make any more noise because he was a stranger here and felt vulnerable. The sword he carried may be formidable enough to keep enemies at bay, but how long would it take for a predator to realize that he lacked the strength to wield it? Wouldn't the item perhaps be a temptation in itself for certain beings to own? He honestly couldn't answer these questions, but his logic told him that it must be so. The old man at the mosque had suggested he try to hide it.

He heard a sniffle—or was it a snort? He wanted to avoid it, but the noise came from everywhere. He kept moving towards one of the doorways, drawn inexplicably there as he looked for a way out. If he could avoid a battle he would; he did not want to fight anymore.

Unlike the mosque, this place reeked of pain and suffering. The mosque felt safe somehow. At least it had felt safer than outside of the mosque. Maybe it was the old man or the twin guards? Maybe it was the vulnerability of the murdered woman and her seemingly peaceful existence?

He heard the jingling sound again. He focused on not shuffling his feet as he moved. He tried not to make a sound.

The silence was stifling. He had no doubt that he had heard something nearby, but he didn't know from where. He tried to shift the heavy sword to his left hand for comfort, only to feel it fall loudly. The sound echoed throughout the silence and seemed to reverberate forever.

It was the dog's bite. His arm seemed festered and black in the darkness. He became aware of a bone-deep pain that screamed up his forearm and into his shoulder.

Everything inside of him told him that the sword was extremely important and that he should not part with it. He cursed at it in his mind, though; he resented its weight and its size. Mostly he loathed the noise it was making.

Nothing moved. Even the rats had gone quiet. The sound of water dripping was all that remained.

He pulled the sword back up from the floor. With a sudden flash of insight, he positioned the side of the blade across his shoulder. He slid it forward until he found a balance point. It was still heavy, but balanced this way he could manage to carry the item in larger spaces. If the sword was as recognizable as he believed by others, he might be able to give the impression he could manage the weapon. He would attempt to walk in such a fashion as to give off the aura of casual battle readiness with a heavy dose of cockiness. He had no idea if such a feint would be successful here, but he could lose nothing by trying. It was better than showcasing he was a weakling in a land of predators.

He moved forward once more. He became aware that the boxes, which were now everywhere, were some type of stone coffins. They appeared to be very old and severely distressed from the moisture in the space; some sort of slimy algae covered many of them.

He stepped through one of the doorways and into a narrower passageway. This room was far darker. He stepped ahead slowly and carefully.

A scuffing sound. Nearby.

The pit of his stomach turned. He was not alone. Something was very close. He had not imagined this noise, and it had been too loud to be a mere rodent.

A step with his right, a step with his left. Slowly, carefully.

A clink of metal.

He thought the sound came from just ahead where the darkness was thickest, behind the next stone pyre. The buzzing of fear raked his mind.

Right foot. Almost there now.

He moved slowly to peer around the corner into this blind spot, where the shadows seemed darker than Indian ink on a moonless night in the desert.

There was a dark form in the corner. Was it prepared to leap at him like a coiled serpent? Was it another hunter? Was this an ambush? Why was this happening?

He leaned towards the shape, trying to make it out. What was it? Was it a statue? Where he imagined a head to be were sharp, irregular features.

He couldn't help himself. He knew that he should stop or turn around. He knew this was no time for curiosity or false courage.

The figure was the size of a child. He could see square patterns across its back, in varying shades of grey.

Left foot.

The being twisted and sprang at him with a fury that sent him on his heels. A ghastly white face with eyes as black as midnight, an open jaw with rows of teeth and a red bubbling mouth. There was a hissing sound where there should have been some sort of a scream or a cry. Somehow the soundless voice was extremely disturbing. Clawed fingers reached towards him.

Suddenly the creature was yanked backwards in midair. There was a clink of metal as the chain that held it in place became taut. The sudden tension threw it backwards from whence it came.

He realized that he had fallen backwards and dropped the sword once more. He struggled to gain his feet. He rolled onto one of his knees.

He expected it to fly at him again. The creature was still, though, back in its sitting place. It was much further from the wall, more visible, and was now facing him. It held its head in its hands in apparent dismay.

He stopped on his knees, trying to understand the creature in front of him. For some reason he felt pity for it. It appeared to be crying, although there was no sound.

The creature was small. *A demon child?* He studied it for a moment and noted the rise and fall of the being's chest, as if it were in fact sobbing. It stopped and slowly lifted its face to look at him.

The face was impossibly white. He could see this even in the darkness. The jagged eyes were twin pits of blackness, and the lips were black as well.

He looked deeper into the orbs of blackness and was surprised when he saw the reflection of very human-looking eyes inside those circles of darkness.

"Can you talk?" he asked.

The creature stared at him for a long moment before shaking its head back and forth.

The gesture was very human-like. In fact it *was* human. He studied the being some more and determined that it was in fact a child. A child with some sort of a mask on, perhaps?

He realized that the being had responded to his question. It understood him! He saw that it stared at him the same way that he stared at it.

"You're a clown!" he spurted out suddenly and uncontrollably.

The being didn't respond to the statement. He looked closer. No, that wasn't right. Not a clown. More like a joker from a pack of cards.

"You're a jester!" He said it so loudly that his words echoed.

The jester nodded his head, and there was a slight sound of bells ringing from somewhere on him. The black and red hat's many arms bobbed with the motion.

"But from your makeup I see that you are a sad jester. What kind of a king is amused by a sad jester?"

The harlequin stared at him blankly. The soldier felt the last remnants of fear leaving him. He was excited to meet someone, anyone, even if they couldn't talk.

"You really can't talk?" he asked.

The jester shook his head. He then pointed to his mouth and made a scissor motion with his fingers. The action, perhaps the lazy flop of it, suggested that this child was a simpleton.

The soldier looked closer and realised the mouth makeup was mostly dark, coagulated blood. The jagged black makeup around the eyes became clear as well. Tears from crying had made the streaked pattern beneath those orbs.

"What are you doing here?" he wondered out loud more to himself than to the mute in front of him.

The jester held up a chain with a drunken gesture. He could see clearly now that the chain was attached to a metal collar around his neck. The other end was fastened to a ring in the wall. Who would chain this child here and why? It seemed especially cruel. Wouldn't he have been an easy target for one of the hunters? It seemed that there was no end to his questions.

"Should I try to free you?"

The boy sprang upwards so quickly that it startled him, and he almost fell back down from his knees. The jester stood in front of him with his hands locked together in a praying, begging gesture. He stood up and saw that the small man, or boy, only stood up to his chest; he seemed very small and frail.

"I will try to free you, but I will need your help," he stated hopefully.

The jester seemed to be listening.

"I need you to help me find my way out of here."

The fool nodded his head in ascent.

He picked up the sword once more and stepped past this new friend. He swung the blade downwards. The chain flew apart with a shower of sparks.

Before he had a chance to react, the jester had wrapped his arms around him. He could feel the jester's hug and the shake of his body as he started to sob into the front of his cloak. Unsure how to react, he put his hand, the wounded one, on the back of the clown's hat and patted gently.

"If you trust me, I can try to make the chain shorter. We can rest it on top of the stone here, and I can break it." He pointed to the top of one of the stone graves.

The jester stepped back and looked up at him for a short while with eyes that looked dimwitted. After a moment, the child seemed to realize what the soldier was saying. He then seemed to have concluded that this would not be a bad idea and that he could in fact trust this strange soldier.

The small being fell to his knees once more and dramatically gripped the neck ring with both hands. He bent back his head and seemed to be exposing his throat for an executioner.

The gesture made the soldier very uneasy. He had killed in his life, that was true, but never in his life had he killed an innocent intentionally. Never in his life had he killed anyone that wanted him too. That was, he suddenly remembered, a regret of his too.

The Jester had recovered a sceptre of sorts from the corner that he'd been chained in. He now walked with head up high and chest puffed out, with the item tucked under his arm beneath the armpit. His strut as he walked ahead, leading the way by several meters, was that of a triumphant king.

The soldier had no idea if he could trust him. He hadn't a clue where he was or where he was going. It turned out that the tombs he had found himself in had been beneath a very old church. The jester had taken them through a secret door and into a cellar. A spiralling staircase had brought them to a passageway, which had led them to a large room of worship.

He had pulled up the hood on his cloak and repositioned the sword on his shoulder. The facade of power was all that he had. He was a stranger here, completely unaware of the rules. The old man in the mosque had suggested he would be hunted but was safe in holy places. He had also suggested that he should have a plan, but the notion had completely baffled him. He had no plan that he knew of, but he could only suspect that the wolf had brought him here for a purpose.

It suddenly occurred to him that he was dead and that this was no dream. He had not been given a moment to mourn his passing, however, because fear had promoted survival as his first priority.

His only intent right now was to try to discover who he was, but his mind seemed to be getting foggier all the time. He needed to remember.

In the process of remembering, he would try to understand his situation with a little more clarity. Why was he here? What had happened, and who had told him to resist that golden light? *Was* there a specific reason that the wolf had brought him here? Could the jester help him?

So many questions but the last one held the most weight right now. He remembered how the jester had initially leapt at him and started to second guess his decision to free the harlequin. Maybe he wanted the sword? Maybe he would simply wait until he slept before he took it? Did he even need to sleep?

He sized up the jester walking in front of him and leading the way through the dim candlelight. Someone or something had felt the need to chain this little spirit up. People were usually imprisoned for only two reasons that he was aware of. They either posed a threat to someone, or they were being punished.

Long dead monks stared at them stoically from behind statues of saints. A lone praying family, obviously living, were hunched in the shadows. The youngest child seemed to look up at the two spirits as they passed, and he felt himself become slightly fatigued. Small winged beings crawled across oak leaf vines carved on the upper walls. These seemed to whisper to one another and tracked their movements. His eyes soaked in everything nervously.

He was safe in a place of worship from the hunters because of some treaty, the old man had said. What about the occupants, though? Was he safe from them too?

They came to a door that was partly opened. The jester turned sideways and slid outside. The soldier pushed on the door, but nothing happened. It was a tight squeeze, but he followed suit and found himself outside of the church with the waiting jester.

The clouds were partly obscuring a full moon. A wind whispered through the leaves of giant oak trees. He felt himself being observed from everywhere. Despite the quiet, they were not alone. He tried to make lifting the sword back onto his shoulder as natural a movement as possible.

The jester had his head thrown back and seemed to be laughing, though no sound came from his mouth. He hoped that the joy was the response to freedom and nothing more. If there had been some other joke, he had missed it completely.

The jester gave him a bloody-toothed grin before moving across the courtyard towards some separate buildings. He followed behind, curious as to where he was being led. A stone archway gave passage through a high wall. A cobblestone path led into a labyrinth of buildings. He realized a few minutes later that pathway had probably marked the boundary when they had left the sanctuary of the church.

He continued to follow, however. Nothing had happened, and he had nowhere else to go. He was curious as to where this jester was leading him. The promise to get him out of the church had been fulfilled. The fool was now on his own journey. He chose to follow, for now.

Dark, ominous shadows hung thick to the buildings and maze-like streets. The jester seemed to know the area well, however, for every turn he took seemed automatic and without hesitation. He eventually led them to a door that was hard to see in the darkness. He tried to pull it open but nothing happened. He then stood silently, looking up at a high window.

A man opened the door after a short while. He was different than them—like the praying family, he was obviously living. He did not seem to notice them or pay them any heed. He was a very fat man, and his face seemed wet from sweat. He stood in the doorway and lit a cigarette. The jester slid past him into the building, and the soldier followed behind.

The door slammed shut behind them. There would be no easy escape if things went awry. That particular thought was smothering.

The smell of cheap, sweet perfume washed over him. Old band music played from somewhere upstairs and carried down the staircase. The only light source seemed to be from burning candles. Two World War II American soldiers sat on a couch with short glasses in their hands that looked to be filled with whisky. They stared blankly at the duo. One of the men seemed to have a chest wound that was soaking through the front of his jacket. Rifles leaned against the wall behind them. Having apparently been interrupted, the two men started to converse with one another once more, ignoring the newcomers.

The jester led the way up the stairs. The soldier followed him, lifting the sword a few steps at a time by the hilt, almost like he would a walking stick. From up above he could hear the sound of a woman's laughter.

He followed the jester warily. There was a presence nearby that unnerved him; something powerful and perhaps deadly was up ahead. The patterned carpeted stairs seemed to be as foreign as anything else he had seen this day, despite the likelihood of the design being based on reality. It was multicoloured with lots of sharp angles set into the pattern.

The carpet ended after a slight curve in the steps. There was then a long, red carpeted hallway before them that stretched past several doorways lit by coloured glass oil lanterns. He could hear moaning, sensual and hushed. The doorways lined the hall but were covered with red fabric. He could see candlelight through the thin cloth emanating from each room. The big band music stopped, and a new song started to play. He recognised this one. It was the song "The End" by the Doors.

He sensed that this was a busy place but that the voices were kept low on purpose. He became aware of a wet slapping sound that could only be described as bodies colliding rhythmically in sex. He could smell tobacco, thick, foreign and sweet.

The jester moved towards the end of the hallway. His movement caused one of the door sheets to flutter. Inside the disturbed room he briefly saw an old man on top of a naked young woman. Her legs were wrapped around him as he pumped furiously. His potbelly swung heatedly in the bizarre picture of sexuality. The woman was giggling and moaning in joy, which made no sense to him because of her extreme beauty. A second image of her seemed to be partway out of the smiling image of her. The second image was crying and looked up at the soldier.

"Help me!" she was whispering to him loudly.

Strangest of all was the beast that stood at the head of her bed. Similar to the Minotaur of Greek legend, he looked like a bull on his hind legs. There was nothing human about him except for hands where the front hooves should have been. Both of these pulled a massive penis in a frenzied masturbation over the girl's head. There was a snorting, laughing sound that came from him as he did this.

The soldier quickly focused back on the smiling girl's image, the living one, one more time. He was confused by her. She was whispering yes over and over now to the old man. She looked to be less than twenty years of age, while potbelly must have been in his midsixties. The curtain fell back over the scene and shut him out once more.

The jester was almost at the end of the hallway, and so he sped up to catch him. He held the sword off the ground slightly to make more progress. He caught up to the jester just as he was entering a large room. Two pieces of fabric covered this doorway; the sheet was split in the middle. As the jester went through, there was a wind chime sound of beads musically banging together. The soldier followed him through.

    A gorgeous brunette woman lay on a large bed. She was completely naked and spread out above crumpled sheets, undignified. Her mouth was open, and her head was to the side. Her breasts fell to each side of her ribcage, a telltale sign that she was probably at least thirty. Her legs spread wide to reveal moist lips, preciously pink. There was no hair anywhere on her body. The long, straight black hair on her head cascaded over the pillows beneath her. One hand rested over her heart, and the other was thrown far to the side. Her fingernails were deep red and matched her toes. Arching eyebrows rested on a graceful face. Her eyes were hidden behind closed lids.

    "Balzola?" A woman's thick, sensual voice from the other side of the room asked in surprise.

    He felt something stir in him even as he saw the track marks on the sleeping woman's arms, and he did not look up at this new speaker. There was something void about the woman before him, but he didn't care. A discarded syringe lay on a night table beneath a candelabrum and a few discarded books. He noticed some rubber tubing beneath the outstretched arm. Still, she made him hunger for her in a thousand previously unimagined ways.

    "Am I being too cruel? I think your friend likes her," the voice said.

    He was knocked from his trance and finally turned around to view the speaker. She smiled suggestively at him. It was if she had shared a million secrets with him. She knew him. He could trust her. He loved her.

    The jester clung to her left leg, hugging her. She leaned back in a chair smoking a cigarette through a filter akin to those used by beautiful women in movie classics. Her eyes danced with mischievousness as her teeth clenched onto the plastic end between full, yet somehow pouty, lips.

    He was not prepared for her beauty. If the woman on the bed was beautiful, then there were no words to describe this creature that flooded him with electric desire and need. She most definitely was not human.

    Her hair was long, jet black and curly. Her skin was brown and her features Middle Eastern. Her eyes were the lightest mint green that he had ever seen, shining almost neon and very large. Her cheekbones screamed nobility. A tiny nose held a silver ring in the right nostril. Her ears possessed several earrings.

The grace of her neck drew his eyes slowly to large, well-placed breasts. A white silk robe was partly opened and barely covered her nipples, which could be seen slightly through the fabric anyways. She wore arm coverings from her knuckles to her elbows that at first glance appeared to be long, fingerless gloves. They were black and the same green as her eyes. He could see that they were laced from inside the arm. The top of her flat stomach was exposed in a V pattern above the robe's tie. Her feet were spaced shoulder width apart on the floor and were bare. She wore an anklet of silver. Her toe nails, like her fingernails holding the cigarette, were again the same green as her eyes.

The depth of her eyes was not the only indication that she was not human. He had initially thought the silver above her head was something on the wall behind her. Then he had thought it was a crown of some sort. Now he saw clearly that the silver metal was a type of jewellery that fitted over the two small horns on her head. They each erupted an inch from her hairline, directly above her eyes.

He swooned for a moment as if drunk on the perfume she wore. He felt powerless and wanted to go to her. If the jester was not there before him, he would have done so. His pride was slightly greater than his desire; he did not want to share her with this slight, unworthy man. He did not know how long he could fight this urge, though.

She let out a little laugh that was both playful and cute.

"Well, Balzola, who is this new friend of yours? Was it him that freed you? All the whores in heaven know that I've tried more than once."

The soldier swooned and swung the sword forward like a cane to rest upon. He needed to keep his feet.

He noticed her rise suddenly and stand somewhat defensively.

"Who are you, and why is that blade in my house?" she asked in a suddenly commanding voice, dropping all light-hearted pretence. The question was not fearful or unkind, but it was urgent and hurried. He felt his reason coming back to him, and the spell seemed to lift.

He looked back up at her. He still wanted her but was no longer drunk from lust. He realised that on some level she had released her grip on him.

"I don't know my name. I don't remember," he responded. He felt himself trying to make his voice deeper somehow, as if this would impress her. "I followed the jester here from the church. I'm lost."

She looked at him with a very serious expression. She was still gorgeous even without that mischievous smile upon her face.

"The jester's name is Balzola," she said before sitting back down.

"Who is he, and why was he chained up?" He swallowed hard, coming more and more to his senses every moment.

"*He?*" she asked, pausing with one eyebrow arched for some time. "Yes, Balzola ... well that is a story in itself, isn't it, and one worth sharing. I will help you, forgetful one, *dark mind*, but perhaps you will then answer my questions. Also, there will come a day in which you will need to help me In exchange ... when the time comes."

"Help you? Should I be making deals with devils?" he asked excitedly.

She laughed lightly. "Hardly a devil, *Darkmind*; you may call me Bali for now. Besides, you do not look to me to be someone with a lot of options. A man without a name is either twice the man or no man at all. You look like you need friends."

He was happy she put the argument to him. In his heart he wanted to owe her favours, he wanted to make pacts with her. Devil or not, he wanted a reason to believe in her and to somehow taste her.

He nodded at her to indicate that they had a deal. She smiled a closed-lip smile.

"Balzola was a harlequin for a minor king here in Italy several centuries ago. *He…*" she paused as if considering something, "was one of the greatest that has ever lived. Balzola could breathe and juggle fire, perform all sorts of magic acts, read the nobles fortunes, act, sing and perform any part in any play. His jokes were always light in nature, though, so that everyone was spared injury to pride, which was what truly made him great.

"Balzola had many secrets and never ceased to amaze the king or his court. It seemed like his luck had finally ran out when it was discovered that one of the knights had lost a valuable family heirloom. When Balzola returned it, it became apparent that he had stolen the item in extremely difficult circumstances. Balzola, as sometimes happens, had a compulsion to steal that could not be sated. He did not truly wish to own the item, however, so upon seeing the pain that the missing item had caused to the owner, he had returned it.

"What should have been the very end for Balzola was actually just a new beginning, for the king marvelled at how the jester had managed to steal the item through impossible odds. Those were strange times and strange people. The court started to revel in the thefts as long as the items were returned. It became a game. No matter how ridiculous of a test was left for the jester, the theft would be completed. Snakes, poison, dogs, falling weapons, darts, fire—there was no end to the ingenuity dreamt up by the ruling class. It became such a sport that the nobles would actually leave bonuses for the thief. A cup with the face of the joker on it would be beside the item with a gift inside. It was a tithe of sorts.

"The king eventually started to send Balzola on missions to steal from his enemies. They knew of course who was behind the thefts, for the legend of Balzola had grown far and wide. At one point accusers went to the church and accused this little one of witchcraft and of being a demon. In all of their corruption at the time, these priests simply recruited Balzola to do jobs for them as well. Assassination was eventually added to his resume, and in this he was perhaps peerless throughout the world."

An Arabic melody now replaced the song by the Doors. The music drifted in from down the hall. Bali put the cigarette out in an ashtray on a table near her. She blew out a stream of blue smoke before continuing.

"Balzola knew all the riches, fame and respect that anyone could ever ask for. This was especially true of someone with such humble origins. However there was one treasure that was, though unspoken, understood to be absolutely off-limits though. That was the king's 15-year-old daughter."

Bali let out a long breath and continued. "His luck had finally run out. Both the church and the king were enraged. Balzola was found in the daughter's bedchamber. His tongue was buried deep inside of her gyrating hips. His arms were both up her blouse, and his hands were fondling her young nipples. Out of shame the daughter turned on Balzola as well. She accused him of casting a spell on her to make her weak. She said he also took her by force.

"A public killing would admit to the world what had transpired. This heinous crime had to remain a secret, especially from prospective suitors and their families. The king consulted the priests, and within hours of the incident the jester was chained to a dark corner of the old burial chambers. His tongue had been cut out. He was then given a slow-working poison that is said to weaken the person to the point of paralysis. Finally prayers, or spells if you will, were cast over the imprisonment to bind him forever.

Balzola had no strength to get out of the chains because of the poison. Without food and water, it was only a matter of time. When his higher self went on, he was left almost completely without intelligence.

"In life, Balzola spent a significant amount of time here, even though my home has changed faces many times over the eras. Over the years I have gone to see him in the dungeon, visiting the once proud jester and given what pleasure I could with soft hands and tender kisses. I have been Balzola's only friend in life and in death since the betrayal. That is, until you came."

The soldier nodded his head slightly, as if the tale were completely normal. He tried not to get fixated on the hand pleasure part. Why was he still jealous? This was ridiculous.

"Why did the hunters not come for him? Is it because he was in the church and safe because of some agreement? Why haven't they come now?" Darkmind asked.

"They still might," Bali answered, heavy with concern. Balzola had wandered over to the bed and was staring down at the heroin-induced woman with the spread legs.

"He has probably been forgotten for now," Bali continued. "Maybe the circumstances of his death left him earthbound, like my guards downstairs."

"What makes someone earthbound?" he asked.

"It usually happens when a relatively insignificant soul meets an untimely, unplanned death. Suicides and murders especially fulfill this requirement. Then the hunter, or collector, goes to pick up the soul at the *scheduled* time of death if they are unclaimed by higher beings. If that soul is not there when the hunter comes, because they got off the bus too soon, so to speak, the reaper often will not bother. These earthbound spirits usually lose their mind quickly and settle into a predictable pattern of life that part of them feels they are still living. They wander like drunks or simpletons and spend all of their energy trying to be noticed until they fade out completely. The energy they have left is usually not significant for a hunter to even bother."

"They usually lose their minds?"

"Yes, though not always. Some seek power. Some manage to do so before their life's memory is completely gone. They can gain great power in the spirit world. It is especially so if both parts of the spirit are present."

He caught himself staring down the front of her robe and quickly pulled his eyes back to her face. "What kinds of power?"

"They can open doors, move objects, enter people's dreams or even manifest. They can sometimes have conversations with the living, protect loved ones or kill, although this is supposed to be forbidden. They are always ambitious, at least at first, and are usually killed by those that have gained the power before them if the hunters don't get them first. There are a few who become masters, though this is rare. The powers of these are usually of extreme good or extreme evil. You will not be able to understand now, but basically all things are possible from a high place of power, including body possession of the living or the dead. The goal at that point as the masters become more powerful is usually to be worshipped by the living to sustain that power. To become some sort of god so that they may spend energy and have it replaced. It is always about power ... for all of us."

"The hunter that came for me was wounded when he killed another hunter, or collector as you suggested. It was a winged warrior woman. I picked up her sword and finished him. What does that mean?"

Bali's eyes became slits.

"That most likely means you will be hunted until you are destroyed."

Darkmind looked over at the jester Balzola, who was standing at the foot of the woman's bed. He was rubbing the end of the sceptre between the woman's legs. He had a large, open-mouthed, bloody grin. Darkmind felt disgusted. Was he so compromising to befriend hell's rejects?

"You want this weapon, don't you?" he asked her, fearing the answer.

"I cannot pick the sword up. It is a violation to whatever agreement allows you to keep it, I would think. Whatever hunter group that lost it would likely swarm me to take it back as soon as I was vulnerable ... and justifiably so."

"Why has this not happened to me?"

"I can only speculate, but my best guess?" She paused for a moment before continuing. "The hunter you describe is most likely either an angel or a valkyrie. They are both winged warriors who were both likely present at the battle you were in ... based on geography, culture and each warrior's personal beliefs. Destroying its enemy, avenging it, has probably bought you some mercy. I can only speculate, as I said. It is possible that they do not know what to do with you and are debating this even now. These high beings, both the angel and the valkyrie, honour courage in battle."

"I can hardly wield this weapon, though! Whatever happened to my rifle?"

"You appear as you believed you appeared in your final moments. You are taller and bigger than most, which says something in and of itself. Most are very small. Their image reflects an end of self-pity and powerlessness. You did not see yourself with your rifle at the time, so you do not get to keep it."

Bali pulled another cigarette out from somewhere inside of her robe and attached it to the end of the filter that was resting in the ashtray. She lit it with a flame from the end of her finger.

"Can I learn to use the sword?"

"Yes, and I think I know one who could teach you," she answered, staring off into space. "There is one who owes me a favour and should honour it despite his dislike of me. He was my lover at one time. He has a very powerful weapon as well, but his is quite different. He trains certain soldiers. I can introduce you."

"Why would you help me? Why are you doing this? Can I even trust you?" His voice sounded like a child's, even to him, as the words fell from his mouth.

"Why do you feel you cannot trust me?"

"You are a whore!" He regretted saying it even as the words left his mouth. He had not intended on being cruel. For a man who had sinned so much in life, he had an acute sense of right and wrong. He had often been uncompromising in his approach to living life, or so he liked to believe. Some would have said this was his greatest of flaws.

She smiled wearily but did not look offended. "All women are whores. All women have both lust and a price. They also have a need for power, the same as men. A cheap woman will give herself freely and casts aside her power. She may do this for money or even for food in desperate circumstances, or for drugs if she becomes an addict." She pointed to the woman on the bed whom Balzola continued to molest.

"A woman's value is increased the fewer men she has been with. She can go after stronger men to bear children with, to be protected by and to perhaps marry. The cheap woman believes that there are secrets in the land of the living, but there are not. When two people meet, there is always an exchange of information. One's higher spirit will know everything about the other's even from past lives. Whether that person is enlightened enough to pay heed is another matter altogether." She stood up and began to pace before continuing her speech, holding the cigarette up with one arm while her other hand rested beneath the elbow.

"Physical beauty makes the formula more complicated. The most desired woman in the world is the virtuous beauty, but these are rare. A very beautiful woman will be accepted even after being with many men because her presence gives men power. Living on her back gives her a very short window, though. Most women have ten years of high beauty before they start to deteriorate. Then they start to grasp and to settle. They will think that they *still have it* when they land a man, but in fact a man will usually fuck anything and will settle for the best that is presented on his plate in any given moment."

He responded anxiously, "You said that there are virtuous women, though, waiting for the right man? How does that make them whores?"

"What mother would not suck a stranger off to spare the life of her child? Is this not noble prostitution out of desperation? Do you know how many women have been whored out of love to the wrong man? Pure and beautiful women have been sold to slavery at a young age with little control over their destiny. In most third world countries, women meet with tourists in the night to feed their families. These may seem like extreme examples to you, but all women have a price. For some it is one drink and a little bit of attention. For others it's a new sports car. Every woman has a self-imposed value, a tipping point if you will, where she decides she will have sex with a man."

He had a flash of a woman's face, a memory of the woman he had loved, and these theories seemed flawed. Bali looked at him knowingly, as if she had read his mind.

"This is my paradigm, Darkmind, and does nothing to explain the concept of honour, which I have struggled with for over a century or even of a man's price. If you wish to know more about honour, the one I will introduce you to will teach you. This will hopefully be before you lose the last of your memories. I only wish to defend myself to you for reasons that will become clearer in time ... if all goes well."

He felt bad. He had spoken without any regards to her feelings. He would not have thought that a succubus had feelings at all.

"I am sorry for calling you a whore."

"I *am* a whore, my friend. The one I will introduce you to would agree, if he agrees to meet us at all." She looked at him with a smile, slightly sad and contemplative.

"Who is he?"

"His name is Hachimantaro. He is a samurai."

4

They moved down the stairway cautiously. Bali had transformed and left a second mirage image of herself in the bedchamber. She now rode on the shoulder of Balzola in the form of a raven.

She had explained that she did not want to be seen leaving her abode with the strange soldier carrying the sword. He thought that the raven's mint green eyes seemed like a beacon, of and into itself, to others who knew her. He noticed the raven still wore the anklet, though a much smaller version, above her talons.

The guards, the drinking soldiers, paid them little heed as they left. The door opened in front of them without her having to physically touch it. The fat man, an apparent doorman or pimp of sorts in the physical realm, seemed unable to see them and cursed at the door before lumbering up the few steps to close it once more.

The night had grown foggy, and he pulled his face deeper into the shadows of the cloak's hood. Bali had explained the unlikelihood of any beings attacking the duo while they were in her kingdom. If they had been followed, however, or betrayed by an observant spirit, an enemy could be waiting outside.

Apparently Balzola felt indebted enough for his release to come along. Darkmind was sure there was more to it though. Balzola had been a daring and reckless being once. He hoped that the jester would somehow also gain back some of his lucidity. Darkmind hoped the eccentric simpleton's presence would not be a hindrance. Truth be told, he welcomed the company for he truly did not wish to be alone.

Balzola led the way through alleyways and dark, unlit streets. The pale faces of the once living stared at them out of windows or darkened corners, whimpering while clutching comforting blankets that seemed to cover them with denial. Things moved in the dark that no living person would want to know about or believe in—vampiric beings feasting on the thoughts and hearts of the living chased each other, and the emotions of those living, in and out of doorways and through walls.

They took a wide and circular path to a cemetery that was attached to the church. Bali spoke in whispers to them of a side gate seldom used. It was a gate she did not believe existed anymore in the land of the living but that they could access on this plane.

A shadow stepped in between them as they neared the despairing iron gate. The humanoid figure was extremely tall and lean with limbs as thin as toothpicks. His face was relatively normal except for large, bulbous eyes. A long, thin moustache hung below his chin. His eyebrows were permanently shaped in a serious expression lifted into his greasy hairline.

"You pay the toll!" His words lacked a depth of intelligence.

Darkmind reached for the sword handle with the wounded arm. Holding the sword with two hands might show the toll collector he was not prepared to bargain. Bali remained quiet, in doing so condoning his actions.

The tall man opened a wide mouth with impossibly tiny lips, which shook with disbelief.

"It okay this time! You go free!" He moved aside and pulled the gate wide as he did so.

Darkmind was glad at the easy entrance because he was aware that they had nothing with which to pay. He imagined that any price would seem too steep for someone with only a few items to their name, especially since they might not acquire more items again. They pushed past the gatekeeper without offering any thanks.

The yard was surprisingly deserted. Here and there lone figures roamed either contemplative or confused. The foggy wind moved slowly around rustling trees and over patches of long grass between unkempt grave markers. Italian crickets sang a haunting melody that seemed to come from the mouths of angel statuettes. Vines clung to trees, and a faint smell of smoke came from somewhere nearby and mingled pleasantly with the perfume of night flowers.

The raven cocked her head back and forth before throwing out a throaty caw. She swung towards a short stone wall and plucked a cricket into her beak. She then held the thin, almost translucent, squirming insect in her mouth for a long moment before swallowing the struggling creature. She seemed to position herself to wait.

He heard the howl of the wolf, deep and haunting. It echoed off of the fog and seemed to come from all directions. It seduced him with its call and began to swallow him whole. A mist rolled around him and into him. It swirled and foamed like a wash of ocean water between two craggy seaside boulders.

He could also suddenly hear the call of a magpie. He saw its face flash into his mind; it seemed to be smiling. He thought for a moment it was wearing the jester's hat. An image entered his mind of the bird hopping alone on one foot.

There was a fluttering of what sounded like many wings. His fingers felt soft fur between them once more, and again he felt drunk and incoherent. His mind faded deeply, as if to a restless sleep. He knew no more.

He became aware that he was on his knees and swaying back and forth drunkenly. He looked over and saw Balzola on all fours in a similar state. The raven was no longer present; Bali had returned to her human-like form and was standing nearby, patiently waiting for her guests to compose themselves.

She looked shorter somehow. She wore a long gown of black and mint green. It appeared to be silk and was as he imagined a geisha's dress would look. Her hands were hidden in the folds of her sleeves, and her feet were hidden beneath the gown. Her face was powdered white, and her eyes, although still piercing green, had somehow become slanted. Her hair was tied up with several varnished sticks protruding out of it, which seemed to be holding it in place. Between her horns was stretched a green silk cloth with black borders. Japanese kanji characters were written in black on the flag. He was surprised he could read the characters for *demon* and for *angel*.

She stared silently at them while she waited for the pair to collect themselves. Darkmind leaned down to hoist back onto his shoulder the heavy sword. There was a jingling of bells as Balzola dusted himself off.

"I don't speak Japanese," Darkmind stated flatly more to himself than anyone else.

"The curse of Babel has been lifted from your brow, my friend." She explained. "All the earthbound speak the same language, unless of course your words are not meant to be heard by one who listens uninvited. I use speaking as a metaphor because you choose to interpret communication as language." She paused for a moment. "You will be able to understand Hachimantaro, do not worry. Do not be disappointed, though, if he will not see us. It has been a very long time, but he may still be angry at me. Unless he has changed greatly, however, he will feel bound to an old promise. In a way I am using you in a final attempt to make peace."

They were in a graveyard of sorts. Stone walkways overrun with grass led up stairways and between torrii, Shinto gates, into gardens of stone artwork and burial markers. Tall trees were everywhere, making the night-time landscape seem a gothic, manmade jungle of sorts. Paper lanterns were held in the arms of motionless, staring Asian people in various types of dress. A warm breeze that did nothing to warm him came from an ocean nearby. A bird sang unnaturally in the night from a nearby tree. A living monk was somewhere in the shadows, whispering prayers for either himself or a loved one. In the end they were perhaps both the same thing.

Darkmind was very aware of his wounds once more.

"Everywhere that I go, it is night," he said casually as he and Balzola followed her.

"Time is not as linear for you as it once was. It would also cost you a lot of energy, that you have no way of replenishing right now, to appear to someone. It is easier to hug the shadows. It is apparently a difficult thing for the earthbound to walk in the day. There are many living, children and old people especially, with the ability to see you. You would leave an imprint upon them and shed a lot of your energy. Too much energy spent, and you would simply cease to exist. Only the very powerful walk in public places or during the day, Darkmind. Less populated places are another story altogether."

He could not help but watch the sway of her hips as she moved in front of him. The smell of flowers radiated from her. "Thank you, Bali. I don't know why you're doing this, but you've answered a lot of questions for me."

"You have honour, Darkmind." She fell back a few paces to walk beside him. Balzola stepped further to the front with a wide, toothy smile, moving quickly ahead. "You will help me when I ask ... if you survive long enough. The chances of your not being destroyed soon are very low. However, I believe that you may have the ability to survive all of this. It is not anyone who happens upon the sword of one hunter and destroys another."

"I do not understand the hunters, which you have also referred to as collectors. Why do some seem evil and some good? And what is the gold white light that I saw?" He felt like a child asking her so many questions, but he couldn't help it. He needed to know.

"If you have not learned the answers to these questions here, then I will explain these things to you sometime. I am afraid that we do not have that opportunity right now, however, for we are near." She stopped before a gateway of sorts where Balzola had been waiting for them.

A building was in front of them with beautiful concaved wood beams pointing towards the heavens. Wooden walkways ran the whole front of the structure before paper sliding doorways. Candlelight made its way through the thin paper and cast ominous shadows across the grass before them. Cherry blossoms floated over the structure from the gardens hidden behind it. A strange-looking cat the size of a lion sat silently watching them from its resting place upon the walkway. It looked to be made of stone with a wild mane and demonic-looking eyes. He sensed it was not evil but very dangerous nonetheless.

The glint of another set of eyes, off to his side in the tall grass, caught his attention. He stared for a moment and then realized that hidden in the shadows was a second one of the catlike beings. Its eyes were like twin flames hovering in the darkness.

Bali quietly took the stairs with Darkmind and Balzola in tow. They had clearly been expected because as they reached the top of the steps, the paper doors slid outward. Two men had moved the doors smoothly and in unison.

The two men wore Japanese World War II uniforms with samurai swords in their belts. Both wore white scarves around their heads with a red design on the front of them. Darkmind thought for a moment of the two American soldiers he had seen in the house of sin and wondered if there was any significance to them being in pairs.

Both of the men bowed in unison. Bali bowed to them in return. Darkmind decided to do the same and noted Balzola did so as well, though Balzola had an air of mockery.

They stepped through the opening and into the waiting area as the doors were slid shut behind them.

"I will go and meet with Hachimantaro. It has been a long time, and like I said he may still be angry with me despite what I believe will be a great curiosity. I am quite certain that he will be very interested. Wait here. Someone will come for you when he is ready to see you."

The two guards opened a second set of doors, and the lady stepped through them.

Darkmind and Balzola were led through a garden of trickling brooks that were gently being rained upon by thousands of cherry blossom petals. He noted that even in the darkness he could distinguish the bright colors of koi fish swimming beneath walkway bridges and resting in pools. Here and there stood intense-looking Japanese spirits, both men and women, staring at the two guests and the escorting guards.

After a short walk they came upon a clearing. On mats sat several people upon the manicured grass. Bali sat off to the side facing inwards. Two mats were placed before her, but instead of facing her they faced the host. The two guards bowed before the host and his council. Again the guests, Darkmind and Balzola, followed suit. Everyone including Bali repeated the gesture.

The guards motioned for the guests to sit down. Darkmind's movements suddenly seemed very awkward to him. He sat cross-legged and tried to lay the sword before him delicately. He then looked more closely at his host for the first time.

Hachimantaro sat upon a bamboo mat on his knees. He looked far younger than Darkmind would have expected; he appeared to be barely out of his teens. He had a moustache that came to his chin and jet black hair that was tied up into a bun. He had two swords attached to his back, with the hilts sticking above his shoulder blades. The weapons, he noted, were not laid out before him like most of the other samurais' weapons were.

Except for the swords, Hachimantaro did not look as Darkmind would have imagined a samurai would look. His dress, although appearing traditional, was very humble. He was not wearing any armour or flashy jewellery. His eyes looked soft and unintimidating, but there was something piercing about his gaze.

Several men sat around and behind him in similar dress and fashion. Most had two swords in the grass before their mats; in samurai fashion, there was a long one and a short one. For the most part the weapons looked intricate in their design and seemed to have an aura of intrigue.

All of the men were interesting to Darkmind, but two stood out to his eye more than the others. One was a white man with closely cropped hair who seemed slightly out of place despite his calm outward appearance. The second looked very similar to the others but had several facial piercings and seemed to have dark-coloured makeup around his eyes. He also had an elaborate neck tattoo of a dragon.

It occurred to Darkmind that there were other powerful beings nearby that he could not see. He had to trust Bali's judgement that he would be safe. At this point, he supposed, he did not have a choice.

Hachimantaro made a gesture, and a woman, one of several nearby, brought Darkmind and Balzola cups of tea. Darkmind nodded to the man, his host, before taking a sip.

"You should not take food or drink in your new world so freely, Darkmind." There were no breaks in his sentence, and his words were smooth and confident. "I am Hachimantaro."

"Nice to meet you. I don't call myself Darkmind, but it's what Bali's been calling me. I don't remember my name."

"A name that has meaning is hard to find in the world nowadays. If you do not mind, then I too will call you Darkmind." It seemed to be a question.

"It's as good as any other name, I suppose."

"And this must be your retainer, Balzola. It is an honour to meet you as well," he said politely.

Balzola smiled a toothy, somewhat bloody smile. Darkmind did not know how to respond. He did not consider himself samurai and so did not see Balzola as his retainer, even if there was a debt of sorts. He decided to wait for Hachimantaro to speak first.

"Do you know what Hachimantaro means, Darkmind?" It was a question not meant to be answered, for there was only a moment's pause. "It means son of the war god. It is a nickname I acquired in life but one that I despised in death. Do you know why? It is because the name suggests that somehow I am great. Eventually I came to terms with it. I am not great, nor am I the son of a war god. I simply am. In this realm a label is as important as it once was in the last realm. This label reminds me every time it is used that I need to remain humble. For now, you too may call me Hachimantaro."

Darkmind nodded and took a slow sip of the warm tea.

"I would prefer the name Darkmind," the samurai continued. "It indicates one that has been able to destroy oneself, for in the end there is nothing and no one. Do you understand?" This was a question that Hachimantaro wanted to be answered.

"To be honest with you, I don't. I do not understand." His voice was filled with sincerity.

"Perhaps I expected more from you in your current state of innocence, but you have come in good faith, it would seem. It is unimportant for now. In this realm your old name, your birth name, should not be given freely if at all. For one who is attached to the world and things of the world, a name can be more deadly than the sharpest blade." Hachimantaro himself took a sip of tea before continuing.

"I lived a long and fruitful life once. Every deed I enacted was in the name of honour, as the spirits of the land may bear witness. I was bold and I was reckless. I treated the less fortunate with respect and honoured every spirit that I learned of with the utmost reverence. There was nowhere that I went without the sword that was given to me at an early age." He let his hand touch the right hilt behind him as he spoke. "Even when it was presented to me, I was told that this sword had great power. With every action I believed this, and so the weapon gained power throughout my life.

"Secretly I wanted to die in combat. I never strayed far from my path of righteousness, but in my heart I prayed that my lands would be beset upon by demons and evil men from faraway countries. The mortal hordes never came, but my eyes started to open, and some evil spirits did in fact come to answer these prayers. I fought battles alone in my old age that many would dismiss as fantasy. With every victory my sword grew stronger. With every kill I felt energy fill me.

"I was an old man when the shinigami came for me. I was deep in meditation. I saw the approach of the demon after committing seppuku, ritual suicide, and he was horrible to behold. He wore the mask of the night ninja with his skeletal face partly exposed. His black robes flowed around him and did not betray either movement or size. He wielded a great katana with which he meant to strike me down. I was very afraid, but I lusted for the battle and attacked the being with ferocity. My weapon was startling to him and my strength underestimated. I often tell the story as if the battle was short, but it was not." Worry lines appeared upon

Hachimantaro's face as his eyebrow creased with the telling of the story. His eyes were far away.

"We fought long enough that reinforcements could be seen coming to join the battle. Truth be told I had been aided at one point where I was sure to have been killed. We had both been wounded, and the battle seemed very even. I saw that part of him was relieved that other shinigami were coming. I had a moment where I had to decide to run or to fight. I decided that I was ready to die here and die as a man. A part of me surrendered to something that had been building inside of me my whole life, fierce and divine. With a mighty roar I cut the head from the being. His sword had barely touched the earth when I grasped it in a forward roll. I came up running with two swords in hand. I ran at the other approaching shinigami. I now had *two* swords." Hachimantaro pointed to the hilt above his left shoulder.

"Hunters are proud beings immune to pain and suffering as we know it. Some would say that the divine, those spirits that have never lived, are courageous, but I have learned to scoff at this. Courage can only be possessed by those that are intimate with fear, not those born without it. The Greeks at Thermopylae; Queen Boudicca's rampage against the Romans; the last charge of the Australian light horseman; the Americans, British and Canadians storming the beaches of Normandy on D-Day—these are men of courage. All of them possessed the spirit of samurai even though they were not Japanese or even Asian. Every one of them had hopes and dreams. Every one of them had business that they had left unfinished within their homes and within their hearts. That is courage. The hunters, good or evil, do not know courage because they are immune to fear ... but they are not strangers to self-preservation." He took another long pull from his tea.

"I rushed them and they retreated. I had killed their brother with a mortal weapon, and now I had an immortal one as well. I cursed them as they disappeared. When I came back from my battle trance—and strangely it was calm instead of a rage—I felt a new wave of power in me. In this new state I wandered and fought all manners of beings for a very long time. With every kill my power grew, and so did my power over the physical realm. Many times they came for their brother's sword, but never were they even remotely successful."

Darkmind held onto every word as he occasionally sipped his tea.

Balzola likewise seemed intrigued, even if the meanings of the words were possibly lost on him.

"One day, Darkmind, I felt a new wave of energy enter me. It was refreshing and youthful. I contemplated the source and discovered that someone was trying to contact my spirit. I approached and was startled to discover that I had become a legend of sorts. A young lad was praying to me! Can you believe this? I was no god!" His voice suddenly became softer. "But here was this lad asking me to show him honour and the path of righteousness. I was touched, and at the time my ego was elated. I whispered to him in his dreams to be strong and to walk the path of righteousness, and he did. He was not samurai but was from one of the ninja clans. When the hunter came for him, I struck it down too and handed the ninja that hunter's sword. He joined me. Since then there have been several more. Some of them have been able to acquire weapons beyond their earthly blades. As they say, though: many are called but few are chosen. Those you see around me are the bulk of those who have survived the wars. Our numbers are few, and few call to me anymore. More tea?" Hachimantaro asked suddenly.

"I am fine, thank you." To Darkmind's side, Balzola put a hand over his cup as well.

"The story that Bali tells me about you intrigues me a great deal. There are very few stories that I am aware of regarding the acquiring of weapons such as yours or mine. She did not share many details, but I would ask you more. If we help you, you will either need to do something for us, a favour of sorts, or join our cause. This may be a greater burden than you realize, for if you choose not to join us, you may find that when the favour is asked, we are not even friends anymore. I would still expect you to do the task asked of you at the time, however. So you will need to decide whether you will join us or swear to help us sometime; I will leave that decision up to you." Hachimantaro nodded as he finished speaking.

5

"Can I learn to use this sword? It seems heavy and awkward." Darkmind was still very confused.

Hachimantaro made a gesture with his hand, and two old men approached the inquisitive cloaked soldier. The first fell onto his hands and knees before Darkmind and began to measure the sword with a string. He seemed very careful not to touch the weapon. The second approached him with a small, elongated bundle.

"Consider this a small gift," Hachimantaro said as the second old man unwrapped a dark silk cloth to reveal a samurai sword about the length of his arm. It was a much smaller weapon than the one Darkmind had taken from the hunter.

"It will be much easier to wield. At one time it belonged to a very special person who shared a very complicated understanding of life with me. I wish that you carry it with you for now. It will not be as bulky or awkward, and you will find it is much lighter than your other weapon. It is called Black Dragon." The old man that was measuring the longer sword got up and left at a jog. "He will retrieve a sheath that will fit that one as well. It will not be an exact match, but it will do until he is finished making you a proper one."

"I can't repay you," Darkmind said in awe as he inspected the black-handled, lighter weapon. It had dragons carved into the blade.

"Do not worry about that right now; you will decide whether to join us or to owe me that future favour. We will have an understanding, agreed?"

"Agreed," Darkmind responded firmly.

"You have lived before." Hachimantaro stated.

"Excuse me?"

"We were not always friends, Darkmind. In fact our previous relationship was very complicated, and we fought against one another as often as we fought side by side. When I first discovered you approached my sanctuary, I thought that this was a trick and that you had come to try to kill me."

"What?"

"Do not be alarmed, but you have lived before."

"I have?" Darkmind's mouth was ajar.

"It was a long time ago, but we knew each other well. We were not friends, but we had a mutual respect and an understanding. This is not the subject I want to discuss right now, however. The point is that when you remember, you will remember how to use the hunter's sword. As you gain power, the weight will not seem so significant."

Darkmind sat dumbstruck. He looked over at Bali for a sign that what was being told to him was some sort of trick. She met his eyes and smiled at him. He felt his insides flutter as she nodded that this was true. The fluttering had more to do with the smile than the answer.

"The next while we will spend training you, but it will be extremely difficult. You will be guided on journeys to try to discover your past and remember before it is too late. You will be taught to heal." Hachimantaro pointed to the dog bite on Darkmind's arm. "And you will also be taught to meditate in this realm to prepare you for the time of punishment."

"What is the time of punishment?"

"Are you cold?"

"Yes."

"This will become unbearable before it becomes better. There will be pain as well. You will feel the pain of rigor mortis as your body dies on a cellular level. Then you will feel the insects tear into and through you. You will also feel the sting of acid as your body starts to decompose. It is a long, painful process. In the end I cannot say that the pain ever goes away, but it becomes somewhat tolerable when you are nothing more than a skeleton in a coffin. Some gather energy and power simply to alleviate the pain."

"What about cremation?" Darkmind was horrified. The black blade rested in his hand, temporarily forgotten.

"Are you to be cremated?"

"No."

Hachimantaro let out a gentle laugh. "Well, if you would have chosen that path, then ... let's just say it is painful during the process. They scream for a very long time, and the sound, if you have heard the spirit cry, does not leave you quickly. This I know from those who have been burnt as they screamed out to others and even described the pain. They say the fire rips into you and around you without a care in the world for your well-being. It consumes you and eats away layer upon layer with no sense of urgency. This process leaves very few here. We are not so sure why the earthbound generally leave after being cremated and have debated this often. No one who is burnt and leaves is ever seen again. It is believed that somehow they are destroyed. The screams are long and are unbearable to be around.

"Some cultures leave remains to nature. These seem to be some of the more gentle ways. Stands in trees or the casting into the ocean leave one with a feeling of oneness. Those eaten by wild animals have it the best of all. They become as one with the new host or hosts afterwards and gain many of their powers. Of course the meal itself and the digestion are not so pleasant, but the process is over much quicker."

"How come nobody living knows this?" Darkmind asked almost panicking.

"But they do, Darkmind, they do. Any culture that has studied the afterlife knows that it is important to preserve the body as long as possible. Basic cultures did not know how, and so they left gifts to be given for the spirits in the after world during their journey. More advanced cultures mummified their dead, and modern ones embalm them to give the spirits as much time as possible to complete their journey."

"What journey?" Darkmind was far from calm.

"The journey that all must take."

"I'm on a journey?"

"Yes, you are, Darkmind." There was a macabre smile on Hachimantaro's face as he said this. "We are all on a journey. For some, those who go towards the light, the journey takes but a moment. For others it never seems to end."

Darkmind looked over at Balzola and imagined for a moment the pain that he must have suffered as he decomposed slowly, as he was eaten by insects, as he was chained to a floor unable to move. He then suddenly wondered at what must be the disappointment of a suicide. To be released from life only to discover that pain hadn't left you at all. Hadn't Bali said that suicides were often earthbound?

As the old man returned, Darkmind tucked the dark sword known as Black Dragon into his belt beneath his cloak, the way that some of the samurai sitting nearby were wearing theirs. The old man bowed and presented the sheath to him. Darkmind nodded back and accepted the sheath and belt. He managed to slide the sword into the sheath from his sitting position without too much physical strain. He was surprised at how well it did in fact fit.

The sheath was completely black and unassuming. This would help hide the weapon from any unwanted eyes. It would not give him the advantage necessarily of intimidating other entities that might wish to bully him, but he would learn to use the other blade before he left the sanctuary of this place. He left the sheathed weapon in front of him and pulled his cloak tight.

He was feeling very cold. He also noticed his limbs were aching slightly. He wondered if his mind was playing tricks on him or if the time of punishment was entering its more interesting phases.

It moved like a snake, swift and fierce, back and forth, rapidly through the wet grass. Its motion was like that of a fish, water effortless and lightning quick. It carried itself with great confidence, yet it somehow appeared unassuming.

It looked more like a worm than a snake. It had no head, simply a front end that led it forward. Its body was fleshy pink with a thin, clear skin that revealed arteries and veins. It dripped mucus filth into the path that was woven through the grass. A very small earthworm-like tip bent extremely out of each end's movement before the body shifted towards the other direction.

Over headstones and short stone walls it swam. Occasionally, it would leap and dive into the earth only to reappear a few moments later out of the ground several meters away. It moved with speed and with purpose.

The two lions, which were known as shishi, could barely react as the creature sped towards them. One of them leaped and threw his paw over the worm. He was too slow and missed completely. It had burrowed into the earth at the last moment with an impossible speed. It tore through the ground and leapt out on the other side of the complex.

It was a testament of fearlessness that this beast would choose the front gate to enter Hachimantaro's sanctuary. It had no fear, however; it had a mission and it would not fail. The scent of its prey was close and brought forth the hunger that was hard to sate. The graveyard was supposed to be immune to hunters, but there were some creatures, older than time itself, that hunted before mankind had spirits. These beings were from a time before the idea of a treaty was something that could even be comprehended or understood. In the quest for power, nowhere was completely safe for anyone or anything. There would always be something stronger, faster and more ruthless that simply needed to feed.

Deals were often struck. Powerful beings exchanged mass amounts of energy, information, knowledge or goods for deeds or offered future services in a bartering system that was often composed of tasks both owed and completed. The worm too had a price.

Older than the gods that mankind called upon, the worm knew no fear. It had nothing to be afraid of, for it couldn't be killed—and it had never lived.

The Shishi screamed in rage. All heads tilted up at once, knowing immediately that something was amiss. With his left hand Darkmind held onto the new sheath that wrapped his weapon. It was a natural reaction from years of combat and predeployment training. He was not always as afraid as he had been since he had died. He had considered himself a brave man in life not so long ago.

He felt the pain of a lightning bolt strike him in the back of the head. A scream ripped from his chest that he would not have known was possible. The whites of his eyes filled with blood, and pain exploded from inside of his skull.

Despite its impossible size, the worm burrowed into the back of his head and struggled fiercely to gain more ground, oblivious to the man's screams. Darkmind could feel the creature gain purchase. He knew that something dark and foul had entered him and was destroying him. The scream of pain did not leave his lips as he staggered to his feet. He tried to look outward for the coming of aid, but his hopes were crushed by what he saw.

The ground exploded everywhere as the undead ripped from beneath them. If they were physical beings, they would have been the zombies of the movies that he used to watch as a teen. They were not zombies, however, because they had no physical substance at first; they seemed to become more solid with each passing moment.

Everywhere the samurai drew weapons with exploding speed.

With his free hand he grabbed onto the impossibly large tail of the slime-dripping worm. His fingers struggled with the ooze to grab hold as he dug with his nails and spun in circles, screaming. Small worms started to explode out of his skin everywhere with eruptions of pus and unclean blood.

Monstrous blue beings appeared throughout the clearing with large spears. The weapon, known as a naginata, had a six-foot shaft with large sabre-like blades on the ends of them. These beings wore rough, mean pieces of traditional armour, battered and beaten with age. They looked like oversized samurai warriors themselves, but with blue skin and wild blue flame manes of hair upon their heads. Their eyes were sheets of ice.

He continued to scream even as the carnage began. He fought for self-preservation and a need to end the pain. He hugged the sword close to his body with his left arm. He cursed whatever whimsical gods he had once believed in under his breath.

Swarms of beetles erupted from the earth behind the undead. Some flew and some slithered, but they were all intent on killing everything before them. The roars of the lions in the distance became cries of pain, and one of their screams ended abruptly.

He saw one of the large spears rip through Balzola and fling him into the air as blood flew from everywhere. The jester's face was a mask of horror as the being spun and lopped off his head. The undead spectres ripped the flesh from his body before he had even fallen to the ground.

Bali tried to cover her head with her arms as flying insect shapes of all sizes tore her apart piece by piece. An arrow ripped through her, followed by another. She screamed as several of the undead clung to her legs with teeth and claws, ripping the clothing from her body. Only barely able to care through the pain, Darkmind saw one of the decaying men entering her from behind as he started to rape her. Others tore the remnants of her beautiful dress from her body. She fell forward onto her arms and knees as the being pumped madly. It was laughing so hard its lower mandible fell off. *Certainly she has the power to defend herself! Is she startled so completely that she cannot even escape?* Darkmind wailed inside his mind as he saw her head pulled from her body. The spine was attached to the once beautiful woman's face, which was now an inanimate mask of sheer horror.

As he spun he saw the unseen archers now hurtling rusty missiles into the survivors. Darkmind dropped the great sword from the valkyrie. His left hand now joined the right in trying to remove the parasite. He continued to spin as the creature pulled itself further into the back of his skull. He tried to keep his feet.

The archers were skeletons with strips of meat and pieces of hair clinging to their bones. Half-rotting scalps clung greasily to the heads of these distance fighters. Sinew and muscle, which did still exist, were pulled taut as the archers moved chaotically, throwing volleys into the samurai, their servants and the guests.

Arrows and insects tore through them. Blue demons rained down upon them with sharp, pitiless steel. The two men with the World War II uniforms took one of the lumbering creatures down together, having rushed into the space to aid their master. Darkmind watched as their limbs were ripped from the bones and cast aside for the growing melee of feasting and scratching hordes. He could not distinguish their screams from anyone else's—or from his own.

Hachimantaro was wounded badly. He had lost one arm above the elbow and had half a dozen arrows protruding from him, with bugs clawing all over him. Several corpses from the undead lay around him, and at least one of the blue beings had been killed. A second one was on its hands and knees, vomiting out blackish red blood from a chest wound.

"Run, Darkmind!" he screamed. "There is no coming back from this!"

The thought was beyond unsettling. Everything that he was watching was another power struggle in an incomprehensible realm. Beings were feasting upon one another to increase their own strength and omnipotence.

There is no coming back. There was no afterlife for the afterlife.

It was the most disturbing of thoughts; for all of his years alive, there had always been the idea of an afterlife. It was a sort of backup plan. Even the idea of hell and the damnation of fire for all of eternity held some sort of allure to him. In one way or another, for good or for bad, he would continue to exist. Death was just the beginning of something else altogether.

Now as he witnessed the destruction of the allies he had managed to collect, he feared what waited. Beyond this immeasurable pain existed a deeper level of permanent suffering or an end altogether. He panicked. The end he could handle; it would be over and he would be free from this meaningless existence. If on the other hand this was just the beginning of whole new levels of torture, like that which he was currently experiencing, he needed to escape. He could not risk it.

The last few samurai were being ripped apart in front of him. There was no way that they could survive this onslaught. The undead raped the lower part of Bali's torso as they feasted upon her. They would grow rich off of her ancient and powerful energy.

"*I come.*" The voice was both familiar and alien. He realized that his mind had screamed for the wolf. He realized that this was in fact a way out. He was not sure if it would work or not, but he had to try. Maybe the wolf could destroy the worm? Maybe the worm could not go on the journey with them? Except for the feasting of the worm inside of his head, he seemed to have been wounded by the other creatures very peripherally if at all. He had been the one chosen to feed this worm, and everything else had left him alone.

As the mist swirled, Darkmind saw. Even through his strained eyes and even beyond his screams, he saw the final moments of the great Hachimantaro. The samurai was torn apart, and his body was fought over by creatures behaving as if they were starving. He was a great prize, this son of the war god. It belittled him to not have had a nobler ending. At least he had fought and died beside his friends and with his weapons in his hands. For the soul of a samurai, there could be no greater death.

He felt the fur between his fingers. He felt that the worm was no longer inside of his head or had at least stopped inflicting new pain upon him. He felt a dull, cold hurt though that radiated pain beyond measure. He stopped screaming and started to whimper, a broken man. In life he had been the strong one. He was a rock of fearlessness some had told him. They had been mostly women, held in his sweaty arms after a desperate, needy, passionate encounter in those years between his two significant relationships. They were mostly cheap women, as lost to him at the time as he was to them. He had been the strong one, they had said.

He pulled his face against the running animal and sobbed like a child. He had liked Bali and even the eccentric jester Balzola. He had dreams and hopes beyond measure as he had listened to the words of Hachimantaro. In this strange new land, he had been most afraid to be alone. Now without the long sword, which had been with him from the beginning and had seemed like a silent friend, he felt more alone than he had ever felt before.

He thought for a moment to return to the mosque and the old man that had shown him kindness. He dismissed the idea because he remembered the hunter that waited for him there. He did not want to make a decision. He decided to surrender to the spirit of the wolf once more and let it carry him where it would. He wondered if he could stay on its back forever, safe and somewhat warm.

These too will pay, that distant voice in his head stated with pitiless hate.

There was something else that he focused on and became aware of. Something was pulling on him, demanding his attention. He became curious through his misery and his pain, and he let the wolf carry him in that direction. Once more he began to lose the ability to witness the journey as he fell into a state not so dissimilar to unconsciousness.

Even in that state, though, he wept.

6

His head hurt and he was cold. He rose from one knee and tried to get his bearings. Where was he? Who was he? Why was this happening to him?

The room he found himself in was dark yet strangely familiar. A humming noise came from the corner. He looked over and saw through the darkness that it was a freezer, and he suddenly knew where he was. He was back home in the garage.

Technically it had stopped being his home some time ago. He lived on his own now with Shelly—or that was where his mail went anyways, and that was where he paid the rent when he was overseas.

Under this roof, though, Mom had fed him cookies, and Dad had read newspapers and filled his head with half useful trivia. Under the ash tree in the back yard was where Sammie, his childhood best friend, was buried.

There in the corner was the dog house that he had never let his parents throw away. Out of love for him they had kept Sammie's less than aesthetically pleasing home for over ten years. A few tools had made their way into the doghouse's doorway. His dad had probably placed them on the freezer after some minor household or yard repair and intended to put them away later. His mom had then probably moved them when she had taken something out of the freezer to thaw for dinner. It was an old ritual that spanned as far back as he could remember.

The garage was tidy in its own way but held a lot of clutter. Every year his mom got his dad to organize it enough so she could park her car inside on the coldest of winter days. It never lasted long, though. Like almost everyone else in Canada, they had too much *stuff*.

He looked over at his hockey net against the wall. He had had that net for a very long time. His dad used to play goalie and let him shoot the rubber ball at him for an hour or so after dinner when he had time. On weekends it would get dragged onto the street and become part of an epic game of street hockey. Kids from all over the neighbourhood, even some of the girls, would come and play. Those had been some of the best times of his life.

A dartboard was above the freezer with a half dozen darts nonchalantly stuck into it. Nearby was a poster of the hockey broadcaster Don Cherry wearing one of his famous plaid suits. Beside all of the bottles for recycling were his golf clubs. They were leaning up against his dad's. Both of the sets sat inside a little red wagon that he had pulled around religiously as a child.

He saw the room through eyes that had never seen it before. His parents still saw him as a little boy, and the collection of items honoured his very existence. They also loved him more than he had ever realized. His mom had always seemed like such a nag. *Don't drink and drive; that girl's been around the block; you should give Angel a call; keep it easy on the junk food; come to church*—these statements had not been meant to torture him but were testaments of her love.

His dad on the other hand had always just raised that one eyebrow over his newspaper. He too worried about his son, but it was more important to him that he was the cool parent than anything else. A part of Darkmind smiled at this epiphany for a moment.

He held his hands over his face after a time, and tears came swiftly. His parents were going to hurt so much. They had paid the biggest price possible in a land of freedom and democracy. They had stood proudly behind their son, and even though they were filled with fear for him, they had sent him off to war. In their hearts neither wanted to see him go, but they would not oppose him. They would support him.

And so he went, to a land he had never learned of in school before September 2001 to fight an enemy that had pledged to destroy him, his family and their way of life. He had gone because fellow Canadians and thousands of other people, mostly American, had been killed in the two towers of New York City by terrorists trained in that faraway land. That land was the very ground that had blessed the King of Islamist Terror by giving him men and women, by making weapons deals with him and providing sanctuary for he who spilled a Westerner's blood.

Those same men would provide sanctuary for the Chechens who had planned or escaped the massacre in the Russian school in Beslan, where 186 children were slaughtered and some 150 teachers and parents were tortured and killed. The King of Islamic Terror would say that this was a practice run for what was coming to the West. This king, a coward born, was known for his patience. He had never made such a promise that he did not keep.

So Darkmind had gone to fight in the desert, for that was the front line for the King of Terror. It was a new age of evil unprecedented, and the public were for the most part apathetic. They wondered why the soldiers were there. The events of 9/11 were so far away and so very long ago for a fast food nation to remember, and some even claimed that it happened in the United States and that the Canadians killed and the fact that it was the *World* Trade Center—these were just useless factoids, and those radical Muslims were probably good guys and Canada should leave them alone.

The Beslan school massacre had taken place in Russia, to Russian people, so why should they care? Who cared about the subway or dance club explosions in other places of the world? The Internet executions of aid workers or the bombings of school children who only wanted to read and write because their families knew in their hearts and minds that someday that would bring them food? *Who gives a fuck?* the public asked, or at least most of them. *Not our war, not our problem and not our business.*

Sure, they had learned since the seventies not to be mean to the soldiers and to be "supportive," but they had no problem running their mouths about events in which they obviously had no idea. He wondered how that was being supportive. It reminded him of the redneck kids he knew in school who were racist as hell but always followed it up by saying, "But I'm not racist; one of my best friends is black."

They lived in a dream land where women had rights, where children ate and where gunshots and explosions were rarely heard. They had forgotten that at one time all they had known was war, and it had been necessary to preserve that dream and to make it a reality. Now in a land so foreign to all of them, this king and his kin had declared war on them and vowed to wipe them off of the face of the earth, and it didn't matter to them whether or not they thought he was a good guy, or misunderstood, or simply needed a few good hugs. If they were patient enough, Pakistan maybe, sooner or later they would get their hands on nukes and then they could truly do the service of god and eliminate the infidels, bringing the kingdom of Allah to the land of the Earth.

His logic had holes in it, but he was still young enough in some ways to be radical about his beliefs. The one thing he had learned, though, was that the more he learned about the situation, and the more he experienced and did, the less black and white it really seemed. At least he had been there, though. Those who had an opinion based on television and books were the biggest fools of all. He had seen the reporters write from the safety of coffee shops out of KAF (Kandahar Air Field) "reporting from Afghanistan."

There were others like him, people who would fight and people who would support those fighters because they could not do so themselves. While some hid their fear in conspiracies of oil and world domination, others acted. The world had changed, and people either knew it or tried to continue normally in denial.

He had given up so much to join the army. It was the only thing that his heart had told him to do, and his heart needed to be made right. His parents and sisters had stood by, afraid for his safety but aware that in a sense they too had been called. In their hearts, however, they only wanted him to come back to them safe and in one piece.

He tried to wipe the tears from his eyes with the back of his hand. He had known in his heart when he had boarded that plane that he was not coming back. Something had told him that he would die and that his parents and sisters would be okay. Here he was, however, back in a place that some part of him believed he would never see again and concerned about those he had told himself would be okay. The sacrifice they must now make for their country with public grief and heart-wrenching loss was probably a far greater cross to bear than his. If they could know what was happening now to their precious brother and son, then it would be all the worse still.

"What are you doing here?" a sweet-sounding woman's voice asked.

He had not noticed, but the garage door was open into the house. His parents often did this in the summer to try to pull a cold draft in from the garage. There in the doorway stood the silhouette of a woman that he did not recognize.

She looked familiar. He realized right away it was because she looked very similar to his mom's sister, his aunt. She also looked a lot like the older of his two sisters.

"Who are you?" he asked.

"I am your great grandmother, whom you never met. Your mother called me here just now." Her voice was kind and soothing.

"Are you like me?" He meant an earthbound ghost, and she seemed to understand the question.

"No," she answered calmly. "I am not earthbound, but your mother's faith allows me to come at this time. Someone from your regiment has arrived, and they have just found out. Your mother's faith is being tested. She prayed for you every night."

He didn't know what to say, and so he paused for a very long time as she waited.

"I'm so confused," he finally said, misty eyed.

"Most of the earthbound are, but you seem quite aware."

"Why is that? Why is this happening to me?"

"There are many parts to a person, but I will explain to you what little I know about the process of death." She looked at him lovingly and gave him a gentle smile. "If one has lived a balanced and complete life and has no great unforgiven sins or karmic debt, they may join the great light and become one with everything. It really is all about love.

"If one has lived a life where they have harmed others and have a large karmic debt, then they will not be able to fit completely into the great light, so to speak." She walked down the few steps to the garage floor and came closer before continuing.

"Predominantly everyone has two spirits. You have a great spirit and a lesser spirit that coexist in almost flawless harmony. Your great spirit has lived many lives before while your lesser spirit has only lived this one. These are often referred to as the life soul and the death soul by tribal people who know of their existence." She reached out to him and held his hand. She started to guide him towards the steps.

"If you have lived a truly good life, then both souls are joined to the great light. The new soul, the lesser or *one life* soul, will join with the light forever and become a part of all things and everything, which is natural because that is where it came from originally.

"For the old soul, on the other hand, the soul of many lives, this may be simply a staging area before his or her next incarnation. It will leave the light when it is born into the physical realm again.

"So at death," she continued to patiently explain, "If the lesser soul is not good or suitable, it will be abandoned outside of the light. This then becomes a ghost. Without the great soul, this lesser soul will have almost no intelligence. If it is not harvested or collected immediately, this soul will wander or perform patterns in confusion without thinking, becoming weaker and weaker as energy is spent. It may get violent if these wanderings or patterns are attempted to be broken at all by outside forces, but otherwise it is a wasted life, like cast-away garbage."

"What use are the hunters, then?" he inquired with a voice that was finally becoming calm and steady.

"There is metaphor of farming that I will use now for this very complex matter." She paused a moment before going on. They had moved to the steps, going from the garage into the house, and she motioned for them to sit down together. "It is all about energy. The earthbound are harvested for immediate power consumption or to be brought into the darkness, or hell if you will. If they are carried to hell, they are harvested over and over again, forced to release energy. This is done by inflicting pain and terror, both real and imagined, and then manipulating the spirit to become strong again. In this way the soul will be used for all of eternity."

"There seem to be good hunters, though? Others call them collectors of the dead."

"They do a very similar deed by serving the great light. They harvest souls that they feel are not completely without merit and give them another chance. They offer realms of valour and honour, joy and love, passionate lovemaking and heartfelt laughter. It is a cult almost, of gods of every civilization ever known to earth. They believe that if the darkness gathers enough souls, it will become greater than the great light and swallow and destroy it. These kingdoms present themselves in as many different ways as possible to as many different people as possible. Jehovah, Gaia, Allah, Odin, Aphrodite, Father Spirit, Ganesh, the Virgin Mary, and many others are simply various interpretations for the servants of the great light. All of them are real, but in a sense they are an artificial light stepping in where the great light cannot. Some were once people who gained power and survived on the other side, and others were created from people's beliefs and prayers."

"What about someone like me?" he wondered aloud. "Why would I not be a candidate for either light?"

"I cannot tell you why your greater spirit did not go into the light. This happens sometimes, and it is a mystery to me. You are in a dangerous position right now. Most of the earthbound will be collected at the end of their life journey by the great light or by the servants of the dark light.

If they are not at the end of their life, because of an untimely death, the hunters will often not even bother with them. They will forget them instead of searching them out.

"The forces of light will collect any soul they think will bring energy to the great light. They believe in the coming of a great war, and so they collect those they deem to be worthy. The heroic in battle, the virtuous, the extremely charitable, musicians and poets, selfless civil servants, teachers, self-sacrificing mothers and fathers and many others that are not pure enough to join the great light but are far more good than bad nonetheless. Despite the fact that there is a battle going on, there is somewhat of an agreement of who belongs to which side. The selfish feed the darkness, and those that tried but came up short serve the purposes of the artificial light. In a sense it is an arms race in preparation for an eventual war."

She placed her hand on his knee. "You are in an extremely bad position, though," she continued. "The great light—for reasons unfathomable to anyone but maybe yourself, a close spirit guide or the great light itself—has rejected your higher soul. You are a beacon of extreme power, as are all the cognizant earthbound. The great light has spoken, though. The spirits of light have also rejected you now as well, or they would have taken you already. I would have thought that they would honour a soldier such as you, but it is a mystery to me. Perhaps on some level you have rejected them.

"The dark forces will lust after your soul greatly, though. It does not matter if the spirits of light want to claim you; if they have not already they have no claim, unless you plead the circumstances of your case and try to join one of them. For some reason those light beings reject you just like the great light did. For now, you will be hunted only by the dark ones."

"Fuck," he mumbled before looking over at her. "What are you, then?"

"I am part of the great light because both pieces of my soul joined it in death. My life spirit, the lesser spirit with my personality traits from my life, was separated for this occasion, and part of my greater spirit has been borrowed to give me back my earth memories and to give me awareness. It is common enough for aids such as me to be sent to deserving families who pray for help."

"You are alive now, then, or at least your high spirit is?" he asked, intrigued.

"Yes. The greater soul part of me is your younger sister. She feels extremely drained right now from that part of me, of us, missing from her, but she believes it is part of the mourning. She would seem to you as zombie-like, as one of the unthinking earthbound spirits if you were to see her now."

"Is she here? Can I see her?"

"I recommend that you do not. She is upstairs in her old bedroom with your other sister and the baby. They are extremely distraught, and the padre will be going up there to talk with them when he is done with your parents. The men from your regiment are also waiting until some of your family shows up. Relatives are on the way.

"Living people have higher spirits that will be aware of you and may try to communicate with you. There will also be spirit guides and manipulative beings trying to sway some of them towards a dark and selfish path. A being in that group will most likely betray you. I am not sure how it is that you are not destroyed, but I can only imagine that a hunter looking for you would think to start here."

"You said my sisters are with the baby?" He suddenly smiled, completely distracted from the conversation in which he was involved. "My sister had it?" He sounded excited. "She wanted it to be a surprise. Was it a boy or a girl?"

"It was a boy. He was born a few days ago."

He wanted to ask the name, but something held him back. He could have asked all of their names, because he had forgotten his sisters and parents as well. Somehow it brought peace in this moment for them, and for him, to remain nameless. He felt weary, but the news of the child brought him some measure of joy he could not explain.

"Why do I lose my memory? It almost doesn't fit with what you've explained."

"There seems to be a birth into the earthbound role. There is a time of confusion for the lucid, but it will not necessarily last. The important things will all come back as power is gained. Because you have both parts of your spirit, you will eventually remember your past lives and know as much as any being that has existed for thousands and thousands of years in countless different forms. What is troublesome for the high spirits that are earthbound is that they do not have their memory or their strength when they need it the most, which is at the beginning. They will usually be harvested before they gain their memory back.

"Now, if you gain power and use it as fast as you gain it, you will never remember more or be more powerful than you are now. And even if at some point you are the most powerful being in the universe, and you choose to use all of your power at once, you will be back to not knowing who you were and being relatively powerless once more."

"That makes sense to me: I need to try to gain power without spending it. How long have I been dead now?" He looked around at the garage as he asked her.

"A few hours."

"A few hours?" he asked, surprised. "That's it?"

"It has not been long at all. It hardly matters, though, for time is an illusion in which you are still trapped. That too will be easier to manipulate with an increase of power."

"A few hours? Fuck my life. That is the longest few hours I could even imagine! Why did I never experience this type of memory loss in life?"

"Living fuelled you, but even that was only minimal. Eating, breathing and sleeping are all ways to gather energy. Your spirit needs basic amounts of energy for maintenance, to keep it going. If a living person taps into more energy, they will often remember past lives, gain extra abilities and be able to see into the future. This is not common, but it is not uncommon either."

There was a loud knock on the door that he could hear from inside of the house. Whisperings and crying that he had not noticed before suddenly became apparent. He recognized the voices of an aunt and uncle. His mom started to wail loudly now.

"Soon there will be too many people here, and a curious entity may wander in. Reporters and friends will come, and something attached to someone will betray you. It is too dangerous. I can leave with you for a little while, for it will be conducive to your mother's praying, but we must go now."

"Where would we go?"

"You need to say good-bye to your fiancé, Shelly. It should give you peace and a sense of closure. Trust me."

7

The dresser was cluttered. Cosmetics were lined out chaotically from one end to the other. A vase sat on the far end of the counter with a half dozen roses, which were starting to wilt. Candle plates collected the dripping black wax that formed the base to several thick, lit candles, placed sporadically amidst the chaos. An ashtray with several cigarette butts in it also held a burning stick of Nag Champa incense.

The window was partly open, allowing a strong, warm breeze to blow into the room. The thin white curtains fluttered across the framed vintage painting *Tournee Du Chat Noir* by Theophile Steinlen. A large bed held several pillows, and a crumpled, unmade duvet covered in black satin. The foldout closet door was partly ajar, and various clothing items lay scattered on the floor of the room. The bulk of the discarded clothing, however, lay on a red armchair in the corner by the bathroom.

The mirror of the bathroom reflected back into the bedroom the flames of several more candles that burnt inside. This flickering light revealed that the room also lacked organization. A partially eaten piece of pie sat on the vanity and could be clearly seen from the bedroom. Apparently it was the towel on the floor that prevented the door from closing all of the way.

His fiancé sat at the end of the bed with her head down and her elbows on her knees. Her long hair hid her face, and he was not sure if she was crying or listening deeply to the meditative world music that drifted into the room from outside the closed bedroom door. She wore only a black bra and some sweat pants that she liked to sleep in or wear just around the house.

Her big toe made slow circles in the carpet and seemed to be the only part of her that was moving. He could barely even see her breathing as she sat there in the semi-darkness. He looked over at the nightstand and was surprised that the picture of them was not there.

A part of her seemed to move slightly out of her body and look at him.

This vision of her did not look sad or distressed in any way, but it did not look happy either.

"I am sorry," she said to him. As she spoke, the shape of a woman floated across the doorway in the bathroom. It looked like a woman about her age but with shorter, dark hair. Even though she was only visible for a moment, he knew this to be a spirit protector.

"No, I'm sorry, honey," he said. "I'm afraid I've ruined everything."

"You do not understand," Shelly responded. "I'm sorry for cheating on you."

He looked down at her hand, resting on her head over her hair, as he felt the ache in his chest. He saw that the ring was not there. He pulled his cloak tightly around him to prevent the chill, and so that his arm could cover the throbbing wound deep inside of his chest.

"How many times?" he heard his own voice ask sounding flat and dead.

"I don't know. But it was mostly with the same guy."

"Mostly?"

"I was lonely."

"Who?"

"No one you would know. Mostly a guy at work named Nate."

"Who else?"

"The army sent a counsellor. I didn't instigate that at all, but I didn't resist very hard, either."

"Anyone else?"

"A couple from the bar. I was drunk and didn't let my friends know I had given my number. I pretended to go home to take your call and met them after."

"Didn't that higher part of you try to talk you out of it?"

"You're speaking to the higher part. I am telling you what happened so you know. There are no secrets after death and no true secrets or successful lies during life, either. The physical world is an illusion that only the weakest and most vile take literally."

"So you do not agree with her actions?"

"They are still our actions collectively, but my voice is hardly listened to. If it had been, I would have won when I suggested we steer clear from you in the first place."

"What've I ever done that makes you say that?"

"You left for one. You died for another. She was always a liar since an early age, you knew that, yet instead of accepting her, you were inconsistent and sometimes cruel. You think all of the horrible things you did are a secret as well? I saw this coming. I saw it all and warned her. Now she will be consumed with guilt as she goes and sees your family with another man's cum still dripping from her. She will pretend to grieve but she will not. It will be guilt. You know how she will cope with this guilt? On her back. She will become such a spectacle that your own mother will eventually find out that she always was, and is, a whore."

"All women are whores, I hear."

"Where did you hear that rubbish fool?"

"It doesn't matter."

"Well if more women listened to their higher selves, there would be fewer whores, wouldn't there?"

"The world needs a few good whores, I think. Sometimes a man just needs a whore." His words were laced with sarcasm.

"A man is programmed biologically to spread his seed to as many women as possible, to create as many children as possible in the physical realm. A woman can only carry one seed every nine months and must care for that one for far longer, which is why a woman is biologically programmed to hold out for the highest bidder," she stated.

"Highest bidder? Like a fucking auction? " He paused for a moment as he collected his thoughts. "Listen, your logic is all fucked up. I sure as hell wasn't spreading my seeds to the masses, and she sure as fuck wasn't still supposed to be on any auctioning block! I gave her my grandmother's ring!"

His movement was swift and merciless. He backhanded the spirit and rocked her head rearwards. Out of the washroom flew the protector spirit with a hell fury rage. She was clutching a knife of sorts. He flicked Black Dragon out from his hip and buried it through her shoulder. She screamed and fell down.

His great grandmother, her presence suddenly remembered once more, pulled at his back, screaming for him to stop. He felt stronger. This was partially due to the attack, but he also realized that even before he came here, he had been feeling more and more strength. His family's prayers and thoughts were giving him power. Now the violence against the two spirits boosted this power a little, even as he expended some of that energy.

"This is not the way!" his great grandmother screamed as she tugged on him. He paused for a moment and looked at the room. He kicked the door and swung the sword out across the dresser before turning around and leaving.

In the physical world his fiancé was suddenly thrown out of her meditations of self-pity. The wind through the window seemed to pick up for a moment and slammed the bathroom door miraculously over the towel that was lying there. All of the candles on the dresser extinguished themselves at once as the vase shattered and fell. The hairs on the back of her neck stood straight up. She knew in that moment that he had been there. He had been there and he had discovered everything.

She had felt a slap across her face so great that it had rocked her sideways. The room seemed dark with anger, and for a moment she was very afraid. She told herself that it was just him, though, and because she did not respect him in life, she hardly was able to fear him very much in death.

He walked quickly down the dark street with sword in hand. He knew the man's name was Nate. He could sense which direction he was in for there was a trail of sorts, of energy from her bedroom into the dark urban metropolis. He knew this trail would lead him to the man.

His limbs hurt and felt afire with cold, and the dog bite felt infected and festering, but there was another feeling as well. He felt raw power coursing through him, and he was drunk with it. In a very real sense it wasn't a lot, but it was more than he had ever experienced in life.

The wounding of the guide had especially been fulfilling.

"Stop! This is not the way! This is not who you are! It was a mistake, I told you to come here!" His great grandmother pulled on him, trying to make him abandon his new quest of vengeance.

He ignored her and pushed forward. One of the mindless earthbound was staggering up ahead of him along the dark side of the street. His pace quickly led him up to the bearded ghost. As he passed by he swung the sword and cut the man's head off. The spirit dramatically spurted blood from the neck wound before slumping to the ground and fading altogether. He felt more power enter him from the killing.

"I cannot be here for this!" his grandmother chastised him as she floated away, most likely back towards his childhood home.

He squinted his eyes with determination and moved steadily forward. Resolve showed upon his face. He knew that every spirit he came upon between him and his prey would fall victim to his blade. Man, woman or child—it did not matter. He needed the strength to harm a living man. Even if it was his very final act, he was convinced that he would do it.

He became aware that he was strong enough now to hear the secret thoughts of the living.

His name was Natraj, but nobody except his parents called him that anymore. He was Nate to anybody who had met him after the third grade or to anyone who wanted to be acknowledged. This change was the first step of many in a metamorphosis that had helped him become who he was today.

It wasn't so easy being the only son from immigrant parents. He was embarrassed to bring people home; they would see that his mother wore a sari and that his father spoke with an accent, which to Nate sounded like that of a dirty rickshaw driver.

The black vintage Trans Am he now drove was purchased by his parents to replace a Jeep that was already two years old. It was the sixth vehicle he had gotten from them since he was seventeen years old. That meant on average he had been getting a new vehicle every two years. His two sisters and his mom would now share the Jeep while his dad would continue to drive his sputtering Oldsmobile.

It was important, his parents had realized, for him to fit in. He had helped them understand this as he had asked them for all of the latest brand clothes, technology and toys. They didn't understand at first why he needed nicer things than everyone else around him, but he convinced them that being a brown man in this new land left him with a very serious disadvantage indeed.

Nate's parents were relatively happy with their 29-year-old son. He had been a child with only one friend until he was in his late teens. He hadn't gotten any attention from girls and did poorly in school. He never really did much better in school, but when he shed 20 pounds of fat and his geeky friend, he had started to become popular. As long as he continued to make people laugh and buy them things, he would remain so.

He was a very expensive child, which meant that his sisters often went without so he could impress as many people as possible with bottles of Alize and Cristal. It was networking, he had told his parents. With great relief he had seemed to prove his point when he got the job as a bank teller. They were just happy that he would be helping them pay for things around the home like everyone else, but even what he did contribute failed to cover his own personal expenses.

Nate was constantly changing and adapting. He discarded friends as fast as he made them by trading up for cooler associates who liked his lavish lifestyle. Truth be told. though, as many of them were glad to be rid of him as he was of them. He was a guy that always had a bigger, faster and more important story. He was selfish and nothing more than a charismatic user, with ambitions only slightly greater than his ego.

He was the kind of guy that men who had made their own way in the world hated. He did not have calloused hands or even a basic understanding of real work at all. He was the first person to chip in and help—if the right people were watching—but the last person to anonymously do a good deed if no one was. He wore too much cologne, told too many questionable tales and did almost everything in a conniving and premeditated manner. He did things in such a way that it was near impossible, for anyone who saw through him, to confront him without it being socially awkward.

His greatest gift, if it could be called such, was that he could see weakness in other people. He was always there for the woman with low self-esteem, for in the end this was what was really important to him. He wanted the conquest of women and did it in the only way that he could. He chased after the stragglers, the struggling and the weak. He went for the girl who he could tell stuck her fingers down her throat after every meal. He went for the girl with the lazy eye. He went for the girl who was twenty pounds overweight, because he knew too well what that was like. He also went for the girl whose boyfriend or husband didn't give them enough attention or simply wasn't around. The only catch was that they had to be a believer in his stories.

The white furry dice bounced from the rear-view mirror as he cruised down the boulevard from another night of banging the soldier's girl. "Red

Rooster" by Alice in Chains played on his stereo, and the street lights slid across the front of his black hood as he geared the car up to take the next yellow light. Nate wore his sunglasses as he drove even though it was closer to dawn than it was to dusk. A piercing less than three weeks old could be seen above his jet black eyebrow. He figured that it showed people that he was a bit of a wild card, that he knew how to party and have a good time.

The night seemed darker than most. It wasn't because he wore the sunglasses; he wore them all of the time. It was because the bitch had been a real downer after she had gotten the call. She had answered the phone and then asked him if he could give her a ride. He was finished with her and was looking for a way out anyways, and so he told her he had things to do.

He had crushed out his cigarette on the dresser and pulled on his clothes before donning his leather jacket. She seemed like she was upset with him, but he didn't really care. There was another teller at work, a new challenge. The soldier's girl had cost him an ice cream cone, two lunches and a Led Zeppelin CD in order to sleep with her. She had been a real freak, and so he had kept her around. Maintenance on her had cost him two nights' worth of drinks at the club, one semi-expensive dinner, a Tiffany's heart pendent, and most recently a bouquet of roses. The seduction had taken him two weeks. The maintenance phase, as he liked to view it, had taken place over the span of a couple of months. She didn't seem to mind that he wasn't around except when he wanted to fuck her. She was a good plan B when everything else fell through.

He sniffed hard through his semi-decongested nostrils. The line of coke he had done when he had gotten into the car left him feeling pretty good. He worried a little bit though; he had never really meant to start using. A guy he knew had told him that coke was the fasted way to get a girl into bed, and he had been right. If a girl used coke, he could throw a little powder on a pillow and then do anything to them he wanted to as they leaned over to snort it. The best part was that every user he had ever met was in denial. They would tell themselves that they were just partying even if they ended up getting gang banged by Frankenstein and the seven dwarves. How much better would they feel about themselves when they looked into his dark eyes? He was a handsome stranger who only wanted to party with them because they were beautiful and interesting ... and oh, what a surprise, a little coke was suddenly on the menu as well.

He touched his right hand up to his nose tentatively before pulling it away to look at it. *Fuck*, he thought as he saw the blood there. It was definitely time to quit. He hoped he wouldn't get any blood on his clothes or inside of his car as he took the turn a few streets away from the house he shared with his family. If he got blood on the seats of his car, he would have to get one of his sisters to clean it up.

Strangely, the car started to sputter and choke for no apparent reason. He had never had a problem with the car before; it was in mint condition with a completely rebuilt engine. He was glad that he was close to home so that he could walk as the car started to die. He'd deal with a tow truck in the morning.

He managed to pull the car over to the side of the road before it came to a complete stop. He turned the key again after disengaging it and gave the car some gas. Nothing happened. The car made a grinding sound as it tried to turn over.

For some reason the hairs on the back of Nate's neck suddenly stood up. He looked over his shoulder into the back seat of the car, almost expecting to see someone there. It was the coke, he told himself. Coke made everyone paranoid, didn't it? He would wake one of his sisters when he got home and get her to google it for him. He would tell her that a buddy had told him that coke made a person paranoid, and he didn't believe him.

There was no one in the back seat. Of course there was no one in the back seat. He took off the sunglasses and threw them onto the dash. He sat back for a moment with both hands on the steering wheel, trying not to lose his temper.

He heard in the sudden silence the wind in the nearby trees starting to howl. He quickly opened the door and got out of the car. He did not want to get rained on.

He saw something out of the corner of his eye as soon as he closed the door to the Trans Am. He turned quickly and saw that nothing was there. He quickly looked the other way, sensing something was there suddenly as well.

"Burn!"

He thought he had heard a deep, demonic voice. It was not in his head. It had to have been in his head. No, he had heard it. No, he hadn't. His mind was playing tricks on him. The wind in the trees blew hard again, and he thought he felt a drop of rain.

The homes in this area were for the affluent. They were well-spaced apart with tall fences and lots of large leaf bearing trees. The houses that he could see from the curb had the lights turned off for the night as their lame owners tried to rest before another day's work. He suddenly felt very alone as he started to walk the few blocks home.

He heard something nearby and paused to listen. He realized it was a dog crying in a nearby doghouse on the other side of a fence. It was probably scared of the wind or wanted to be sleeping inside with its masters. He wished he had a dog with him right now—a pit bull like the dealer had. That would make him feel safer and give him status.

He glanced back and forth nervously as he walked. His eyes suddenly darted back to a shape between two trees. It looked like the shadow of a man. He knew it was a trick of his eyes, though. No one would be standing outside by himself in the dark. Too afraid to look away, he stared at the shape as his eyes tried to make sense of what it really was. He laughed to himself as he realized that it wasn't moving. Damn, that had scared him. Why was he so jumpy? It wasn't anything.

Then the shadow did move. It turned to the side and walked into the shadows of a large tree and out of sight. *Freak!* What kind of a weirdo would stand in the middle of the grass like that? He started to walk faster.

The wind picked up even more, and he found that he needed to lean forward to get moving at all; the gust was so strong that his foot even slipped. In his head he asked the guru for protection. In that moment he promised that he would burn a stick of incense when he got home. He knew deep down in his heart that he would not, however. He was pretty sure that God and the gurus could see this as well. He knew they would appreciate the sentiment nonetheless.

There was a loud crack as his face was slapped. His hand reached up instinctively and held his cheek. His mouth was open in a state of surprise because he could see plainly that no one was near him.

He started to run.

All around him he heard laughter. It was deep and ominous and did not sound very human. He made a promise to himself that he would never do blow again. He reminded himself in his panicked state that it was a tool. He had no business messing around with it. His parents thought that it was cute he was somewhat of a womanizer—as long as he married a nice virginal Indian girl at the end of the day. They would never accept the drugs, however. He would be in rehab or he would be disowned, only son or not, there would be no other way.

He lost one of his $300 dress shoes, but he dared not stop. He didn't care anymore if a neighbour saw him and he looked the fool embarrassing his family. He was in a state of panic. Something was wrong.

He was nearing home. He would cut through the Johnston's back yard and enter through his back door. It would bring him to safety 30 seconds sooner than the longer way around. The wind whipped him hard in the face as he started to move off of the sidewalk and into the grass.

He felt the air rush out of his lungs, and he fell forward as he became aware of a cold, piercing sensation go through his stomach. He felt his bowels release and the fluid running down his leg. He tried to get up.

A choking sensation crushed into his throat. In horror he realized he was being lifted from the ground. He could not breathe. It was all in his head—it had to be! Why then did he feel like his feet were off of the ground?

There was nothing in front of him. There was no one there. He heard a clicking sound and an inhuman laughter. He heard the wind and the leaves in the trees. He could not breathe. He felt the stabbing sensation through his stomach again and again. There was a crack as his neck snapped.

His high and low spirit started to leave his body and separate. His awareness saw a hideous-looking man with a burnt face and stone-cold eyes. There was a moment in his consciousness that he knew who it was in front of him.

The phone call and the need for a ride suddenly made sense.

He did not realize yet that he was dead, but he panicked as his lower spirit was hacked apart. His higher spirit tried to move upwards, but this too was attacked. He was in a state of disbelief. This was not supposed to happen! This was against the rules! He knew that he should have a protector spirit here as well. He sensed the guardian was already dead. His entourage of personal demons that had made him feel so invincible in life were gone as well.

He knew they were all dead.

As he received blow after blow, the being that had once been Nate ceased to exist on every layer and level that there was.

There was dead, and then there was dead dead.

Darkmind spun around in anticipation of a hunter. There was nothing but the wind. He realized that he was safe for the moment because this death, Nate's death, was before its time. He sensed he had broken a very fundamental law, though. He started to run. He didn't know what would hunt him now, and he wasn't sure he cared. He now had his revenge. He would now find the military councillor.

The police investigation was quickly completed in the days that followed. The case ended up being somewhat of an urban legend in the department for years. The 29-year-old male had apparently died of a heart attack caused by an overdose. He had stopped his car in a state of delusion and had initially decided to walk home. Maybe he had decided he was too far gone to drive?

He had apparently been experiencing an advanced state of delusion at the time of death. The look of horror on his face, even from photographs, caused police officers and medical examiners to have nightmares for years. *How terrifying must those delusions have been?* was the common question that came to investigators' minds.

Case closed.

The strange thing, however, the thing that got people talking, was that at least three dogs and a cat had coincidently died in the neighbourhood on that same night.

The Johnston family moved very shortly. They claimed the handprint mark in the tree—which only looked like a hand mark, of course, where the bark had peeled—was only part of the reason. The real reason for them moving was the death in which their neighbour had died in their back yard. That sweet little boy Natraj, who used to play on their grass and bring Indian treats for the smaller children in the neighbourhood, had become a drug addict and had died beneath their master bedroom's window.

Neighbours called in for months, complaining of dogs howling in the night. It was a mystery to the police. They would hear the howls as well when they first arrived, but these would often go quiet immediately. This made solving the problem a little tricky. They could not find anyone left in the neighbourhood who owned a big dog. All of the big dogs had died. This was a very large problem indeed, for the howls clearly belonged to larger dogs.

8

He pulled the cloak around him to keep the cold away. His limbs were stiff and his joints ached.

He could feel new energy pouring into him and knew that it was the power being given to him from a nation in mourning. Despite the recent expenditure, he felt strong. It was a murderous strength coupled with a disregard for what could become of him. In this state of anger, or self-pity perhaps, he had transformed from a fear-filled child to another predator in a sea of predators.

His left hand clutched the front of his cloak and pulled it closer yet. His right hand still held the brandished sword. A dark substance oozed slowly off of the weapon as he walked with the point downward.

"What are we going to do?" Lupa asked him as they walked along a deserted street.

Her name was Lupa. He was strong enough to hear her now.

"There is one more I need to kill," he told the wolf walking beside him. She was twice the size of her earth kin.

"This is a dangerous path. The fool you killed, he had done enough evil that even his great soul would have been rejected by the light. His soul belonged to the dark."

"So does mine, apparently."

"More so now." She padded along beside him, becoming his voice of reason. "There are those sworn to protect the living. They will come for you now. You have also robbed the great light the final decision for that which belongs to her, the higher spirit. Even the hunters know well enough not to harm the high spirit until it has been rejected."

He looked over at her with an expression that asked, *Really?* They both knew of the situation that had brought him the sword, the sword that he had now lost, in the first place.

"That high spirit should have offered him better council, and perhaps it would still exist," he answered.

The wolf did not respond for several long minutes, scanning back and forth for any coming threats as they made their way. "Where are we going?" she asked at last.

"I'm not sure. I feel compelled to move in this direction. I must follow this path. There are things we must do before the killings start. I do not remember, but I sense my path." He found talking to Lupa was calming him, and he had subtly shifted away from moving towards the military councillor's whereabouts. "Why have you not come to me before now, other than to help me move from place to place?" He asked after several long moments.

"You did not have the power to summon me. Even if you did, you did not try."

"Can you fight?"

"Can the sparrow fly? Can the salmon swim? Can the rain fall?" Her voice was that of a teacher and lacked any sarcasm.

"Was that you by the lake that time?" he asked remembering the fishing trip again.

"A friend of mine."

"Were there other times too?"

"Many."

"Like when?" he asked, intrigued.

"I bit you once."

"You did?" He actually started to laugh. "When?"

"When you were playing cards."

His laughter ended abruptly. He knew immediately about which incident she spoke.

Steve was supposed to be staying with his family, and he was supposed to be staying with Steve's. Almost every weekend they had spent time at each other's houses since they were ten. It would be a gamble that they figured was likely to work. Each set of parents trusted the other enough not to bother asking. There was almost an obligation of privacy that came along with their children's friendship and staying at each other's homes; the parents had never become close themselves but had remained respectful acquaintances.

Steve had just gotten his first car, an old Toyota Corolla. They all knew it would be a risk to get it out to the cabin because it always sounded like it would die. Over time it would prove to be almost unnaturally reliable however ... until the very end.

One of the other guys had a similarly unreliable van and would bring some of the girls. Darwin, his Sioux friend, would meet them there as well, but he wanted to drive his equally questionable bike. Darwin of course had sped past them on the way to the house. He had wanted to show off to the girls in the van, and so he passed them and fell behind over and over again. Every time he passed them, he gave them the finger, and his ear-to-ear grin could almost be felt through the dark-faced helmet.

It seemed to Darkmind like he was watching an old movie. He was a silent spectator to events that had transpired so long ago. It was Friday, he remembered.

He watched them arrive at Steve's parents' cabin. The sun was just starting to set, and frogs already sang into the growing darkness. Darwin leaned on the bike with his helmet under his arm. He was a dark-skinned teenager who always sported slicked-back, curly hair and a big grin. He was large for seventeen and was already over 200 pounds.

"What the fuck took you guys so long?" he asked sarcastically in a deep voice that sounded like more of a man's than a teenager's.

"Shut up and help us unload this shit," Steve answered cockily, his messy blonde curly hair bobbing with his head movements. He pulled out a bag of hotdog buns and threw them at Darwin. "You didn't carry any of this shit up here, Dar, so you can sure as hell help us hump it up the stairs!"

Darwin never stopped grinning as he put his helmet on the bike and freed up his other hand.

The living boy, who would one day be known as Darkmind, made eye contact with his Native American friend, gave him a secret smile and rolled his eyes.

"I saw that!" Steve said, although it would have been impossible for him to do so.

Before too long they had unloaded the liquor and the food from the vehicles even as a few other cars started to arrive and pull into the gravel driveway. Soon everyone had drinks in their hands and the barbeque was fired up. A medley of Metallica and AC/DC played on the stereo. The energy was high and positively buzzing. They were all thrilled, he remembered, to be together in a parentless environment with a place to sleep indoors. Weekends like these had been rare at the time for the underage drinkers. It was hard to find a comfortable place to party, and they had often ended up drinking around a bonfire somewhere, even during the winter months.

The boy walked through the house past wood paneled walls and towards the back door. The smell of cooking burgers and overly perfumed teenage girls greeted him as he slid open the door to the patio and stepped outside.

"Where've you been?" Angel asked with a shy grin as she put her arm around his waist awkwardly. Her blonde hair was pulled behind her ears, and her high cheekbones seemed accented by a large, toothy smile that glowed against her tanned face. Her thin, dark eyebrows gave her a look of nobility.

Neither of them knew if they were boyfriend and girlfriend yet, but over the last week they had discovered that they enjoyed kissing ... a lot.

"Just taking a leak." He smiled as he put his free hand on her back. The comment had sounded adult to him then even though the memory of it now made him feel a slight embarrassment.

The boy had felt elated at knowing that they would probably be having sex soon. He had only been with one girl, once, and it had been an awkward situation. She had had a lot of experience, and he had convinced her that he had his fair share too. When it came down to it, though, he didn't really know what to do. She had expressed her dissatisfaction openly. He had later felt both dirty and awkward. He was not sure how it was supposed to be, but had been pretty sure that it was not supposed to be like that.

Here was a chance at something a little better and hopefully a little more fulfilling.

Angel playfully punched him in the shoulder. "Can I get you a burger?"

The boy filled with pride in the way that she had offered. No one that wasn't related to him, other than maybe Steve's mom, had ever offered to make him food. "I'd like that," he said.

She smiled and stepped away to grab a paper plate and make him some food.

He knew she was trying hard. They both were.

"Wahoo!" Darwin raised his drink to the slowly appearing stars and yelled in joy. A nearby girl, a small brunette, echoed the chant and held up her drink. Someone turned the music up a little louder.

Beers were passed around, and in their teenage state they tried to talk louder than the person next to them in a peacocking manner. Some of them started to do shots of vodka, and a few of the guys started to wrestle in the living room. The boys figured that if they completely ignored the girls for a little while, the girls would like them even more.

They were all in that teenage stage of alcohol discovery, where the goal was to get as drunk as possible as quickly as possible. It didn't take them long because most of them had only been drinking for under a year.

Holes were burnt in the carpet by careless smokers and glasses were broken. Someone who didn't make it to the deck or the bathroom quickly enough vomited in the hallway. Another boy had his eyebrows shaved off and a Hitler moustache painted on in marker.

The night became a blur and was over as soon as it had started.

He woke the next morning as the bright, sunny day began to pour through the window and over the dead flies on the ledge beneath it. He could barely remember what had happened the night before.

He woke up beside her, beneath a musty-smelling quilted blanket in the spare room. She was in his arms, but they were clothed except for their shoes and socks. He looked at her and smiled to himself at her messed up dirty blonde hair and smeared make up. She seemed to sense that he stared at her. Intuitively she squinted open her dark, glistening eyes and looked at him with her face scrunched up.

"Hi," she said softly.

"Hi," he answered in a whisper. She felt so warm and alive inside of his arms.

The two of them decided to go for a swim. Before Steve's parents had sold all of their land, this had been a farm. Now they pretty much just owned a few acres around the old farmhouse and called it the cabin. They had running water from a well, but there was an old dugout on the back of the property that was there to catch rainwater. It was the remnant of a time before technology, where a farmer's livelihood could depend upon that very rainwater supporting his crops in the driest of times. Steve's dad still stocked it with trout in the spring to give him something to do if he got bored in the late summer. It was a beautiful and meditative pocket within walking distance from the old house. There were a few ancient fruit trees around the water and a little wooden dock that reached like a lonely finger into the micro lake. The long grass and the dip in the ground offered even more privacy as the pool became further invisible from the house.

They leaped into the water in their underwear, screaming even as his heart raced to see her in bra and panties. It was deep enough that they were forced to tread water and make wide circles with their arms. As they did this, they slowly neared one another in sudden silence. There were no words as they shared a very long moment of silence. Navy blue dragonflies hovered and buzzed above the water in search of prey. The dock made a hollow slurping sound as the motion from their jump into the water beat over it in waves. Despite these sounds and the singing of nearby songbirds, there was a hush of silence that came over them and felt just like a dream.

They slowly moved towards one another until they were only a foot or so apart. He hesitated a moment out of fear but realized that he was already committed. He made the move after his mind realised that there was nowhere left for him to run. She met him halfway.

Her wet lips brushed his, and he felt electric fire pour through him. Her hand cradled his face and he fumbled for her bra as their legs kicked to keep them afloat. She ended up having to help him; they were close enough that the garment landed on the dock. They kissed heavily and fumbled awkwardly with each other's bodies as they moved closer to shore where their feet could at least rest upon the bottom of the pond.

Afterwards they lay in the grass for a very long time, wrapped in the blanket that he had the foresight to bring. They used colourful beach towels as pillows.

He told her of his dreams to be a police officer someday. They laughed together when he told her how he had once wanted to be a priest when he was a kid. She told him she wanted to be a Hollywood actress. He didn't think that she was quite pretty enough, although she was beautiful in her own way to him, but he knew that she was well-respected in the drama club. The hours passed as they shared a lifetime of secrets on that afternoon beneath the sun and the white puffy clouds that would occasionally pass by. They both had a sense that they belonged together, that they were meant for one another, that they would always be together. Forever.

That night the boys dragged the kitchen table outside and lit it with candles. They pulled out the cards and started to play beer games until the night fell dark. They then decided to gamble.

Darwin pulled out a box of Cuban cigars that he had squirreled away for such an occasion. He handed one to the boy who would one day be called Darkmind. Angel sat on his knee, placing two newly poured drinks onto the table. The Smashing Pumpkins were playing in the background.

The blue coloured cards were faded from use and were thrown across the table towards players who made comments laced with pride and with cockiness. The light was dim, and they had to squint to see the cards sometimes, but they were content to be in the semi-darkness so that they could comment upon the northern lights dancing above their heads.

They started to play for nickels, and then it moved to quarters and finally to paper money. Darwin would place huge bets. He would be up everything and then be down to almost nothing over and over again. Steve was doing fairly well and was definitely up. Even with Angel as his good luck charm, though, the boy seemed to be just breaking even.

Steve had his girlfriend near him as well. She was a blonde curly haired cheerleader with smiling round cheeks and mischievous, sparkling blue eyes. Her fingers danced through the back of Steve's hair, which seemed to cause his chest to puff out. A pretty little brunette, whom Angel knew from drama class, sat on Darwin's knee, apparently not wanting to be left out. A couple of the other guys were part of the table as well and held cards either against the table or clutched close to their chest. Other people were either in the house or watching the game, or at least this round, from the sidelines.

"I'm out," Became the mantra of the young men around the table one after another, except for the three close friends.

"I will double that bet!" Darwin said loudly as Steve threw down some money.

"With what, dummy? You're broke!" Steve said, laughing at Darwin's uncustomary frown.

"Fuck you," he responded brooding.

"I take IOUs," Steve stated cockily.

"Okay." Darwin dramatically reached for the pad of paper and pen that were cast in the corner of the table. He scribbled something on it and tore off a page. He folded the paper in half and kissed it before slamming it down on the table.

"Now that's acting," Angel said into his ear loud enough for only him to hear.

"What's the bet? We need to know for how much," the boy asked.

Steve reached for the paper, and Darwin grabbed his wrist.

"Show him the damn paper," the boy stated authoritatively, trying to impress Angel.

Darwin released Steve's wrist while he pulled the paper towards him. He took a sip of the drink Angel had brought him as he rolled his eyes at his friend's bickering.

Steve looked for a moment down at the note, his eyes squinting in the darkness as he tried to read what was written. He suddenly spat his drink from his mouth. He bent over in extreme laughter as great as anyone had ever seen from him ever. His face turned red as he half stood, losing complete control and composure. His curvy blonde girlfriend sitting beside him was forced to stand as she was almost knocked from her seat. She had a confused look on her face from reading over Steve's shoulder what was written on the piece of paper, but she started to laugh nervously. Some of the people around the game started to laugh pretty hard from Steve's reaction, even though they did not know the source of his emotion.

"Fuck you, man," Darwin said stoically.

The boy shifted Angel slightly on his knee and reached for the paper. He turned it over in the hand that held the cigar and read it to himself. He had just taken a pull from the cigar and found himself spitting the smoke out as he too started to laugh uncontrollably and cough in discomfort. Angel laughed more at the fact that he was laughing than the content of the note.

Not wanting to be left out, one of the other guys took the paper from the boy's hand and unfolded it. This youth started to laugh hard as well, and started to tear up, but he was a little more composed than the others. The whole table was laughing now, including the spectators that didn't know what was going on. The people inside came out to the patio to find what they were missing.

"Fuck you, guys!" Darwin said again as straight-faced as when he had written the note in the first place. He crossed his arms across his chest. "That's a serious bet!"

"I'd say!" Steve said before everyone started to laugh even harder.

More than a few people were near tears now.

"Okay, Darwin." Steve laughed almost snorting. "But we have to match your bet."

With that the three friends still in on the round wrote the bet and their name beneath it. None of the other guys were still in, and so they watched with confused and sceptical faces.

A sharp pain suddenly erupted in his hand, and he dropped the cigar for a moment. In his remembering, Darkmind felt the pain once more and pulled his hand to his mouth quickly.

"Fuck!" he yelled.

"What is it?" Angel asked.

"Something bit me!" He shook his hand.

She raised his hand and kissed it gently, seemingly assuming that he'd been bitten by an insect of some sort. He looked under the table half expecting to see a neighbour's dog.

"Fuck, that hurt!"

"Get over it!" Steve smiled at him. "Are you in or what?"

"I'm in," he answered.

Darwin won that round. It ended up being a good night for him after all. He walked away with a couple of hundred dollars and two IOU papers placed neatly in his wallet. He was now the future proud owner of Steve's, and of course the boy's, immortal souls.

Darkmind flexed his hand as he walked along, remembering the bite that seemed so very long ago.

He was drawn into the night, the wolf padding along beside him. He knew that it would've taken days for him to walk to the reserve from the city when he was alive, but the time passed swiftly even though they had seemed to move at a very casual pace towards their destination. At some point he forgot about the military councillor altogether. At another he sheathed his sword.

The leaves in the tall trees scraped against each other and seemed to speak, while the crows called into the darkness unnaturally. The undead were everywhere. Never could he have imagined a place with so many untimely, uncollected deaths. Everywhere they stood and stared accusingly at him as he passed. Their faces were white with the pallor of death. They were from many eras, were many ages and were male and female alike.

He remembered this place from the few times that they had visited Darwin's grandparents growing up. It had seemed like a sad place even then. Darwin's grandparents were kind people but had lived long and difficult lives. Both of them had been raised in the missionary schools, where torture and sexual molestation were the norm. They had both encountered hundreds of incidents of racism and hate throughout their lives as well. They loved one another, though, and had never been seduced by the allure of the drink. They loved their kids and their grandkids. They saw people as individuals and had never succumbed to racism against any of Darwin's white friends. Darkmind was glad; Darwin's grandmother had made the best pecan pie he had ever eaten in his life.

He passed by the unnaturally large white birch tree in the curve of the road. The skin of the tree was peeled back and seemed to bleed into the night. Swinging from a large branch, on the hangman's rope, was a native wearing cowboy boots, dark pants, a flat brim cowboy hat with a feather in it and a black vest. The rope creaked from the weight of a man as he swung, as if dead still.

"They are as they see themselves when they die," the dark wolf purred to him the answer to his unasked question. "If the high soul leaves, they are left with little room for reason."

"There was a folk story about this tree that Darwin once told me. He said that it was haunted by the soul of a man who had stolen horses from a white rancher."

"Not as much of a fairy tale as you once thought," Lupa responded. She changed the subject. "The hunters here are wary of you. You reek of death, and they follow in the woods hesitant to attack, though they won't remain cautious forever. We are nearing holy ground, and so we will be safe from them soon."

He became aware of beasts that circled in the woods just out of sight.

"I know we're not going to Darwin's house, which would have been the other way down the road." A few years ago Darwin had moved into the home of his now deceased grandparents.

"We are here to find out about the deed to your soul, I would imagine. Perhaps this was why the great light rejected you."

"Perhaps," he replied, almost sounding bored, for in truth he knew now that there was more to this visit than that. He just had to remember more, but he knew he was a lucid ghost for a reason. He had things to do in this new realm; he was on a mission.

There were things that he needed to take care of first. Perhaps these things would help him remember.

"We are safe from the Windigo, the hunters here that follow us now. We may have to find an alternative way out, though." Lupa spoke of the gathering hunters in the darkness. He wondered if they left the others, the undead natives, alone because this was their land. Perhaps they hungered for him all the more because in life he had been white.

He could hear chanting and drumming. He was drawn to the sound as it seemed to tug on him. In the darkness he saw what looked like a very large tipi. There were powerful-looking warriors standing around the shelter. A few were on restless horses covered in painted handprints, showing off. The faces of the braves were a collage of fearsome and proud colour. Feathers were braided into the horses' and warriors' hair alike. As he came closer, he noted that some of these warriors were women.

All faces turned towards him as he approached the door flap of the temple.

"They are waiting for you," one of the spirit braves close to the door said. "Thank you for coming." He threw the flap open as Darkmind stepped through it. He knew that the door had been opened in the physical world as well.

He squinted into the darkness and saw several spirits of wise men in the circle of people praying.

"We pray in this darkness; this darkness is sacred!" one man chanted.

"We pray in this darkness!" several answered at once.

"Brother, even as your spirit has left your body and returned to the great one, the grandfather, we ask that you find peace and happiness that was never yours in life."

"Aho. All my relations," several answered again.

"Grandfather, help our brother to find you. Help him go back home to the fields of plenty!"

"We pray in this darkness; this darkness is sacred!" the room chanted.

Darkmind saw that many of the men were in tears. He knew intuitively that Darwin had called them together at the news of his death. Darwin had become much more spiritual with age, and with each passing year this seemed to have cost him his smile.

Several of the men looked directly at him as he stepped inside, and he knew that some of them actually saw him while others merely sensed him. There was the taking of his energy when they did see him, but there was also the energy from the ritual given back to him.

The drum was a water drum made from a cauldron of sorts with a hide stretched across it. There were also gourd rattles with feathers of bright colors. Surprisingly, a Bible lay near the man who seemed to be leading the ceremony. A cup with powdered-looking chunks in it was being passed around. He knew that the sacred medicine, peyote, was considered an illegal drug in most places.

In the center of the circle was a fire with several logs on it. The flames danced with many spirits of animals and summoned ancestors. In front of the leader, the highwayman, was a crescent of hot coals in a moon shape.

"We pray in this darkness; this darkness is sacred!"

Darwin looked directly at him. His higher spirit seemed to be in union with his lower one, and they were not separate as he spoke. Darkmind knew, however, that the words he spoke were not uttered in the physical world but only in his new one.

"Brother, I am sad to see that we will not be going on any fishing trips again soon."

"I'm afraid you're right, my friend." Darkmind noticed a familiar shadow sitting beside his old friend. It was the ghost of Steve.

"I have told Steve often that he is free to go, that the wager of the soul did not mean anything. He does not speak. Even the elders have tried to help me, but to no avail," Darwin answered his unspoken question.

Darkmind looked at the mindless apparition. "I'm sorry, my friend, but he won't understand you or the elders. I'm afraid he is as connected to this sickening plane of existence as I am."

"Perhaps if we destroy the contracts somehow?"

"I think it's more complicated than that. The great light has rejected me."

"I am sorry, brother. Perhaps if I kill myself? I will make this sacrifice for you and for Steve."

"We pray in this darkness; this darkness is sacred!"

"That will not help, but thank you."

"I am sorry we summoned you, then," Darwin said reverently.

"I needed to see you. I'm starting to remember. There is a path that led to this temple but returns to the darkness. Whatever binding you have over Steve seems not to affect me."

"Where does this path lead?"

"Lupa, the wolf, says to me now that it goes towards a new master. I'm being pulled. There is a woman brushing her hair before a mirror. Her hair is jet black, and her face is as white as snow."

"We pray in this darkness; this darkness is sacred!"

"You see many things in riddles that I would have thought you would be capable of deciphering easily," Darwin stated.

Darkmind swiftly pulled his sword out and pointed it at Darwin's throat. The fire erupted into a larger flame, and several spirits suddenly stood around him with weapons drawn. Darkmind seemed unconcerned, and held his face stone cold.

"What riddles, old friend?"

Darwin's high spirit stared at him sadly for a long moment before lifting his arm up as a gesture to the surrounding spirits to lower their weapons. The entities stepped back, but their glares were fierce and menacing.

"You have changed, but I will give you the information you seek. Not because you demand it, but because we were once friends." Darwin's words seemed weighted with sadness.

Darkmind sheathed Black Dragon in one swift motion. It was the motion of someone who had practiced such a move for a lifetime—lifetimes perhaps.

"I no longer have the paper," Darwin began. "Before everything started to go bad, even before Steve died, I gave it to Angel. She begged me to give it to her. She said she wanted to *set* you free, and so I gave it to her. She got me a new guitar case for my birthday that year." Darwin smiled at the old memories. "You were jealous, and everyone else thought the gift was unusually generous. We never talked about it or anything, but it was a sort of thank-you, and I think she saw it as a payment of sorts as well.

"I haven't spoken with her since Steve's funeral. I have no idea where she is." Darkmind sighed.

"She calls the wife sometimes, but she usually talks to me longer than her." Darwin had married the little brunette, and they now had a couple of kids. "Angel always asks about you."

Pangs of pain ripped through him. It wasn't the coldness or the ache in his bones, nor was it the headache from the parasite or the bite from the dog. It was not even the final pains of life, the burns on his face and the marks on his body. It was a pain that felt ancient and all-consuming. His eyes filled with tears. He thought for a moment of Balzola and the insane smile of the mute jester, and he realized that even in death his losses mounted.

He realized that he had wasted his life. He had never really thought of how finite things were. Sure, he had sacrificed himself for his country, but she had slipped from his grasp far before that. He had let her get away, and now she was gone forever. He had always thought that someday the stars would line up in such a way that things would be good again. He remembered the day on the blanket. He remembered that there had been no last words between them. They had stood, both in black, side by side above Steve's coffin, and they had held one another's hand wordlessly one final time. There were black roses there. So many black roses.

He roared in pain.

"We pray in this darkness; this darkness is sacred!"

"We should leave." Lupa sounded concerned.

"Where is she?" Darkmind demanded.

"She is in New York right now. She is an actress working on a play. Your vision is right: she has black hair again. It suits her role, she said."

"Again?" Darkmind sounded somewhat subdued but confused.

"She had always died her hair blonde. Always the coloured contact lenses and the bright makeup and accessories. The theatre was always her calling, I suppose."

Darkmind offered Darwin a smile once more. "You know her better than I, old friend."

"One never knows. I thought that I knew you above all people, but even in death you have a mean and selfish streak." Darwin looked at him sternly.

"I'm afraid, old friend. I'm afraid of what I am and what I am becoming. Perhaps if I return, I will know how to free Steve, I will know about myself and I will know how to be a better friend once more."

"If you do return again, Darkmind, you will leave your weapon outside. You will leave your weapon outside, or you will not enter at all." Darwin's words were cold and had the air of finality to them. The use of his new name, Darkmind, did not escape his notice.

9

Lupa brought them to this city far from where he had grown up. Every time that he had traveled with her was different. Each time the journey seemed less painful than the one before and affected him less.

His power had grown great. He knew things that he did not know before and understood things that had yet to be revealed. A dark confidence grew in him even as he felt the knives of autopsy, in another far off place, carve open the flesh of his long lost body.

Lupa was a part of him; she was not separate. She was a conduit and a creation of his high spirit. She was a doorway to animalistic powers that were granted to all high beings. She could just as easily have been a panther or a moth, and perhaps at times in his life she was. She served him as he served himself. If he had great enough power, he could bring her forth a hundred times over and create an army of dark canine.

"Release these despairing thoughts before they destroy you!" Lupa scolded as they moved through the cross-shaped building. Depressing organ music cast an air of reverence.

"So it's you who will act as my voice of reason, then?"

"Of course; I am your guide and your helper."

"If I die, then you die with me. You seek to escape this road I've chosen?" His voice seemed to echo from between the tall white pillars. Votive candles burned brightly throughout the building. "What happened to my guardian spirit? Did I ever have one? Was it the shadow with the sword?" Darkmind asked as they passed a statue of the Mother Mary. Her head was down, but he could see teardrops of blood running down her cheeks.

"I do not know," Lupa responded. "If you had a spirit guide, he may have been destroyed or called home. Maybe he joined the great light so that he could be born once more."

"I have to find out. I have to know who spoke to me and why I was supposed to resist the light. Beings have suggested that the great light cast me aside, but there was a moment in which I could have entered—my higher spirit, anyway. It seems that the fate of my lower self has been avoided as well." He contemplated this. His lower spirit was his identity. This lower spirit had fear, judgement, anger, lust, impatience and ego.

"You will not survive this," Lupa stated plainly as they passed rows of praying spirits. The organ music continued to be melancholic.

Darkmind fingered his sword nervously as great, winged guardians kept pace with him nearby. Beautiful stained glass windows cast strange patterns of light across the marble floor. He viewed these images suspiciously, as they seemed to be acting out the events that they portrayed. "You say this only because I believe it."

"That makes it twice as likely, then."

"I have nothing to lose."

"You lie to yourself," the shadow beast said.

He did not disagree.

Sacred places and those of religious importance were easy to find in the cosmic web. That was why travel between such sites was easier than following the web line of a significant event, object, person or place. It was much more complicated than this, but he could sense that the woman he had once known as Angel was not so far away, at least physically. Crackling with intuition, he sensed that she was somehow distant as well though.

He could feel her when he left the sacred ground. Unlike the other places he had been, this particular cathedral offered safety only up to the huge doors that he exited. Outside those doors was the madness of a congested and active city.

He was enlightened enough to understand that the sacred ground that he stepped upon did not actually offer the sort of protection that he had imagined. This was an agreement made by beings that had found it necessary to coexist with laws and order. There were many beings that would gladly break such rules, but the repercussion would likely be swift and devastating if they were found out. Unless the forces of darkness decided to ignore the custom collectively, the infractor, and perhaps the infractor's whole association, would be destroyed forever by the collective.

He knew he had less than ten blocks to travel through the city to the theatre. He stayed in the dark patches as much as possible. He could feel people sensing him, and snippets of his power would fall away as if a bite had been taken from him.

He knew he had different ways to view his new landscape. He could view the spirit world only, which was abstract and disconnected from the land of the living. He could also see the living only, which was in a real sense like walking blind into a closet filled with vipers. His third option was that he could view his universe as a sort of blend between the two. He had already been naturally doing this. It was a feeling, pushing, pulling sensation based on what needed to be seen, what could be ignored and what he desired to see. As he walked into the dark and wet night, he continued to do just that.

It had rained recently, but the clouds were parted for the moment to allow the brightness of the moon to shine down in patches. Cars splashed by, carrying both the living and the dead. Confused beings walked the sidewalk beside teams of pedestrians much the same way as they had in life. Dark beings stalked the living, trying to convince them of the fruition of their selfish deeds.

For the moment he minded his business. The dark wolf moved loyally beside him. For the first time since his passing, he wished that he had cigarettes. It seemed to him like the very thing that he should be doing as he walked these busy streets. For whatever reason, it seemed like it would be a very New York thing to do.

The smells of food cooking mingled neatly with car exhaust and the clean scent of the rain. The sounds of the night seemed to be the hum of man alone. He looked at the cathedral behind him. As imposing, jagged and sharp as those towers seemed, they were dwarfed by the buildings that surrounded them.

This is why, he thought, *the sacred ground around the building seems so limited.* Even as he thought it, however, he was forced to admit that the church stood grand, somehow above its height.

He moved under awnings and fire escapes and hanging flags. He clung to doorways and buildings and the darkest of shadows available to him. Occasionally it would be unavoidable that he brushed against someone. When he did so, they seemed to shiver suddenly. Sometimes they would comment that they were cold or that there was a draft. Every time it happened, he felt a slight drain of energy. He knew this would have been a more drastic amount if he had been weaker.

A woman approaching slowed in her step and stared at him.

"Good evening, ma'am," he said to amuse himself as he passed. She had stopped dead in her tracks. He wasn't sure if she could hear him or not, but the drain of power was much more significant. It was barely anything to concern himself with, however.

The apparition of an Irish policeman in an old uniform passed him by. The officer was whistling to himself and seemed to be one of the confused ones who were unaware that they were dead. The ghosts from hundreds of violent crimes walked wailing, crying or sulking quietly down the streets. He looked up at the taller buildings and saw gargoyle shapes perched or hovering everywhere. He believed he had as much reason to hide from them as the living. All the while the wolf followed along protectively.

Cars were parked facing him up both sides of the one-way street. The building was nested up against a hotel where a superstitious valet seemed to be looking at him. Cigarette smoke, from a long dead ticketholder still waiting for his date to arrive for a show, clouded the sidewalk. A loud pub across the street drowned out any of the more subtle noises around him. People inside, the living, seemed to be screaming or celebrating pretty hard.

Three sets of double doors stood in front of him. He passed through them with relative ease.

"Your power is not endless," Lupa cautioned him. He knew he was being frivolous overall, but he had seen no other way to enter the building.

"I will find more if I need to."

"From where? Your country mourns for you now, but soon only your friends and family will remember you. Eventually even they will forget you or pass on to death themselves."

"There are other ways," he replied, throwing the thought out there: he had gained most of his power on his own.

"You were once reluctant to kill," Lupa purred, motherly.

"Look how that worked out for me," he stated bitterly.

Lupa seemed silenced for now, almost as though frowning. She must have known he was right, though. He had tried to live a decent life; in the end it had amounted to nothing.

He had been under the impression from Darwin that Angel had become a successful actress. As he entered the theatre, he was aware that this was not the case. The building that she was in was not even an actual operating theatre. It was old and had resident spirits. Performances were rare there these days, except for private events and stand-up comedy.

It was not an unhappy place, though. He was sure that it attracted almost as many former patrons as it had the living in days gone by. He saw, strangely, the earthbound dancing and socializing. He saw these people laughing and smiling upon their wedding day.

Every day was their wedding day.

He walked down a short hall past the lobby. He could tell that there were very few living people in this part of the building; almost everyone had left except for some hotel staff who were tidying up in nearby adjoined rooms. A single beam near the stage was the only light on in the relatively deserted theatre.

The room was like a dream. The red curtains over the stage and the viewer boxes stood out from the gold trimming that lined it. That trimming seemed to be sparkling with jewels. He walked upon purple carpet and past luxurious red seating to see these more closely. The illusion was caused by fine tiles set into the gold work. Shadows clung to the spaces around the pillars that framed the boxes and the stage itself.

As he neared the stage, he became aware that the small theatre had three levels. He could see that a few of the upper seats were taken by confused spirits that seemed to be awaiting some performance. They were almost hidden in the shadows beneath an intricately shaped ceiling.

Darkmind avoided the light and climbed to the stage on a short set of steps to the far right. He then led Lupa across the dark wood stage towards the curtain. They moved through the fabric and into the darkness, causing the curtain to visibly flutter.

He knew where to go. The door was closed and he moved through it. He found her as he imagined he would. She sat in front of the mirror brushing her hair. Two candles were lit, one on either side of the mirror, and they gave the illusion that her face was floating. A silver, handheld mirror that matched the brush she was using sat face up beside an open makeup box. A single peacock feather rested lightly upon the vintage dresser. A bouquet of flowers sat on a nearby table.

A cat meowed. He saw a small black cat advance towards him with its tail up; the living creature clearly saw him and did not seem afraid at all. He felt it soak in his energy as he crouched and pushed on its whiskers. The room made him feel at ease.

Lupa sat by the doorway, out of the way, as Darkmind approached the girl.

She wore a dark-coloured medieval dress that pressed up her breasts, giving them volume. Her skin seemed somewhat light in the darkness, white at first despite its natural tan color. She had always looked more

Caucasian to him when she had blonde hair than she did now. He thought it strange he had never really seen her before this moment. He thought of her parents and how obvious it should have been all along.

Her eyes were large and dark, yet they seemed to lack their usual sparkle. She smelled like he remembered summer to smell. He wanted to laugh and yell, cry and sooth. It washed over him how much he had loved this woman and how much he had thrown away. If things had worked out, though, would she still be chasing her dream? Would he have ever been chasing his?

He reached out to stroke her hair and allowed his fingers to physically do so. She did not pull away; in fact she leaned into them, closing her eyes and smiling a bit before speaking.

> "Now o'er the one half-world Nature seems dead,
> and wicked dreams abuse The curtain'd sleep;
> now witchcraft celebrates Pale Hecate's offerings;
> and wither'd murder,
> Alarum'd by his sentinel, the wolf,
> Whose howl's his watch, thus with his stealthy pace,
> With Tarquin's ravishing strides,
> towards his design Moves like a ghost."

He had never been that into theatre per se, but he had been around Angel and her friends enough to realize that she had quoted some famous line, from some playwright, that some snooty professor somewhere decided had something important to say. He did not understand what it meant on a surface level, but on a deeper level he realized that she was reaching out to him in her own way. For some reason it felt like he had just been chastised.

"I'm sorry, Angel. There were so many things I should've done differently." He rested his head on the top of hers while his second hand entered her hair.

"When our actions do not, our fears do make us traitors." She responded in that same tone that told him she was still quoting some play.

He nodded his head with more understanding than he would have given her in life. He smelled her soft silky hair and pressed his lips to it. She tasted like sugar and soap.

He knew a part of her felt him even though he had not shown himself. She was sensing him somehow, but she was also very vacant on another level. Her eyes were still held shut. She gently placed the brush onto the dresser top.

"The sleeping and the dead
Are but as pictures.
'Tis the eye of childhood
That fears a painted devil."

She knew he was dead. On some level she had to be aware of the state he was in. He held her close for a very long minute before standing up and looking at her. After a moment she picked up the brush, opened her eyes and began to comb her hair once more. There was something robotic about the movement.

"She is not here. Not all of her," the cat said from its resting place on a nearby chair.

Surprisingly he wasn't startled. "Where is she?"

"She went in search of you."

"And who are you?"

"A piece of her spirit protector—a very small piece, I must add."

"Where's the rest of you?"

"With her. She is in a dangerous situation right now, and she needs all of the protection that she has."

"She seems ... confused or drunk."

"Like one of the wandering dead?"

"Yes, but smarter than most of them." He made a contemplative nod as he said this.

"The power of the lower soul determines the intelligence of the ghost."

"Which is why some can speak or act somewhat intelligently?" He thought of the jester Balzola and the strangely tall man asking for the toll at the cemetery. Balzola seemed very confused but could still function somewhat and interact. The tall man was able to speak, although he sounded very unintelligent when he did so. He knew he had already realized this himself at some point on his journey.

"Exactly," the cat said seductively. "Angel just gave an entire rehearsal performance this way. She tripped going out, but this is thought to be good luck during a rehearsal anyway."

"So she is in a play here?"

"She will be. It will be one time only. This theatre is rented out for private parties. An eccentric old millionaire wants to give his wife this gift for their 30th wedding anniversary."

"That's romantic."

"It would have been romantic if he chose one of Shakespeare's more romantic plays." The cat started to lick its paw.

"Like which one?"

"Not the Scottish play, that's for sure." The cat seemed to smile at its own joke despite the fact that Darkmind had not been able to grasp it.

"So where do I find her?"

"You risk harming her unless you wait for her to find you. You stay here, and her barely functioning self will be a target to your enemies—and an easy one at that."

"I'm confused."

"Go somewhere and lay low. She will find you. Just because they have not acted yet, do not think you are not being observed. Every word I speak endangers her. All will reveal itself in time." The cat stopped licking a paw and looked up at him as she said this. She did not have to say anymore.

He realized that he had kneeled down beside the cat and let go of Angel's hair during the brief conversation. He stood up quickly and kissed the woman's forehead before moving for the door. She had closed her eyes and smiled as he planted the kiss.

"Turn, hell-hound, turn!" the cat said as way of farewell in a Thespian voice.

He moved quickly away from her and out of the theatre. He would never risk losing her in any way again. He was excited by the idea that she was looking for him, but this joy was short-lived. It was worse than it would have been if both of them had gotten married to other people. She was alive and he was dead. Even when she did die, if she lived a good life, she would join the great light. An untimely death, at the very best, would give him a theatre-quoting spirit to take care of. That was the very best-case scenario, and it was the one most selfishly in his favour.

He was excited that perhaps he would get to make amends and see her one final time. He could then ask her to relinquish any power she had over his soul. Then he could say good-bye for the last time. Any other arrangement would be too painful for both of them.

His few moments of hope had been washed away by an eternity of despair. It was hopeless. He felt heavy and depression hit him hard. A deep sadness washed over him even as he felt more and more poking and prodding tools enter his physical body somewhere far away.

He pulled his hood up and stepped into the very chilly night. He did not know where he should go from here or what he should do. He walked with Lupa and searched for the darkest places he could find.

10

They had walked for a long time. The cat had spoken the truth; he felt that he was being watched but that the beings observing were weak and inconsequential compared to the monster that he had become.

As he moved through the busy night, his desire grew more and more intense for a cigarette. At first it was little more than an annoyance, a scratch he could not itch, but eventually it became a need. He *needed* a cigarette.

He wondered about the cigarettes that Bali had smoked. *Did she buy them? Did she have a regenerating smoke pack? Or was it merely cosmetic?*

He had tried to bum a smoke from the ghost outside of the theatre, but that one clearly couldn't see him. He then tried a couple of more times with other nicotine using spirits but met with equal results. The entities he came across simply lacked the ability to see him or, in some cases when they could, even comprehend what he was saying at all. He wondered again if their packs continued to be full indefinitely. It was a thought that bounced around in his head regarding firearms as well. *Would the bullets keep returning?* "You are as you see yourself as you died," Bali had said. *How exactly did it work anyways?*

His thoughts were hopping around quickly now.

He started to think about the cat. The cat had occupied a physical body despite never seeming to have ever even lived as a cat. Could he himself possess a cat? What about a dog ... or even a person for that matter?

How much better would an actual cigarette be through an actual set of living lungs?

"Don't even think about it!" Lupa said with a scolding tone.

He had always had a problem with authority and disciplinarians, even in the military. He was never disobedient per se; he just hated feeling as if someone was telling him what to do. Lupa seemed to be taking that role right now, and it annoyed him. As a living person this had usually left him feeling weak on some level. Now it made him want to contradict her even more.

He could possess a person. The idea had been born from a wandering mind, but now it had stuck and he couldn't seem to shake it.

He still felt powerful. He felt that he could do whatever he wanted. It wasn't like he was going to kill someone; he was just going to take them out for a little joy ride. If he could pull it off, he could have a few cigarettes, a couple of drinks, maybe go see some strippers or pick up a girl. He wished he knew when Angel was going to be around. He had an idea that this plan forming in his mind would help him out of the depression he was sinking into, but he didn't want her to necessarily know that he had become the seedy sort since he'd died. Not so long ago, he liked to think, he was a nice guy.

Maybe this was the teenager phase of being dead. He was exploring his boundaries, rebelling.

He wasn't even sure if it would work, anyways. He would probably need someone weak. He thought for a moment of trying to find a drunk college girl to possess so he could touch himself but ruled that out. He didn't want to be a girl.

A child seemed like it might be somehow funny to possess. He could pull all sorts of antics in a kid's body like looking up skirts or trying to buy a bottle of bourbon from a liquor store. But he wasn't sure if he was in the practical joke mindset at the moment. He was more nostalgic than anything else.

Nostalgic for life.

He still felt cold and his body ached all over. Maybe a possession would relieve the pain for a while.

He could take over a street person like a druggie. A junkie seemed like he would be easy to take, but he didn't want to smoke a cigarette through a junkie's mouth. It would seem dirty somehow.

He struck down one idea after another until he eventually decided upon a male as close to himself as possible, who was in a vulnerable situation. He didn't even know if the target needed to be vulnerable, but he thought it would be a good starting point. He could be more and more experimental in the future if he was successful. For some reason, though, he knew that it was going to work.

"The cat said to lie low!" Lupa nagged.

"Fuck the cat!" Darkmind retorted, his mind made up.

He continued to walk in the same general direction, away from the theatre and even further away from the cathedral, scanning pedestrians for a possible target. He felt dragged in a certain direction almost beyond his control, and so he surrendered to the feeling and went with it as he continued to seek out a target.

Eventually he saw some Goth kids dressed all in black moving down the street. One of the kid's spirits was floating out of his body dramatically and trailing behind as the boy slightly staggered. He could see that drugs had left the dark-haired half Asian boy in a vulnerable state. Darkmind became excited and moved quickly towards the target.

Entry was even easier than he had thought it would be. He simply stepped into the boy's space and willed it. He felt the release of a large amount of power though and understood that he would need more if he was ever going to do this again.

A boy. Hardly a boy but more of a young man. He seemed like a boy even though he was probably around the same age that Darkmind had been when he died.

"I need a fucking smoke," he said heavily through the stranger's mouth.

"You just got some, Shadow!" replied Indigo a little too sarcastically. She looked like what he imagined a corpse would look like if the corpse was a slut. The black veil didn't help.

"Yah," seconded Jinx. He was very small in stature and had his dyed black hair pulled into a ponytail. He had a smile that was a little too contagious and eyes that sparkled beneath his horn-rimmed glasses.

So his name was Shadow? That didn't sound like much of a name, but who was he to judge? He seemed to be going by Darkmind these days. He found the smokes tucked into the front pocket of his jeans, which felt two sizes too tight. He fumbled for his lighter and lit a smoke. The first drag tasted even sweeter than he had imagined it would.

Shadow scanned over his new crew. There were five of them including him, two other guys and two girls. His eyes went wide when he looked at Zarah, who looked to be a 300-pound female version of the much sexier, but still slutty, Indigo.

"What's that for, boi?" Zarah asked in a heavy voice. Her face was painted white, and her hair was jet black. She tried to show as much cleavage and leg as Indigo, but the result was frightening. Her image was completed by a spiked dog collar that she wore around her neck.

"You just look a little thinner, that's all. Black's good for you," he uttered from Shadow's lips.

"Fuck you, weekender!" she roared back.

The second male was a bigger guy and looked to be more like a punk than a Goth, with a tall, spiked mohawk. He started to roar in laughter at Zarah's expense.

"Fuck you too, Thorm!" she lashed out. This only made him laugh harder.

"Damn, this is good," Shadow stated more to himself than anyone else. He knew as soon as he said it that they would think that he was talking about the weed they had just smoked and not the cigarette.

"What the hell's gotten into you?" Indigo asked. She obviously knew that Shadow had hurt her friend's feelings and seemed to want to lash out at the unusually quiet and melancholic boy.

He gave her a look with a cocky smile that he hoped would tell her he was just playing around, even though the sight of the big girl had truly shocked him.

"He's too mundane and boring, never high; now he's trying it out, and you're beating down on him!" Jinx said with his very un-Goth permanent grin.

"Fuck you too, insta-Goth with lifts!" spat Zarah. Darkmind knew she had confidence because she was part and package with Indigo. She was used to a little harshness from the guys, but they never went too far, for if they lost Indigo they would lose them both and lose status as a group. Darkmind saw all of these dynamics through Shadow's perceptive eyes.

Not that they were a solid group anyway. Thorm was the only one in the group who had maintained a consistent image for over a year. The six-foot-four Goth looked like he should be a football player rather than a Goth, and truth be told, he actually was more punk anyways.

Jinx went silent at the heavy blow. At five foot three, he did like to wear lifts in the subculture that found them fashionable or at least accepted them. The fact that Zarah pointed them out, Darkmind sensed, reminded him of how hanging out with other people used to make him feel.

"Mellow!" Indigo said forcefully, seeming to realize that she would have to be the mediator. That had usually been Shadow's job. He was the level-headed peacekeeper. She was the bitch, Jinx and Zarah were the ones that bantered with each other all of the time, and Thorm was either laughing at everything or depressed as hell—it depended on whether or not he was high.

Normally after someone tried to calm the group, someone else would second it with a *yah*, but tonight there were no takers. She looked over at Shadow with a seeming concern of how messed-up he looked. He must have appeared to be having a hard time walking and even focusing his eyes.

"Any of you fuckers got a drink?" he asked through gritted teeth.

"You in pain, man?" Thorm asked as he pulled a bottle out from his cargo pants while scanning for police. "We need to stash this before we get to The Cave anyways." They knew that they would never be able to get an outside bottle into the club.

The other three were now starting to stare at Shadow for his strange behaviour. They had paused at a bus stop, and all of them seemed to be waiting for him to say something.

"Can we go somewhere and talk? Just the two of us?" he asked Indigo.

"What for?" she responded without thinking, alarmed.

"I just want to tell you something, that's all."

"Listen, you're being a conformist prick. You want to say something, say it in front of everyone. We're family, boi!" She had the air of superiority that one often got when dealing with another person in a less cognizant state of mind. She kind of reminded him of a mother figure, the way she was leaning towards him with one hand on her hip.

"It's just, I think I love you," Shadow stated in that same hard voice.

"What?" Indigo cried. Thorm started laughing and clapping his hands while Jinx and Zarah both stood and stared open mouthed. When it was clear he was serious, or at least he thought he was, she continued, "What do you mean, you *love me*?"

"I love you. I always have. That's why I'm acting strange." He took a very long swill from the bottle of Southern Comfort.

"Always! For how long?" She asked seeming genuinely surprised.

"Forever," he said as he sat on a short wall.

"Well ... like, um ... since we first met or what?"

"Yeah. Since that time." He took one more long swig before handing the bottle back to Thorm.

"What's my name, Shadow? I don't even know if you know yours right now."

He dug into Shadow's memory, but the mind was blank because the boy had frozen up in fear. If one thing could be discerned from seeking the information, it was that Shadow was definitely not comfortable at all with what was going on.

"When I look at you, I see a black rose. Perfect and corrupt all at once. Your name is heaven, but it is also the devil." Shadow's lips were pushing hard and seemed to be uttering words he had already thought, as if he was just spouting poetry from out of the boy's mind. Darkmind just hoped that the gibberish sounded romantic and disturbing for the heavy makeup-wearing, low-cleavage horror queen. This might be his last chance at getting any … ever. If this went sideways he would walk away from the group and try somewhere else. He rationalized that the shirt he was wearing with *The Nightmare before Christmas* print on it had a better chance of impressing this group than one of the Gucci dress-wearing honeys he noted passing by.

Her face slackened a bit and her eyes went wide. They were quite a pretty blue, he noted. He also saw that her neck beneath the coat of makeup was blushing. Jackpot.

"Why didn't you tell me this before?" she asked softly. The others stood awkwardly silent at last.

"The pain of not being with you when we were near was bittersweet." He wanted to pat himself on the back for that one, for it was his and not Shadow's.

She smiled and kissed him on the forehead. Shadow got butterflies and started to rise in his pants. He wondered if he, Shadow, had ever been with a woman before. He knew the answer though before he had even completed the thought.

"Let's go, boi," she said as she helped him up from where he had sat at the bus stop. He put an arm around her to help support himself, and they walked away. The other three followed and started to talk about a new CD that Jinx had just bought. The conversation was surprisingly friendly.

* * *

He remembered bits and pieces. He remembered pretending that he was straight at the door to get in. Then there was a lot of close dancing with Indigo, who was just trying to support him—at least that's what she said to Zarah. Thorm knew a lot of people and so was there and gone and back again all night. Jinx and Zarah were both completely subdued, not sure how the evening's festivities were going to change the dynamics of their little group over the next few weeks. The friends moved from one floor to the next all evening, but for two of them, Zarah and Jinx, it looked through Shadow's eyes to be the most awkward night they had shared together so far.

Darkmind reached out with his mind to read the thoughts of these two friends of Shadow. He found it was not as hard to do as he would have expected.

First there was Zarah. She was especially concerned. *What had happened to Shadow?* He didn't look the same, he didn't act the same, and he didn't even smile the same. He was cooler and funnier, but he was clearly very high. Despite her friend's appearance, Indigo was anything but a loose woman. She had seen that look on her face before, though. Her friend was a hopeless romantic. Indigo had told her once that she liked Shadow but had always thought that he was way too shy for her. Zarah struggled internally, trying to understand if she might just be jealous of the possibility of losing Indigo. They had been friends since the third grade. She had always known, though, that Indigo would find love first ... that was a given. Indigo had a couple of short-lived flings with older guys in high school, but this was different! This had potential! Zarah on the other hand had sex exactly three times with three different boys so far. All three had stolen her panties as proof that they had "taken the challenge."

Jinx was also affected by the shift. He now looked at Zarah out of the corner of his eye as they stood beside the dance floor. Nine Inch Nails blared the song "Closer" to "satisfy all of the posers," Zarah had said. He liked the song, though, and it made him think of sex. Zarah was all woman. He imagined burying his head between those massive breasts. He saw them walking down the street together, a complete non-conformist image of sexual compatibility. He wondered if they could ever get along long enough to hook up. The thought had never even occurred to him before Shadow's recent confession, and the new thoughts made him uncomfortable. This night, though, it was all that he thought of.

Shadow woke up with the worst headache of his life. It took him a moment to remember where he was and what had happened. He looked over at the sleeping image of Indigo beside him, and his eyes went wide.

It had not been a dream. He had been possessed.

The sun slipped through a crack in his curtains and fell over the futon bed and onto the hardwood floor. Various articles of black clothing were littered throughout the room that he usually kept immaculate. The dark red walls kept the sanctuary dim on weekends long enough for him to sleep in.

A framed poster of Roland from *The Dark Tower* was the only picture on the wall and was above his bed. A dresser with a mirror faced them. He never really used the space other than to throw his wallet onto, because it was cluttered with various gargoyle statuettes. On the wall opposite the window, beside the bedroom door, was a large Celtic cross. Beneath that cross, sleeping upon the floor was a very unimpressed-looking large dog.

For a moment he was not afraid, for he seemed to sense that it wished him no harm. Then he felt a tinge of terror that threatened to rise out of control.

The beast was a beat-up, mangy-looking dog that looked to him more wolf than pet. It stared at him without looking away or showing any signs that it wouldn't continue to stare anytime soon.

"Good morning!" a voice said cheerily. It was a man's voice, deep and hard. It seemed to have come from inside of him.

"Who are you?" He answered loudly.

"What is it?" Indigo asked, half asleep.

"Uh, nothing ... just talking to myself," he answered as he got up and pulled on some nearby track pants. "I'll be right back."

He walked out of the bedroom and across the wood floor towards a set of glass doors. He then stepped onto a very large stone-tiled terrace with a short brick rail. The city view was amazing from the 19th floor of Shadow's apartment. Even with the weight set, an obviously expensive bike, a mosaic table and chair set, and a dozen or so plants, it still seemed sparsely occupied.

"Who are you?" Shadow asked again out loud. His heart was beating fast and heavy. On the one hand Indigo, the girl he had secretly loved, was naked in his bed. He wasn't sure how he felt about that. Pages of dark poetry dedicated to her filled the lower dresser drawer in his room. These were feelings that made him suffer and experience pain, and so he valued them and their secrecy. He had always known that he was too shy to ever act on them and that he would not know what to do even if he did.

Yet he had acted on them. He had on one hand, in a very real sense, won the girl he wanted. On the other hand, he had barely even been a spectator for the whole experience.

"My friends call me Darkmind," the voice said coolly. Shadow noted that the dog had followed them outside.

"Are you a demon?" Shadow asked, sounding only somewhat concerned. It had not yet occurred to him yet that he might actually be mentally ill.

Darkmind laughed. "You can call me that if you like; I like to consider myself more of a lost spirit on a journey." He basked in the warm light that fell from the sun onto the young mans skin.

"What kind of journey? How long are you, ah, staying?" Shadow asked out loud.

"A journey to save my soul perhaps, or lose it. I wouldn't mind staying for a while. I may never know the pleasures of life again, and the pain goes away when I'm inside of you."

"Laying low?" Lupa asked from the patch of tile that she had decided to occupy in the shade. "Idiot!"

"Did that dog just talk?" Shadow asked, amazed, as if it was perfectly normal for a being to occupy him and to hold a conversation, but unthinkable that an animal entity might be able to speak.

"Not a dog. A wolf. She likes your tattoo, I can tell," Darkmind stated in a voice that Shadow would have never guessed had barely spoken without a note of terror, not so very long ago.

Shadow looked down at the tattoos that lined his arms. He guessed Darkmind was referring to the tattoo of the Fenris wolf on his right forearm. "Thank you, thank you," he said nervously to the wolf, who seemed to bow in return. "I don't know if this will really work out. I have things to do and stuff ... You know?"

"You work as a bike delivery boy, and your wages barely cover your rent here in Hell's Kitchen." Darkmind seemed to like saying the neighbourhood's name. "It's Saturday morning, and you have the whole weekend off. You have no other plans other than that you were going to do some writing. You were going to write on the paper in your journal—how quaint—about a girl that the *forces of darkness* would never let you have. Then you would spend a couple of hours drawing pictures in the margins that I am sure would be extremely dark and memorable. It is pointless really. That girl is in your bed," Darkmind reminded him.

"What should I do, then? Take a back seat while you trash my life?" Shadow panicked.

"Trash? Hey, buddy, I got you laid for the first time—and with the girl you profess to love no less. That has to count for something."

"Sure, but you didn't even use a condom! And you made her suck you off!"

"I *suggested* she suck you off."

"By throwing your hammer down her throat!"

"I was in the moment, okay? Besides, it's *your hammer*, really."

"Jesus."

"No! It burns! Don't say that name again!" Darkmind screamed.

"What?"

"Just joking," he said through the laughter. "You know, *The Exorcist*?" He felt that he needed to explain because Shadow wasn't laughing.

"Oh I get it. It's just not very funny."

"You're uptight."

"You think? You think I might be too uptight for a possessed guy?" Shadow asked sarcastically.

"See! You do have a sense of humour! In fact, that is going to be our first task! We are going to get you to lighten up!" Darkmind stated cheerfully.

"Lighten up? You think maybe that might be a hard thing to do while being demonically possessed?"

"I thought you guys lived for this shit? The undead, demons and ghouls and such."

"It's more of a metaphor really. If it was completely real, we would all just kill ourselves."

"Well the next time you are at one of those Goth conventions, or whatever you morbid fuckers like to call your little gatherings, you can take a survey and find out how many of your friends have ever even spoken to a spirit."

"Tonight's the big night though! Last night was more of a mixed crowd, but people come from all over the State on Saturdays. We were going to hit up some used book stores, drink some wine here or at a restaurant and then go out."

"Well, first we are going to have some fun with Indigo. Then, because you are such a pussy, we are going to read her some poetry, *your poetry*, while we're waiting for the food that we'll order."

"No, please!" Shadow pleaded.

"We will go book shopping if you want. There is a trade-off though. I would rather some live sports, maybe an Islander game or something. But I'm sure tickets would be tough, even if they are playing. I'm not sure if it's during the season or not; I kind of lost track. Anyways, then we will see how the night goes, but I definitely want to pass on the club."

"She doesn't need to hear the poetry!" Shadow was more fixated on that than on the evening's plans falling apart.

"You know, I would find it amusing to help Jinx nail that wildebeest as well. I saw how he was eying her. What do you think? They'd make a good couple?"

"Why are you doing this?"

"Trust me, kid. You keep whining, and you'll get a backseat instead of a side one. Just sit back and enjoy the ride."

"Who are you talking to?" Indigo asked. She had stepped outside without him hearing her. She was wrapped in a sheet that held to her curves suggestively. She was more beautiful with most of her makeup removed than he would have ever imagined.

Shadow looked at her with that devilish grin that seemed so unlike him. He stepped confidently towards her and wrapped her in his arms. She smiled and giggled as he kissed her neck.

"No one, baby," he responded. "Just a bad habit, that's all."

Shadow took her by the hand and led her back inside. He had surrendered to the will of Darkmind because it was truly what he had wanted as well. It gave him the benefit of confidence despite paralysis.

The more he surrendered, the less Darkmind controlled him, until it was *his* shaking hands sliding up and down the girls firm, yielding body. He could sense a deep sadness from this being who now held back and let him fulfill his dreams.

He could not completely ignore it, however. It hung over all three of them. It was a sadness that seemed more profound than anything he had ever experienced in his very short life.

11

Thorm didn't come with them to the bookstores and coffee shops. He wasn't much of a reader, and so he was going to meet up with them for dinner later in the day. He was different from the rest of them, but they loved him for it. Despite being more of a punk, Thorm had charisma that had given the group the feeling of extreme popularity. They had all been going out in dress now for only a few short months, but recently they had all—except for Thorm, who always had—finally felt like they had found their place in the world.

Zarah's quick wit and alpha comments always brought laughter everywhere that they went, and Indigo had the attention of a dozen or more hopeless young men that feared rejection due to her stunning looks. It was a beauty barely hidden behind dark clothing and a bitchy persona.

It was hard not to like Jinx; he rarely didn't smile. Anyone who spoke with him got the feeling that they were truly important, because Jinx had that rare gift of listening to a conversation fully without becoming distracted. It was his size that had proven to be a problem from a young age. Bullies that were not interested in conversation had loved to erase that very smile from the small and defenceless boy. He could remember those dark times before he had become friends with Shadow, who brought with him protective Thorm.

Shadow had been friends with Thorm for as long as anyone could remember. They were different in as many ways as possible, but no one ever dared to mess with Shadow, and later Jinx, even when Thorm wasn't around. Shadow was a reader while Thorm liked to be more active and was really into music. Thorm was the one that got Shadow into weights. He also got him into bands such as the Cure, Danzig, and HIM. On the other hand, Shadow had convinced his friend into pursuing his dreams of computer-created music and video. It was encouragement that landed Thorm into a college program, where he had met Indigo and Zarah.

At the time Shadow and Jinx were off learning how to be better writers and how to tell the difference between a good and a bad blend of coffee. At first they dressed more punk than Goth, but both had shifted to a more Goth look without ever having intended to. It seemed to suit the paths that they were already walking towards—becoming writers and being more than just followers of the angry bands that they had once been more deeply attached to—although both still shared a real love for the Misfits.

In his usual gregarious manner, Thorm brought Indigo and Zarah to meet the duo one Saturday afternoon. Before that moment the two girls had walked a solitary path of Gothdom—if you could call simply wearing a lot of black that. Though the two boys were actually more Goth friendly than actual Goths, it wasn't long before they had made any last-minute tweaks to become a unified group. Thorm didn't change his appearance much, but he had a look that made it easy for him to fit in anyways. Even if he didn't, his personality won him acceptance wherever he went. The exception to this rule was when he wasn't high. He rarely went anywhere when he wasn't because he was moody and depressing, and he knew it.

From the moment that Shadow had seen her, he had wanted her. He was secretly thankful that Thorm had never given her a passing glance. Unlike Thorm, he liked the Goth style and found it sexy. Thorm seemed to be able to get any girl he wanted. He liked what he liked, though. He chose to chase after little punker girls with big boots exclusively; race didn't seem to matter, either.

It had been a few years since they had all met and started to hang out. It had only been a short while, though, that the two girls, who had birthdays a few months apart, had turned 21, the legal age to drink. That was when they had started to go out in dress as a group and had become actual Goths. They usually went to The Cave on Saturday nights.

How Shadow had longed for her those years. He had opened up considerably and began having long conversations with her about spirituality and religion over cappuccino. He could not, however, get past his shyness. He could not tell her how he felt. He had the commonsense to know that a letter was out of the question, but writing for him was a release. He filled pages with reflections of his feelings, which were mostly dark poems dedicated to self-pity. To Shadow, though, they were beautiful enough that he would read them to himself over and over again. He covered the blank patches in his journal with black ink art. Vines and skeletons,

Nordic gods and dragons filled the books. There had been once that he had almost told her, only once, on a swing set in the dark. For a moment he had thought of kissing her.

Indigo was beautiful enough and outspoken enough that she was intimidating to the boys of her subculture. Any of the guys that did step up also needed to accept Zarah, which for some reason was hard for the few that actually did. Miraculously, Indigo stayed single for the whole time that Shadow had known her. Predictably, so did he. He dreaded every time she had a date. He would always smile and wish her luck, though; he was a friend first.

Indigo was attracted to Shadow and always had been. Darkmind could read that now. Shadow lacked the confidence of a man that so many of the boys her own age often did. If she had been outside of the subculture, she would have a boyfriend twice her age already. She had never met an older Goth that wasn't taken or just wasn't plain creepy. She knew that they were out there; she just hadn't found them. So a comfortable stalemate had developed within the group. Shadow had the commonsense not to tell Jinx or Thorm about his feelings. On the other hand, he would come up more often than he knew in conversations between the girls.

This had been the best day of Shadow's life. He had held her hand as they had walked the circuit between bookstores. Their free hands carried coffees, which made them let go of one another as they browsed through the books inside. They would catch each other's eyes and smile. She was as happy as he was. True to his word, Darkmind watched but only interfered when Shadow became particularly nervous. As each moment passed, this was happening less and less.

Surprisingly, Darkmind ended up enjoying the bookstores more than he would have ever imagined. Perhaps it was the access to Shadow's knowledge and the way in which he viewed the world. Or maybe it was the content in which the two entities felt more and more compelled to browse. It was likely a combination of both as they poured over books on the occult and mythology.

Shadow was beginning to like Darkmind's presence. He felt the raw energy of the being that came with a sense of invincibility as he became more and more aware of him. On the night before, Darkmind had seemed more interested in cigarettes and sex alone. Now for some reason, the squatter had taken an interest in his life; his decision to read poetry to

Indigo as they had waited for breakfast had been a shifting point for him. It was clear that Indigo was deeply moved, often to tears, by some of Shadow's pieces. Under all of that makeup was a girl that just wanted to be loved. She had melted before him. It was a very good start.

It was a solid beginning for their relationship. It was also a good birth, as far as trust, for the being who called himself Darkmind. The wolf, who seemed mangier by the minute, was relatively quiet and subdued, but she made Shadow feel safe as well. He could remember no other day greater than the day that passed before him now.

Shadow thumbed through every book he could find on possession, sensing no resistance from Darkmind. Every store seemed a slight variation of the last. They smelled of old paper and dust, but it was a good smell to him. Eccentric storeowners smiled, recognizing and welcoming them like family.

Shadow thumbed through as many books on the topic as he could. He was a man who usually searched for knowledge for knowledge's sake alone. Now he was like a man on a mission.

He had never even heard of a situation where someone was possessed by a beneficial being. Again and again he came upon stories of adolescents being taken over by foul-mouthed, foul-tempered spirits. Darkmind was nice, though. He felt safe.

If he had known, however, of the conversation that was taking place under his very nose, he would have been very concerned indeed.

"You are a bigger fool than I imagined!" Lupa rasped. "You spend all of your energy so you can get laid and party it up!"

"It started that way, but I couldn't let him live life without chasing his dreams," Darkmind answered calmly.

"It is *his* life to live, not yours!"

"And I am letting him do so. He now has the woman he loves. That's a good start."

"Start? What next? Will you rack up his credit card even further than he already has? Maybe he needs a new car? How about a bigger TV?"

"He has dreams. Dreams he's afraid of. Dreams that he can accomplish. He's talented."

"What is wrong with you? What about Angel?"

"I have failed to chase every dream that I ever had. I let Angel slip between my fingers, and that was my only chance at happiness. I should have been a hockey player. I should have at least become a police officer."

"So you didn't, so what! How many police officers have you met that you actually liked? Men that feel small inside and need to compensate, women that want to be drunk on power, young kids that feel that badge somehow makes them a better person than the unemployed mother down the street or the construction worker who has nothing but words of kindness for all of those around him! If there is anything that we have learned, it is that all of that amounts for nothing! Any police officer or hockey player who thinks they are better than a single person around them will burn in a hell more horrible than they could ever imagine, or cease to exist altogether. That is a fact!"

"I would be different. I would have been a good cop."

"You lie to yourself over and over! You have a little bit of power now, and you are drunk with it! You think I don't know what you're thinking? Is killing so easy for you?"

"The Indian deserved it."

"Because he had sex?"

"Because he had sex."

"You have no idea what it was like to be either one of them," Lupa said more calmly but coldly. "You have no idea what circumstances propelled them to make the choices that they did. Besides, who the hell are you? There is already a system in place, a day of reckoning, if you will."

"I didn't want him to fall through the cracks."

"He wouldn't have!" Lupa snapped.

"I did."

"So you feel sorry for yourself and start killing both the living and the dead?"

"I have only killed one person since I died."

"The spirits were not yours to take, either!"

"Perhaps."

"And now you plan to kill again? Who will you kill?"

"I'll find criminals and I'll kill them."

"And when the boy gets caught, as he will eventually?"

"He won't get caught."

"He will never agree," she said more calmly. "He is no killer."

"I can help him gain everything that he could imagine. He will become as powerful as any man alive. If the woman cheats, he can replace her with ten more. His writing will be picked up and published. No one will ever cross him again. He will have an advantage that no one else on earth has."

"No one? Are you so sure? Sounds awfully familiar to me."

"What does?"

"Guy kills a load of people and says the devil made him do it."

Darkmind nodded at the truth of the statement. Perhaps it was not such a novel idea after all.

"I'm sure I could do better."

"Seems like a theme of yours these days, dead less than 48 hours, yet wiser than any other being that has ever lived."

"My situation is unique."

"That may be so, but it does not give you the right to destroy the innocence of this boy. I am more afraid that you will be able to convince him to do it than not to. Besides, you really *should* lay low."

"I am," Darkmind replied cockily. "I'm on holiday."

"You continue to break every rule that we have learned along this road. I would fathom to guess that you create more enemies than the sky has stars. Soon this will all catch up to you."

"Maybe you're right." He let out a long sigh and changed his tone. "I did something good here, though, despite what you tell me. A whole life lived and I amounted to nothing. In a few decades, no one will ever even know that I lived. Which in itself might not be such a bad thing, if I had lived a good life."

"Amounted to nothing? What is wrong with you? You gave your life for the cause of good. If there is a god, which I am not so sure there is anymore, fuck him. Fuck him for not recognizing your sacrifice." Lupa continued to sound righteous. "You gave all that you had, and everything that you didn't, so that strangers you never met could suffer a little less! So what if you didn't play in the Stanley Cup? So what if you never got the girl? So what?"

Darkmind's eyes filled with tears. He had pulled back just enough so that Shadow wouldn't feel it. *So what?* he thought. It didn't matter. He had lived as good a life as he could have. There were regrets and scars, but that was to be expected. He was a good man once—a lifetime ago, it seemed.

He had anticipated a heaven and a hell. He had been ready for either one. He had failed Steve at his hour of need, and that had never left him. He had heavy burdens upon his soul regarding the kid he had accidentally killed and the mourning family. He had failed Angel miserably. Perhaps she was better off? Not failed her, then, but failed to love her the way that she had deserved to be loved.

"You're right, Lupa. I will not wash this boy's hands in blood. He deserves to live a life devoid of violence and horror despite his fascination with it. I will not turn him towards this darkness, but neither will I abandon him. He will live his dreams. He has a great heart but has no one to show him that he can release its power, his power. If it is the last thing I do, I will help him become a man. Perhaps then I will feel that I did something noble during my existence. I do not seek redemption from anyone else but myself. If I am destroyed thereafter, then so be it. It will not matter."

Lupa nodded a very tired head in agreement. To him she looked proud.

"So many magpies," Zarah said in an exaggerated monotone voice as they left the slice of pizza shop.

"We have magpies?" Jinx asked in the same tone as he pulled out a cigarette.

"We have crows too, boi," she responded with slightly less bite than she usually did. A blind man could have seen that sparks were flying despite their attempts at normalcy.

The magpie bounced across the railing of a nearby patio before taking to the air. The bird let out a cry followed by a few chirps. The sounds of traffic quickly drowned the bird out.

Zarah looked over and saw that Thorm was making a pistol with his right hand while trying to follow the creature. He pretended to shoot the imaginary gun before bringing it to his lips and blowing on it.

"Asshole," she said in a relatively normal tone as she hit him on the arm. As usual he just laughed.

Despite his reservations about going back into the club, Darkmind had given in. He was truly starting to enjoy himself. There was no more pain, and the closeness of the crew reminded him of how things used to be before everything had happened. Before him and Angel had broken up. Before Steve had died.

* * *

They had spent the day fishing in the river near the abandoned dam. Everything that they had caught they'd released. It had been a nice day with a lot of good fights as they had landed fish after fish. Darwin hadn't been able to come because his mom had needed him for some menial task around their home.

"What a pussy," Steve said with a smile as he took a sip of his beer.

Their rods had rigs with worms on them out in the river's water and were propped up on the shore. Bells were on the tips of the rods so that they would ring if they hooked a fish and the boys weren't paying attention.

"Whatever," he responded from his nearby concrete perch on the half-finished, decaying dam.

"Whoah! Someone sounds a little angry," Steve joked as he cast a stone from the concrete ledge that they were sitting on. It splashed with a plop into the water.

"Just calling it as I see it." He also had a handful of pebbles that he jingled together in the palm of his hands between throws. Several empty beer bottles sat on the slab between them.

"You know, you used to be happy once," Steve said with a soothing voice.

"You used to mind your business." He regretted saying it as soon as it had left his mouth. It wasn't just the hurt look that Steve tried to hide; it was also the fact that the comment had no basis in reality whatsoever.

"Listen. Whatever you do, I'll support it, okay? It's just ... well, I like Angel that's all, and I kind of feel like you're being too harsh."

"She cheated. I won't go back down that road again. Ever."

"Darwin saw the whole thing. He said the guy took her by surprise and stuck his tongue down her throat."

"She kissed him back man! Everyone saw it!"

"For what, like twenty seconds? She was drunk out of her mind and probably didn't even know what she was doing!" Steve's voice rose as well.

"So? I'm supposed to let that shit slide? I heard from a reliable source that he had his hand on her tit!"

"Reliable source? Shit, man. I would hardly call Shelly a reliable source. She once claimed that we stole her lunch money, remember?"

"That was in grade five. People change by the time they're in high school," he reasoned.

"Some do, but not her. She's a lying bitch. Even if he did grab Angel, she pulled away and left the party."

"It's cheating, man."

"Come on!" Steve barked. "Hardly the same as sucking dick, now, is it?"

"It is what it is."

"You know, man, I can't believe you're going to throw away a year's time invested in a really cool girl. You two are perfect for one another. Everyone else can see that—why can't you?"

He thought about what Steve had said for a moment and realised that he was right. He loved Angel more than he could ever imagine loving anyone else again. There was another voice, though, a stronger voice inside of him that told him that he had to let her go. It was a choice that he couldn't return from. He knew that he would love her forever, but for some reason it didn't seem like it was going to be enough.

"I can't, man. Try to understand. I just can't."

They didn't speak for a long time after that. They just sipped their beers and tossed pebbles into the cold dark water and watched them sink far below into the dark, unforgiving water.

Shadow walked into the club's washroom and stared at his reflection for a long time in the mirror. Darkmind had asked him to and he had complied. The being was silent for a long moment before he spoke. He sounded old and very tired.

"I'll be leaving soon, Shadow."

"Do you have to?" Shadow asked, sounding like a child. Darkmind smiled to himself; he had grown to like the young man a lot over the last day.

"I have to. I'm growing weak."

"Will I ever see you again?" he asked. A few intoxicated patrons walked by, ignoring him except for sideways glances, thinking that he was on an acid trip and was just talking to himself.

"I hope so, kid. If it's meant to be, I will come back again to check up on you."

"I hope you do."

"Hold onto that girl, Shadow, and promise me you'll try to get some of your writing published. It's good, you know. Better than good."

"I will."

"Promise?"

"I promise."

"Thank you, Shadow ... for being such a good host." He let out a weak laugh.

"Thank you." Shadow's life had been changed for the better and he was truly grateful.

"I was wondering if you can do one more thing for me?" Darkmind asked.

"Anything."

"I'm going to show you my memories. Maybe they will help you to understand the importance of living a good life. Maybe I just want to leave something behind, in case I leave *it all* behind forever."

"What are you saying?" Shadow asked, wide-eyed as he stared into the mirror.

"Just say yes, kid. I don't want to do it without your permission. Please?" Darkmind sounded almost human.

"I will, Darkmind ... I will. I'll do it."

He smiled, for Shadow had remembered his name. He then showed him all that he had learned.

Steve's Toyota Corolla sped down the highway with relative grace. The motor made the questionable noises of a hard-driven vehicle, but it persisted. Never had the sketchy sounding machine betrayed her owner through rain or snow or fog. She was, and always had been, a first time car owner's dream.

They had shared few words since the dam. Both of the boys were tired from the long day of travelling, fresh air, exhilarating fishing and reflective conversation. The car smelled of wood smoke from a river shore campfire. An old deck stereo played a cassette, which despite the questionable sound quality managed to make the trip seem shorter.

Jimi Hendrix's "All along the Watchtower" carried them over the rise and fall of the highway, past wooden farm fences and around long gradual turns. Horses pranced over autumn fields, and water foal glided across ponds of varying sizes. Dark clouds raced across the highway as the sun-bleached day somersaulted towards its end.

He took a long pull before handing Steve back his cigarette. Smoke rose from his lips and streamed into his inhaling nostrils before being exhaled once more. Out of repetition he unscrewed the Coke bottle lid once again before taking a long swallow that fizzed through his nostrils and made his eyes water. Dark clouds painted patches of the highway in darkness.

Death came.

He raised his gun. Double tap.

They turned gradually as the pavement wound its way through a valley feature. The stream passed through a culvert beneath the highway. There was a metal railing that offered reassuring security from the slight drop off of the road. The rail caught the sun and reflected it dully.

There was nothing on the road, he remembered. There was nothing on the road except for a pool of darkness. There was no pothole, debris or moisture upon the surface. It was just one of those things, a fluke really.

The tire exploded unprovoked. Valiantly Steve held onto the wheel. There was the sound of metal grinding and a sickening thud as something gave way beneath them. The sound of glass exploding as the car first found her side. A feeling of weightlessness as they were flung. The car rolling, earth and sky over and over. Blackness.

He raised his gun. Double tap.

He awoke to the smell of something burning. He did not remember crawling out of the car. He dragged his useless leg behind him. His face was bleeding.

There was Steve. Metal was thrust through his body. He knew it was metal, but it was red. He could see bone and what looked like strings of blood clot creeping down unspecified white and yellow liquid that dripped slower than its bright counterpart. Glass stuck out of his face like the thousand quills of a porcupine. Steve clearly could not see through these once clear shards protruding from his face and eyes. He coughed blood.

"Kill ... me . . .," he asked hoarsely

Could not move. Staring down at Steve. Rooted in place.

"Kill ... me . . .," he asked again after a moment. "Kill ... me . . ."

He dragged his useless leg to the mess of the machine nearby. There was a filleting knife amongst the scattered fish hooks. He picked up the tool and pulled it from its sheath.

"Kill ... me . . ."

He reached down and pulled Steve's curly hair blonde backwards, exposing his neck. Steve's breathing became hoarser.

"Kill ... me . . ."

He raised the knife. He could see the stubble upon his friend's face when he was this close.

"Good-bye, Steve," he said coldly as he raised the knife.

Steve did not seem to hear him and clearly couldn't see him.

"Kill ... me . . ."

He looked at his friend's throat and saw the pounding of a slow yet steady pulse. He saw the old scar on his chin from playing hockey.

"Argh!" he yelled as he tossed the knife aside. "I can't do it!"

"Kill ... me . . ."

"I can't, man. Try to understand. I just can't." It was the second time that day he had used that line.

Three days. Steve suffered for three more days. A passing farm truck and the squealing of tires as the man went to find a phone. Eventually there was an ambulance.

He never stopped screaming from the pain, and when he spoke, the words made little sense. He talked about demons and brave warrior spirits that protected a tribe of elders. Nothing would silence him. No pain medication numbed him enough. When his doses of medication reached dangerous levels, he would still writhe and twist in the hospital bed and pull out his tubes. His teeth would grate against one another. Still he would scream. For three days he suffered unimaginable pain.

It was three days before he died.

"Kill ... me . . ."

"*He raised his gun. Double tap.*"

Kill ... me ...

A small child. A dusty village in a desert.

Kill ... me ...

He raised his gun. Double tap.

Kill ... me ...

"*So cold...*"

"*I love her, promise (cough) ... tell her.*"

"So very cold…"
"My mom…"
He raised his gun. Double tap.
"Kill me!"
Double tap.
"Guy kills a load of people and says the devil made him do it."
Hahaha!
"So very cold…"
"Kill me!"
Double tap.
"Burn!"
"*The sleeping and the dead are but as pictures. 'Tis the eye of childhood that fears a painted devil.*"

So very cold.

He twitched upon the dance floor. Foam came from his mouth. His eyes were wide and vacant. His friends came rushing to his side. Spectators watched helplessly. Someone called an ambulance.

Far away there was a voice both friendly and strange. The voice sounded as if it spoke through harp strings and satin filled dreams. He tried to find that world in which the voice had come from. He did not, could not understand. She was so far away.

He felt so cold.

"Shadow!" she called.

12

He had not wanted to come, not initially. There were lesser dark spirits everywhere. The living looked like spirits, and the spirits looked like the living. He was hunted. It would not be wise.

He had buckled, though. He had longed for the land of the living, the exhilaration of crowds and the unpredictability of the free-floating night. He wanted to taste the drinks and smell the women. He wanted to see again through the eyes of a life never lived. He wanted to taste cigarette smoke against his lips. He wanted to imagine that he had never killed or had never died.

He felt that this was his last supper. He had tasted the cups of the kingdom of life for the final time. There would be one here, somewhere in this crowd, who would betray him. There would be a Judas somewhere in this throng. He lacked the strength or the will to battle.

It was the night that would be his final send-off.

A part of him smiled inside. A young man had found his love just as he had lost his. Perhaps two more would, indirectly through his actions, find love as well. He told himself that he had done a good deed. A man had been afraid to live and now was living. Another man had been afraid to die and now would do so. He had done good, and the world would be a better place. It had started off selfishly, but he had committed deeds of which he could be proud.

All of these things he told himself as he left the body. He did not look back because he was committed to his path. He felt that Shadow would be fine, though. He had shown him why he needed to change, and his mind had been receptive. Darkmind had no clue what he was doing, how to transfer the knowledge, so he was happy that Shadow could see what he had showed him.

All was well in the world. It was time for him to die.

He staggered through the club and towards the exit. He had lost so much energy that he had to shuffle with the living towards the doorway. No longer could he walk through walls. No longer could he open doors. The wolf was nowhere to be seen.

Pain erupted through him and around him. His joints felt on fire and his insides hurt. He wanted to fall down and scream, to curl up and die. He felt so cold and alone. He was suffocating over and over again.

Faces moved and swirled around him in a dreamtime fog. "Become an Angel" by In Strict Confidence pounded through the sound system, making him feel like he was in some eccentric music video. The smells mingled of perfumes and drunkenness, sweat and pheromones, the living and the dead. There he saw the face of a smiling cactus head, a painted clown, emos and punks and stylish Victorian imaginary vampires.

He saw them too—their grinning visages. They saw that he was vulnerable and alone. Lupa had left. He could barely keep his head up. He was not so sure he could lift the sword. They saw all of this.

They were spirits of this place and were loyal to the hunters. They would never have dared to move against him before, but now in his weakness he offered the promise of great recognition by one of the harvesters of souls. He was a powerful spirit that could now be taken and controlled. He did not know it, but there were few things rarer than a being as powerful and vulnerable as he now was on this side of the veil.

They had long limbs on which they ran sideways, like lanky apes. They shuffled on knuckles and the tips of their toes. They wore faces of gleaming smiles, but in each of their fists was a straight razor, like those used by old barbers to shave men's faces. There were lots of these humanoid creatures. They were everywhere around him, too many to count. Every single one of them was dressed in the clothing of the poor from generations past.

He wanted them to be done with it, to kill him. They were circling like cackling hyena and seemed intent on making this game last. Perhaps they were herding him. Either way his movement outside of the club remained unhindered.

As he stepped outside though he saw the reason. The last part of the trap had fallen into place. There in the middle of the street, flanked by passing cars, stood the towering image of the hooded hunter with the scythe. He knew instinctively that the one he had killed was not this one before him but rather a brother.

The maggot skull grinned at him from ear to ear. The fly black hooded cape floated, buzzing, around him dramatically. The gnarled wooden shaft of his weapon evilly sported the long, silver blade.

In moments he would be dead—or worse, harvested. He could not win this battle. Of this he was more than certain.

Shaun was a special boy. His caregiver was at his wit's end what to do with him, though. He was high functioning for a 19-year-old who had been cast aside by traditional Cantonese-speaking parents. They had never planned on having a boy with Down syndrome. When they had first seen his distorted features, they had been beyond disturbed. A boy was supposed to carry on the family name; he was supposed to marry a girl from a well to do family and inherit his father's knack for trading stocks into small fortunes. He was no son of theirs, and so he had been abandoned.

He was incredibly astute; a person would never have guessed that by looking at the big-boned boy, who was in reality a young man, with the bowl cut and the wet, protruding tongue. White flecks sparkled in almond brown eyes that seemed to question and comprehend the world before him. His memory continued to astonish those around him. His wit made him hard not to like.

No matter how many caregivers, doctors and program specialists worked with him, though, they could not seem to break him from the one persistent, recurrent theme that permeated everything that he did. They could not seem to be able to convince Shaun that the fantasy world that he pretended to see around him was something that needed to be shed. He always would point out an imaginary world of invisible people and magical beings, and he would give it no rest.

This night would be no exception.

His caregiver had figured that a late-night walk might show Shaun that the ghosts and devils that he professed to see everywhere were nothing more than figments of his imagination. It was a last attempt of unconventional practice that would determine if perhaps there was more to Shaun's ramblings than an overactive imagination. More and more, his workers were starting to believe that the special needs boy was also mentally ill.

"They kill him!" Shaun yelled, drooling at his caregiver.

"Who?" the guardian asked, obviously frustrated and annoyed.

"The devils!" His mouth was open, aghast. "They kill soldier!"

* * *

Darkmind had drawn Black Dragon as he stepped into the city night. The shufflers circled him and swiped with precision accuracy. He already had a half-dozen cuts on his arms and legs that had slipped past his cloak. His blade had not scored a single hit.

He let his vision fade the physical world out completely as he focused on the combatants around him. He was ready to die, but he would make them pay as dearly as he could for the violent encounter. His left hand held onto his cloak as his right gripped the weapon comfortably, extended far to his side.

The reaper came in, swinging wide strokes and sending the shuffling beings out of his mighty arcs. Several of the beings closed in on Darkmind's back as he turned to face the greatest of the threats. He spun suddenly and caught one of the henchmen in the throat with a wild arc. Energy flew into him and around him quickly. He found his feet as the creature fell, grasping at its torn and bleeding neck.

The reaper, however, was no minor being and was not alone. Even if the hunter had not been there, the sheer number of his foes seemed insurmountable. He was bleeding energy even as he gathered the power that emitted from the one downed foe.

The reaper toyed with him. Maggots fell freely from his face upon the ground. His wide eyes seemed both amused and soulless at once. The snare that had been set around him was perfect.

It happened so fast that Darkmind would forever be sceptical to whether it had happened at all. One moment the odds seemed so impossibly stacked against him. A few moments later he dared to believe he might survive.

His unreckoned hand shot out from the edge of his cloak. It was no weapon of great reputation, and the beings had not known or considered its existence at all. His K-bar knife shot out in his left hand and slammed into the chest of his nearest opponent. He used the moment of distraction to spin and run directly at the dark-cloaked hunter.

A silver shaft, unrecognizable at first, erupted from the reaper's chest and forced the being to arch his back and thrust out its abdomen. Its arms flayed backwards, the scythe still in his right hand, and his feet seemed lifted from the ground. Darkmind split the skull clean down the middle with Black Dragon as the jaw let out an animalistic, unholy scream that was cut short. He spun around quickly as a razor dug deep into his kidney.

He decapitated the fedora-wearing assailant, sending the head flying into the air. He heard a sickening thud as his unseen ally joined the fray. He split another close assailant from shoulder to waist. With every swing his strength multiplied. His rage increased with every inflicted hit even as he lost energy from every wound of his own.

He dared not stop as he shared a kill with his silver sword-wielding friend. There was no time to ask how it came to be that Balzola the jester, who fought with an acrobat's frenzy, was helping him fight the enemies that faced him now. He swallowed his confusion and fought the horde with reckless fury.

Balzola wielded the oversized sword of the valkyrie that Darkmind had thought lost, what seemed so long ago. Every twist of this blade rained death. Rags flew into the air alongside body parts as the two began to massacre the shuffling beings. Balzola bled from a score of wounds by this point as well.

The reaper crawled towards the battle as its head seemed to be repairing itself. Darkmind rolled in its direction with his sword tucked in at his waist before coming to his feet and executing another downwards stroke. He had no doubt anymore that he had once been a proficient samurai. The blade felt a part of him.

Even as the being slumped once, more critically wounded, Darkmind was forced to abandon the attack.

He knew the reaper was regenerating, but Balzola had fallen under a press of three of the shufflers. Darkmind leapt for them, holding Black Dragon in both of his hands, his knife still in the chest of the first writhing, surprised enemy. A side chop cut a smiling head in half. He crossed the blade back quickly and severed one at the waist.

Balzola, freed, was a whirlwind of destruction. As long as the beings were not too close, they fell like ripe fruit upon a rocky field. The sword painted all with the gore of battle.

Darkmind barely lifted Black Dragon in time to block a heavy swing from the scythe. He kicked out with his left leg as he fell into a back roll, avoiding a barrage of blows. A series of follow-up swings kept him rolling dangerously close to every one of them.

The valkyrie's sword nicked the left arm of the reaper and prevented the advancement as Balzola took a hit from a razor to save him. Darkmind in return lifted a shuffler off of his feet by impaling him with his dark blade. His sword fell from his hands as the weight carried it forward.

Balzola half thrust and half threw the silver blade to Darkmind, who reached for the weapon not understanding the jester's gamble. He understood the seriousness of the desperate move as the performer grabbed with both hands onto the shaft of the scythe.

Darkmind swung downward with a ferocity unknown to him. The sword reeked of power that he had been unable to tap before. Now it felt like lightening in his hands as the reaper's right arm was cut from it. It was forced to let go of the scythe.

Balzola brought the weapon overhead with a righteous spin. The skull separated from its shoulders and bounced even as it melted into nothingness. The being seemed to fall into a puddle and dissolve.

Able to hold the valkyrie's sword with his right hand, Darkmind found and pulled free Black Dragon with his left even as the remaining henchmen fled. He finished the few wounded before facing the scythe-wielding jester, who was doing the same.

They both breathed hard and stared at one another, exhausted yet filled with power at once. Balzola leaned heavily on a scythe that looked far too long and awkward to be an efficient weapon. The jester gave him a bloody toothy smile, and Darkmind saw what he had been too blind to see before.

He was confused. He was afraid. He was exhilarated.

"Balzola," he said with a warm hum. "I'm glad you came."

13

"You're alive!" He stated as he walked towards the jester.

She smiled, and her eyes sparkled with intelligence.

He looked her over with fresh eyes from recent experience. She had appeared a boy originally, but her features seemed so obvious to him now. Her high cheekbones and full lips were hidden behind makeup. Her slender neck had seemed thicker beneath a large collar. The black tights hugged against athletic legs. Slight mounds, almost unrecognizable, marked either small breasts or ones that were held tightly to her body. He could see how the woman could so easily be taken as a boy in life.

He took her in his arms, and they held each other for a long moment before Darkmind pulled away.

"I don't understand. I saw you murdered." The words were more of a question than a testimony of fact.

Balzola shook her head back and forth. She laid the scythe on the ground. He wondered if the hunters would come for that weapon now. He remembered how Hachimantaro had explained how they had premeditated the killing and robbing of weapons from hunters in their own land.

She raised a hand and pointed to Darkmind, and then she held her head and shook it back and forth. Her mouth was an open visage of pain as she imitated him. She then put her hands together and floated the fingers apart from one another.

"I screamed and held my head. Then I disappeared?"

Balzola nodded her head.

"How did you find me?"

The woman mimed that she had ran, grabbed the sword and chased him. Her imitation of wings flapping told him that she had either called her magpie guide or shifted into a bird form. The first seemed more likely. She then held a hand over her eyes and pretended to scan back and forth. She seemed to be following tracks before scanning back and forth once more.

"You followed my trail?"

She nodded again.

"The last time I saw you. You seemed dazed, not lucid."

Balzola acted out a rain falling before being filled with power. She did this a few times before he was able to guess correctly. This had less to do with her acting ability and more to do with the obviousness of the situation.

"Your high spirit came to you? You called it somehow?"

Balzola nodded her head.

"Are the others okay? Bali and Hachimantaro?"

She looked confused but indicated yes anyways.

"Why did you come?" he asked her, feeling suddenly very indebted as the seriousness of the situation became clear to him. Balzola would be hunted now with him.

She put up two fingers. First she indicated that he had broken the chain that had imprisoned her. Then she surprisingly held a hand over her heart and seemed to indicate that she loved him. If he could blush he would have. It occurred to him that the girl simply had a crush on him.

"You are a lesbian, though, aren't you? Bali? The daughter that you got into trouble over? The girl in the brothel?" His words sounded awkward even to himself.

She held up two fingers again.

"You like boys and girls?"

She stopped and looked up into the air for a moment, apparently lost in thought. She faced him and nodded yes. There was something else she was trying to say, however. She smiled largely and then pretended to hug an imaginary person while occasionally feeling breasts. Then she indicated the chain and frowned dramatically. She pretended to hug someone once more and acted as if she was crying while she was chained.

"The daughter?"

She nodded up and down eagerly. Then she pointed to him.

"I was the daughter?" He asked, shocked.

Balzola nodded her head. She then opened her hand before shaking her head to indicate no. He was confused but strained to understand her anyways. Her final hand motions indicated that she pulled something out of the top of her head.

"I am the same *great* spirit!" he said excitedly, knowing that the statement was true. He knew at some point he would have to deal with the fact that on some level he had betrayed and killed her, but the interpretation of information was too important to even focus on any peripheral thought at the moment. He continued to focus despite the very seriousness of that thought and the repercussions of guilt he would probably feel when it all sank in.

"For what it's worth, I'm sorry for being such a bitch."

She looked at him very seriously for a while as if she was unsure how to take the apology.

"Have you, your greater spirit, lived since as well?"

Balzola jumped up and down excitedly and nodded yes. She then flapped her arms back and forth.

"You were a bird?"

She gave him a dirty look and made a face at him before shaking her head back and forth. She then intermittently went from holding her hands reverently across her chest to flapping her *wings*.

"You were an angel?"

Balzola nodded her head grinning widely. She then gave a hand motion that rolled over itself. It seemed to indicate that there was more.

"You were an angel," he said quietly trying to figure it out.

She kept rolling her hand in front of him.

Then it came to him all at once. A warm wave flew into him and seemed for a moment to wash away the pain. A fluttering feeling rose within him and gained momentum as he knew it to be true.

"Angel?" he asked barely daring to believe.

She nodded her head as she leapt into his arms. He knew it wasn't entirely true because Angel was living still. He knew, though, that Angel and Balzola shared the same high spirit. She was her reincarnation just as he was the reincarnation of the lying lover. He knew innately that there were other lives as well. They were ancient lovers.

They kissed passionately for a very long time, unconcerned for the dangers that lurked nearby. The scythe lay on the ground between their feet. His arms behind her back were crossed, yet they pressed her body against his even though both of his hands still each grasped the hilt of a bloody sword.

* * *

Even as an ambulance arrived for Shadow, another nighttime drama played out before the club. A care worker begged passersby to dial 911 on their cell phones. Shaun was partially pinned against the wall, screaming frantically into the night.

"Clowns kill devils, and so does Shaun!" he screamed nonsensically as his tongue flapped out of his mouth. "Soldier and devils and devils and devils!"

"Shhh!" the caretaker tried to hush him.

"I kills him! Ahhh!" he shrieked as his bowl cut hair flopped cartoon like.

"Shhh!"

"Ghosts and devils! Ghosts and devils!"

The caretaker felt the boy shivering in fear beneath him and knew that he had failed. There was no hope for Shaun. He was suffering frightening hallucinations at a whole new level. He would have to be committed somewhere. There would be tests, and perhaps with the proper medications there would be another opportunity someday. Maybe a more patient worker would eventually get another chance at helping the kid.

He could only hope.

Darkmind recognized the sound of baying dogs that echoed into the night and they began to walk. He knew that they came for him once more. They came for her, too. The hunter in the chariot would come, him or another very similar. He wasn't sure if they could kill that one. Perhaps the dogs would fall like the shufflers, perhaps they wouldn't. The demon with the horned helmet had radiated a whole new level of terror.

If he was alone and prepared to die, he would make his last stand here. *If* he was alone. He was not, though. Balzola was also Angel, and in searching for him he had abandoned her living incarnation to help him. She had come for him and had saved him. She had returned the sword and its temporary sheath to him. Even if he hadn't loved her, he would be indebted enough to make sure that she survived this ordeal intact.

If Balzola perished, what would happen to Angel? Would she die as well? Would she remain in her confused and drunken state? Or would she simply cease to exist?

The club was not very close to the cathedral, and he knew of no other place of worship nearby in this strange and foreign city. There had to be another way.

"If I call Lupa, can you follow me?" he asked as he turned to look at the trailing jester.

She flashed her bloody teeth in a wide smile and nodded that she could. Then she shrugged her shoulders as if she was unsure. She trudged alongside him, carrying the long, gnarled scythe over one of her shoulders.

She seemed like she thought that she could but wasn't 100 percent sure. How could she be? As a coherent wandering spirit, he probably had more experience than her at this type of thing.

"I'm going to try," he said as the barking and wailing seemed very close all around them. "We can't stay here."

He felt the energy drain from him as Lupa manifested beside him. She looked healthy and strong once more.

Took you long enough, she seemed to smirk.

"Can you lead us away from here?" he asked. "Anywhere."

"Yes, but if they find our trail, they will be close behind."

"I don't see many options."

"The highways of the spirit world are a maze without a map, a cosmic web that ties all things and should not be hastily traveled."

"Where will we end up?" he asked with a voice ripe with tension.

"There are other planes and dimensions. Time is not linear. Even the most skilled traveler would tread with patience and purpose!" Lupa protested.

"We will let fate carry us, then! To stay here invites certain death, I'm sure! We'll deal with what we have to!" Darkmind decided.

The magpie appeared once more as the world became a haze of fog. He felt they had to travel this way, because he was sure they were out of options. With any luck, however, they would leave their pursuers behind.

If they had to fight, then fight they would, but first they would try to flee. Being a spirit once more helped him to remember on some level that the path he had taken was no coincidence. He would remember first, and then he would have his revenge.

* * *

He felt himself pushing through a thick fog, heavy and deep. He could not open his eyes. He could not breathe. It was as if he was sinking into the thick, salty ocean on the blackest of nights.

He felt as if some time had passed when he began to stir. He did not feel that he had blacked out or that he had lost consciousness. His body ached.

He heard children playing. Then he heard the rustling of leaves as they fluttered dead upon the ground in the wind. A child started laughing, and then there were more shouts of joy and of glee.

Darkmind became aware that he was lying on his stomach in those very leaves. He slowly opened his eyes and began to raise himself to his feet. He was surprised that it was night; the playing voices had made him think that it was day.

He looked up and saw a young boy standing on a ridge a short distance away. The boy was not playing with the others, whom Darkmind could still hear but not see. The small, brown boy stood staring at him wide-eyed and sad. He stood motionless.

Darkmind dared not look away from the child for fear that he would disappear forever. He recognized the boy from another life that seemed so far away from him now. The boy stood motionless with his tiny hands at his side. He did not blink. Two bullet holes were in his chest.

The kids' voices were playing in whispers, but they were somehow louder at the same time. The wind blew leaves into the air between the two spirits who looked at one another. The smell of autumn filled the air.

Darkmind knew that he was alone, yet still he dared not look away. Balzola and Lupa were no longer nearby. He questioned his own judgement for having fled the great hunter. Perhaps they should have made their stand on more familiar ground. He had not wanted to risk losing Balzola or Angel though; he should have listened to Lupa's concerns more fully.

Now he was completely alone.

There was a sense he was in a very alien place. There were stars above him, but he felt as if he were in a cave deep underground. A part of him felt weak and vulnerable. The feeling reminded him of being a child once more, a time when every shadow had held something within it to be afraid of.

The boy on the ridgeline slowly looked up into the tops of the trees. He didn't really seem to be looking at anything but was listening to the sounds of playing. The act of looking up suggested that the children he could hear were playing above him somehow.

Suddenly the boy darted. Like a startled deer, he ran abruptly over the ridgeline and out of view. Darkmind quickly finished getting to his feet and sprinted after him into the forest.

The act itself was not preconceived; it was instinctual. He would not have chased the boy if he had not run away in the first place. Now that he was running, however, he would not consider abandoning this chase that seemed to lack rationale.

14

He moved through the unknown for a very long time, while the forest itself seemed to claw and tug at his cloak with every step that he took. The stars above appeared somehow artificial as he became more aware of them, as if they were painted upon the roof of a very tall cave. The moon as well looked more like a dim streetlight than nighttime's mirror of the sun. However, the illumination was bright enough for him to navigate a path through the bramble.

He could not see the child could but knew that he was close. Always just visible in the distance were shrubs shaking and small trees being bent, as if another ahead of him made the same journey.

At first he thought it was a trick of his eyes in the dim light, a tall black shape stretching from the forest into and across the heavens. As he got closer, he saw that it was not completely unlike a tree. Black Indian ink blew across the canvass of the sky. The branches reached out away from the main body but shifted like black dye in a clear glass of water, or perhaps the poison of an octopus that had been shot out into the betrayal of the sea. Its sheer size was menacing, and he could see no end to the thing's height. He felt a dark and beautiful magnetism as he was drawn towards it.

As he got closer he recognized that there was a light at the base of the obsidian tree. The blue and orange flames only reached up short distances, but their tongues could still be seen from where he was. Their dancing colors reminded him of gasoline spilled upon the surface of the water like dull, burning rainbows.

He heard a steady drumming that came from the same direction as the flame. He also slowly became aware of a singing violin and several hands clapping. Shadows flung themselves across the light's image in a twirling dancing motion, but nothing could be seen of them besides their silhouettes. He felt a strange sense of excitement and exhilaration tremble through his being with every heartbeat that pounded within his chest.

His heart beat.

Darkmind suddenly stepped into a clearing that circumvented the great tree. At this close distance, the entity did in fact look very much like a tree. It was a tree that seemed to dance and move to the music offered before it. The light of the lone fire showed an ancient bark that covered its surface. At the base was the yawning mouth of a very dark cave. He knew that he needed to move through this opening, and a momentary fear shot across him.

Several small-statured people danced around the fire; they seemed to have painted their skin powdery blue. The women wore long braids and the men long beards. They were barely clothed and were both athletic and sexual in how they moved across the space. They appeared to be unaware of him and moved in rapture as if in a trance, with their eyes either pressed towards the heavens or peering into the ground. Long coloured ribbons flowed from the women's hair and were tied around their limbs. The men held cups of gold in outstretched arms.

There was no drummer that he could see. He became aware that the pounding matched that of his heart. He pondered this very thing for a pause until his mind shifted towards the lone violin player. The manlike creature who played with a fury stared intently and unblinkingly at him, smiling all of the while. He was as large as him, or at least his upper body was. His lower legs were those of a forest animal of sorts, similar to a deer's. He wore a loose-buttoned shirt that was partly open, revealing a strong muscular chest. Nothing covered his smooth, hairy legs.

His eyes were blue and very human. He had blonde hair as well as a sharply pointed beard. He was a handsome man, Darkmind was forced to admit, despite the two small horns that protruded from behind his hairline. He was both beautiful and strange at the same time.

Darkmind stepped closer, feeling that he should join the orgy of dance. He moved slowly into the clearing until the dancers were circling him madly, yet still they paid him no heed. The violinist, however, rose and walked slowly towards him as his feet rooted to a single spot. The bow screamed across the instrument hauntingly while the eyes looked the stranger up and down. As he continued to play, he also started to circle him.

Darkmind turned to face the musician keeping eye contact with the musical satyr no matter what position he took around him. He did not blink or let his stare waiver. The two beings studied one another without kindness or hostility but a type of curiosity that is known only to beings so foreign from one another as to never have likely met in the first place. The musician seemed to play harder, as if trying to illicit some sort of response from the wandering spirit.

To Darkmind there was suddenly an understanding. He was a lucid spirit in a place that a lucid spirit had no place being, and yet he knew that other lucid spirits had come this way but had been blind to what he now saw before him.

This place somehow belonged to him. It was his home in a very real way, the gateway of his ancestors into the belly of the world tree. Spirits usually came here in a flash at death, or never at all. Sometimes healers came here to cure the living, searching for lost pieces of their patients' souls.

Darkmind bowed slightly to the ancient being before him. The satyr nodded back before moving away from him in a gesture of admittance and rapport. He never once lifted his eyes off of the newcomer, and neither did Darkmind. The playing never stopped.

"*Have you seen a jester come this way?*" Darkmind asked the stranger without moving his lips.

"*Balzola the harlequin. Yes. She was with a wolf. Two swordsmen pursued her shortly afterwards.*" He continued to play the violin as he walked in larger circles around Darkmind. He did not speak with words either.

"What did the swordsmen look like?" he asked.

"*Like old friends, Darkmind ... like friends that once were.*" There was a momentary pause before the voice filled his head once more. "*They were your Hachimantaro's samurai looking to help you or to kill you. They have been seeking you since the attack.*"

"How do you know so much? Do you know about the worm that attacked me?" Darkmind asked in awe of the musician.

"*I know of your life because I sit at its gate. Your friends came by a very long time ago, but that may not matter as time is an illusion here. You should know that they have lost your path; the wolf refuses to leave her side. You should find them.*"

"Thank you," he answered as he started to move towards the cave opening.

"*Darkmind.*"

"Yes?"

"The attack?"

"Of course."

"You have dangerous enemies ... or perhaps Hachimantaro does. The worm was bribed by the great hunter to separate you from the others. What you were convinced of, the worm entering you, did happen; the attack on the others, did not. Bali-Tali-Andra lives, as do the others. These alliances can protect you from the dark masses that gather. This hunt is gaining purpose and momentum. Your spirit would be a great feast for the dark ones. To let you live risks another Hachimantaro yet a being who plays by his own rules."

"Who are you?" he asked in his head once more, both thankful and reverent.

"I am a prince in the kingdom of the past."

"I have so many questions, though." Darkmind stopped himself from leaving as quickly as he had intended, now that he had an opportunity to gain some understanding.

The forest prince continued to play as he waited for the questions to come.

"Why would these samurai want to kill me if they are my friends?" he asked.

"They do not like the games you play with the mortals. They do not yet see you."

"See me?"

"You do not yet see yourself. The same hand has dealt every card here."

"More riddles?"

"More riddles."

"What else can I expect?"

"Death or life. Death for life."

"The longer I talk to you, the less you make sense."

"Find your friends and fight your battles. Soon the circle will be completed." He winked one eye reassuringly as he said this.

Darkmind looked at the ancestor spirit, this prince, for a long moment before nodding his head. It was clear to him that he needed to carry on and that the information that he was already given would have to be enough for now.

Still, they continued to stare at one another for several moments.

"Thank you," he said at last before stepping into the darkness of the cave. The satyr never answered, and the music faded quickly as he moved into the darkness.

* * *

The air was dank and quiet. It smelled of rich garden earth, freshly stirred beneath a summer's rain. He moved forward into the darkness that he could not penetrate with his gaze. He was aware of a presence on the ground, to his right, lying in an unthreatening manner. He knew this canine being would devour any living soul that wandered into the cave without the right to.

He moved for a long time with a sense of purpose. He knew this path but did not understand it or why he should feel this way. He had been here before, of that he was certain.

He walked into a room that was very much like a dream. It was a voyeur's mirage that would have disturbed him immensely had he still been alive. There before him, like a movie composed of chalky dust particles, were images he knew he could not interact with: they were his parents, wrapped in a sweaty mess of naked youth. The room was obviously rented, a cheap hotel found in a moment of desperation. It was here that he had been conceived.

He had seen pictures before but had never fully comprehended that his parents had been young once like him—young and naive and simple. He marvelled at the passion that they had once shared. It was something he had never even glimpsed for a heartbeat in all of the years that he had been alive.

His mother covered his father's chest with soft, moist kisses every time she rocked past him. His father playfully kissed her neck and fondled her breasts.

"So this was how it began," he stated aloud, confident that his presence could not be felt or his words heard.

He looked up suddenly, aware that he was not alone.

On the other side of the image stood the small, brown boy, wide-eyed, staring at the sexual act being played out before him.

Guilt consumed him once more. It was not the guilt of a man who was showing something forbidden to a young mind two innocent to understand, nor was it the soiling of his thoughts from the same, the destroying of innocence, which Darkmind also considered in that moment. It was a guilty wave of regret for actions that could not be erased. He had stolen the life from this boy, and he had no idea if there was any way that he could ever hope to give him anything of value back, that could ever make up for it.

The boy's eyes were wide with incomprehension. He looked back and forth between the ghost and the image. Not sure which one was more frightening to him, he pulled out of his paralysis and started to run further into the cave.

"Wait!" Darkmind yelled too late. He needed to make peace somehow, despite his unkind appearance or previous role in the child's misfortunes.

He started to run after the boy who disappeared further into the cave through the fog of images. Darkmind could sense him up ahead moving quickly through more pictures of pregnancy, marriage and childbirth. He moved swiftly but had to focus so that he did not move too fast through the movie of his life. He knew that he could move through its entirety in the span of a moment if he chose to do so. The child ran at a human pace, so he chose to run at the same pace as well.

The images curled around him and licked at him like flames—kindergarten, the birth of his sisters, family deaths and dramas, heartache and laughter. The emotions clung to him and made him feel heavy. His times of happiness were replaced and consumed by guilt and misdeeds. Noble acts seemed to shield him somehow from the pain of the viewing, but selfish ones grated into him and filled him with sadness.

There was a path he followed, and he could see it clearly as his life spanned out before him. He was aware that other passages branched away from him into side caverns and rooms. He thought briefly that these were paths not taken, alternative lives never lived. A moment after this epiphany, the pain came tenfold.

He realized he had not felt the physical pain of death in this hall of memories; in fact it had been a reprieve he had not considered initially while stepping into the novelty of the place. The new pain was terrifying to him, though, and he ached for that old, base form of pain that did not consume his soul.

He saw a dance he had been to once in junior high. There was a shy girl he had wanted to ask. He had put it off, building up the courage, knowing that he would ask her eventually. The dance had ended and he had not had that chance. A pattern for his life had been set.

It was an appropriate moment to focus on, for it was these types of moments that cost him the most pain now. Kind words that had been withheld. A handshake or hug to a friend or family member. The pocket change that he had told the beggar he did not have, wanting to return later but not doing it, seeing now that the homeless senior had passed away shortly after. His memories were filled with what-ifs and regrets. It was the opportunities to be a better person that hurt him now.

Then there was Angel, sweet, sweet Angel. The woman he should have been with, the woman who now struggled so hard to move past his memory and into a better life. Still with every action chasing the boy, she had loved with all of her heart. He started to cry.

The small, brown boy took a sudden unexpected turn up ahead. It was into a tunnel that led away from the images of his life path. Darkmind followed him. He stepped through a barrier of some kind and into a dark and dusky cavern. What he saw took him completely by surprise.

The boy stood statue still directly ahead of him in the darkness, paralyzed once more in fear. There were shadows playing against the walls that moved with purpose and seemed to swirl outwards towards them. There was a banging sound that started almost immediately after their arrival. He moved to position himself in front of the boy as a protector. The sound was of metal being banged, like a drum against some old abandoned pipes. It reverberated and echoed into the darkness.

"Close your eyes!" he told the child sharply. The boy obeyed, and he felt him clutch to the back of his cloak while completely forgetting the fear of the ghost who had pursued him mere moments before.

Darkmind drew his blades because he felt that battle was imminent. There in the darkness were the reflections of scores of pairs of eyes. He looked behind him to see if he and the child could back out of the cave, but he saw that there were also sets of eyes coming into focus in the darkness from where they came as well. Now there was also the growling of metal on metal and grinding ancient steel that somehow began to rise from the floor of the cave as well.

He watched as humanoid shapes started to manifest everywhere. The heads were misshapen and smooth and seemed to reflect the light. He could hear heavy breathing and unearthly moans that even in his otherworldly state brought a shiver up his spine. He was aware that the boy behind him was now sobbing.

There were too many of the beings. Scores of them moved around him at once, maybe more. He heard the sound of many swords coming out of their scabbards. The blades were short, and he was aware through the semi-darkness that many of the beings held shields before them.

"Step away from the boy!" a voice demanded loudly, and the words echoed around the room heavily.

"No."

"Do it or die."

"If you want to harm this child, you'll have to kill me first," he stated plainly, trying to sound confident or at least intimidating.

A figure moved out of the darkness in front of him and took several steps forward. A formation of figures behind this leader stepped slightly into his line of sight as well.

"It is you that wishes to harm this child, and us that will protect him."

"Hurt him?" he stated the question loudly to the Roman-looking soldier in ancient armour.

"Were you not just chasing him?" the man asked sternly. He raised his sword arm and banged it against his shield. The clashing and grinding sounds were quickly replaced by an immediate and eerie silence.

"I owe this child a lot, and I wanted to tell him this. I wanted to make amends."

"Amends?" the Roman asked in a curious tone.

"Yes. I was a soldier and killed him by mistake during a battle. He was in a building where we were fighting the Taliban. We found out later that when his family, a group of farmers, had fled before the operation, he had stayed behind because he wanted to see the fighting. At least, this is what his father said that he had believed happened. For all I know he was Taliban as well."

"My father would never fight with the Taliban!" the boy yelled out from behind Darkmind. "They killed his father and all of my uncles!"

"War can be confusing, and it is sad to learn that innocents still die," the Roman stated in a much calmer voice.

"What is your name?" Darkmind asked.

"Lucius," he answered. "We are all trapped here. We can look outside of the mouth of this hole and sometimes view the lives of my kinsmen, but we have never found a way to leave." He sheathed his sword, and most of the other legionnaires did the same.

"You are my relative, then?"

"Yes. I am many generations your grandfather." Even as he stated this fact, Darkmind knew beyond the shadow of a doubt that this was true.

"Why are you trapped here?" he asked as he sheathed his own weapons as well. The boy looked up from the side of his cloak but still clung to him tightly.

"War is confusing, as you said. We were ambushed in Britannia. I led my men into a cave—a bad tactical choice, but the only option because we were being murdered in drones. For some reason I thought we were still alive, even though we were fighting all manner of dark beast.

"Not knowing that we were already dead, my men followed me to a man. We pushed through the visions of my life that were confusing to me until we found this dark and seemingly peaceful spot. Many of my men were torn apart by the canine at the doorway, but we were too many and pushed past. Some of our pursuers—demons of some sort, it would seem—made it past as well, and we fought until many more of my men disappeared forever and the creatures were no more." As Lucius started to relax, his bravado faded from him. Darkmind could see old wounds and broken armour from those days of battle.

"And you're trapped here?"

"Yes. There seems to be no way for us to exit. No one has ever entered here before you. You may be trapped as well."

"How many of you are there?"

"In the space it seems impossible to get a count, but we are sure that there are over six hundred of us."

"Six hundred?" Darkmind asked, shocked.

"I myself thought that only my cohort had followed me, but in all of the confusion most of the whole damn army followed. Ha! Although many, many were destroyed that day. My men trusted me, though, and other platoons and sections trusted me more than their own leadership. Some just followed the mass exodus."

"Are you all lucid?" Darkmind was still in disbelief.

"What do you mean?"

"Can you all speak rationally, have thoughts and opinions, have vivid memories?"

"You speak strangely, friend. Do you have a name? I have given you mine. For now I am forced to see you as a friend, for I am not sure what etiquette to use when referring to a distant offspring."

"I'm sorry. I don't remember my name. It seems that many refer to me as Darkmind." He suddenly turned to the lad beside him. "And this is . . ."

"I don't remember, either!" the boy answered as he started to cry. Darkmind laid a hand upon his head, trying to think quickly in an attempt to calm the lad. "Is it okay if I call you Alec? It's a name from where I'm from."

"Okay." The boy seemed to surrender to the idea without any amount of resistance. He steadied himself and stopped sobbing.

"Alec?" Lucius asked.

"It means *boy* in his language, in Pashto. Even though we all seem to speak the same tongue here, it really is a boy's name in my home as well."

"Alec it is, then," Lucius said, fatherly addressing the child before shifting back to the adult conversation at hand. "Yes, we remember things. We remember our families and loved ones, whom we have not seen for centuries. We remember the blue sky, the green grass, the bright sun, the smell and sound of the ocean birds in flight. We remember a warm bed, sweet wine, the soft touch of a woman and the taste of the loaves from our mother's ovens. We remember everything, Darkmind, but we are doomed to stay here without any reprieve whatsoever. If I had a choice, I would have no memory at all."

"What did the creatures look like that hunted you?" Darkmind asked.

"They looked like the spitting image of Chiron the ferryman himself! There were lots of the bastards. They came at us with long, evil singing spears and were in such a state of frenzy they did not even seem to care as they were killed one by one. Even the last of them fought bitterly to the end without care or consideration for their own preservation."

Darkmind felt his jaw drop, for here were *hundreds* of kindred spirits. He needed to find a way to free them. If he did, there could very well be strength in numbers. They could set up a base over some holy burial ground or in a large church. Maybe they could even organize themselves like Hachimantaro and his crew.

"Do you have any of the weapons from the beings?" Darkmind asked excitedly but without really expecting there to be after so long. The only weapons that he knew that had survived from hunters were taken in the moment of death. Maybe things would be different here, though, or maybe the Romans had used the weapons during the battle as they wrenched them from their enemy's hands.

"We do, Darkmind. Many of them. They are dark and foul things that we keep discarded in the corner."

"*Lucius*," Darkmind seemed to purr. "I am very glad to have met you."

15

"You are right," Katsuo said. "This is a dilemma."

Ayumu, the tattooed samurai with the facial piercings, nodded his head to acknowledge the much older and more traditional warrior.

"If we wait for Darkmind to travel to the end of this path, as he surely will, there will be us two against the three," Katsuo continued. "If we kill the jester now, we will have to kill the wolf as well, and then we are no longer guaranteed that he will come this way to collect that part of himself."

The two men conversed as if they were alone. On the other side of the phantom images of Darkmind's life, however, were the very beings they spoke about. Balzola leaned on the tangled scythe, and Lupa padded back and forth protectively in front of her.

It was as strange a place as any of them had ever seen, for it was the final room in the cavern of Darkmind's life and showed the battle in the desert over and over again. High up on the wall, where the images sprang from, was a shelf of sorts. On this shelf sat a mummified woman at a loom. She worked the instrument tirelessly, and all of the images sprang from her toils and flowed backwards toward the beginning of the cave. Her lips and eyes were sewn shut with thick catgut thong.

So it was like a river that sprang forth from the blind and speechless hag. The powdery coloured scenes started thin and spread out to form the full images before them. On the one side of the scene sat the two samurai, and on the other side were Balzola and Lupa; it seemed like they were in fact sitting across a stream from one another.

All four of them knew that there was an exit here as well, but they waited for Darkmind because it was more likely that he would come this way than any other. They knew instinctually that if someone were to walk into that waterfall of powdery color, they would enter into the final moments of the soldier's life. Just like they knew that there were other people's lives being shown here simultaneously that they could not see. Darkmind's living relatives had streams of images here as well that, unlike his, continued to change with every passing moment and would not have a repetitive ending.

"He has to die, though, of that I am certain," Ayumu responded after a while. "He has no honour and has no respect for the living or the dead."

"I agree. It was you that initially argued with me on the matter."

"This battle bothers me, and I would wish to question him further about it, but I do not trust him."

Both men stared at the strange scene before them. It was a massacre and an unleashing of a lot of energy that was before its time. In fact, none of the soldiers were scheduled to die when they did, which meant that there were beings as evil as Darkmind who had committed greater acts of dishonour.

"I wonder still, in the world of the living, sometimes deals are struck with evil men so that a greater amount of evil men may fall. Maybe we could do such a thing?"

"Once more I agree, but he has slapped Hachimantaro in the face. He used the sword to kill a living man and destroyed his higher spirit. Our code dictates that we either offer our hand in friendship, sincerely, or that we kill him as our enemy."

"Or die trying."

"Or die trying," Katsuo echoed.

Both warriors had tried to reach out mentally to Hachimantaro for guidance or support but were unsuccessful. In fact, ever since they had followed the trio's trail into the realm, they had been unable to communicate. At first it had seemed like a very cold trail indeed, but they had come fresh on the trail of Lupa and Balzola. They had followed them into the tree and caught up with them here.

Lupa had been able to lead Balzola past the canine guardian as her guest, which wasn't entirely uncommon but was not at all common either. The two samurai had used a combination of mental blasts of confusion and speed that no freshly dead spirit would have ever been able to accomplish. The dog had not been able to react in time to kill them. In essence there was the rightful visitor who had been split in half (each half had brought a guest of sorts, if one included Alec) and two trespassers.

The samurai did not know about Alec, however, nor did they know about the Romans. They felt as if they had the upper hand, but in reality they were extremely outnumbered. They were samurai, though, from a code that gave them as powerful beliefs in this new world as it did in their old one. Even if they had known the odds were so badly against them, that would have hardly changed the conversation that they were having now.

"Can you still sense my presence?" Ayumu asked. Over time and with proper training, Hachimantaro's warriors were all connected by thought and energy. If one of them were in trouble halfway around the world, the rest of them, in theory, could be there almost instantly. They were far from safe, though. Enemies liked to pick them off one by one as if they were a herd of caribou being circled by starving tundra wolves. Here those feelings of unity seemed disconnected somehow. It was as if they were the last two samurai left in the group entirely.

"Yes."

"I feel you as well. This is what I propose."

Darkmind sat up against a wall back in the main tunnel beside the boy now named Alec. They had tried everything. They had tried to pull and push warrior after warrior through the opening. Even though they were easily able to step through the invisible barrier themselves, it was as if there was a solid impassable wall for any of the Romans. They had even tried to cut through the barrier with his swords and the discarded hunters' weapons, but to no avail.

"I don't feel good about leaving them here," he said to the boy. "They do not deserve it."

"Maybe you can come back after you ask the pretty lady what to do."

"What pretty lady?" Darkmind asked, intrigued as he looked over at the child. He was just as surprised at the advice as he was that the boy had spoken at all.

"The one with the horns," the boy answered.

"You saw her?" he asked, surprised.

"Yeah."

"How long have you been with me?"

"Since before you died."

"And how come I never saw you before?"

"You told me to hide because there was going to be lots of fighting, and I could get killed again. You told me if I saw you to run away and to hide from the giant dog in the tree."

"When did I say that?"

"When I died."

"That doesn't make sense, kid. I was still alive. Was it my higher self?"

"No, because he couldn't see you either."

"I'm very confused. Are you sure that it was me?"

"I am sure 'cause I was very scared at first ... 'cause you were burned. But you were so nice."

"So what you are saying is that I was still alive, but the burned me told you to hide until when?"

"Until you saw me, or something like that. He said that when you saw me, I was supposed to run. I was then supposed to run until I needed help."

"This is very confusing. Why did you look at me then like you were afraid?"

"I could tell that you didn't know me or remember me, and I was really scared. You felt different, too. You were really mean to people."

"You mean my energy?"

"I guess ... You just seemed a lot nicer before."

Darkmind reached an arm around the boy and pulled him towards the safety of his chest as his own father might have.

"I'm sorry, kid," he said. "I'm a little confused, but you can trust me now, at least to protect you as best I can. I don't really know what is going on or what the rules I am supposed to be following are, but I promise you that I will try to figure it all out. I don't know if I will ever be like the nice lady or as good a man as Hachimantaro, but I will try to find somewhere safe for you as soon as we figure this whole thing out."

There was a long silence between the two beings as they rested there against the wall.

"It's not your fault, you know," the boy said at last.

"What isn't?" he asked.

"When you killed me."

Darkmind tried hard not to weep.

* * *

The two boys stepped over the discarded water bottles and cigarette butts and moved towards the light-coloured mud wall. With surprising agility they moved in the bright sun's heat up to the roof of the compound that was nestled alongside the old mosque. Here there were more cigarette butts and a few pieces of litter.

The boy wearing all grey picked up one of these butts and put it into his mouth before lighting it with a lighter that he had been given by a soldier. Out of the corner of his eye, he saw that his white-wearing friend looked at him with envy and with awe.

"The soldiers are my friends," he said as he took a drag from the lit American cigarette. "They talk to me and give me gifts."

Everyone knew that he now had a lighter and two packs of cigarettes, but all of the other boys were still in disbelief. Canadian soldiers had been up on this roof with a machine gun for almost two weeks before leaving. Other soldiers had stayed behind in a nearby platoon house to try to keep the Taliban away.

"Why don't you smoke those ones?" The other boy asked as he pointed to the butts on the ground. It was plain why he didn't smoke the full packs: once those were gone, the boy would no longer be considered wealthy by his friends; he would lose his status. The other boy thought to himself that he himself would smoke them before a bigger boy took them away, a bigger boy who believed that his Canadian *friends* were not coming back and wouldn't protect him.

"They pissed on those ones," he answered rather cockily.

"Oh." The smaller boy in white nodded his head in understanding. No one wanted to smoke a cigarette butt that an infidel, no matter how friendly, had pissed upon. "What if the Taliban kill you?" he asked. The village had lost many men to them over the last decade or so. The men would disappear at night and would never return. They were presumed dead, but the Taliban would often say that they had come to join their cause for God. No one believed them, but most were too afraid to contradict what was said.

"The Canadians won't leave. They told me they want to kill all of the Taliban," the boy lied. No one would know the difference because he was now the authority on the Canadian military for the other boys of the village.

"They don't seem like they want to kill. They are always smiling and friendly. They don't seem very strong."

"They are very powerful. They are so powerful they do not even care if they seem strong."

"Like the Americans?" the second boy asked.

"The Americans are different. They are very strong, but they are not nice unless they want something."

"That's not true. Those Americans were very nice, too."

"That's because those ones were black and Muslim; they are not infidels."

"That can't be true!"

"It is; the Canadians told me."

"They weren't all black."

"When the American soldiers are mostly black, they are Muslim groups. When they are mostly white, they are Christian groups. Everyone knows that."

"But aren't the Canadians Christian too?"

"Yes, but they are a different kind of Christian. They think Muslims are their brothers."

"I don't know if I believe you," the smaller boy said. "Some of them didn't seem so nice, either. One of them said I was an uncle fucker in English."

"Your English is so bad he probably said something different altogether. He probably told you that God is great."

"He did not! Besides, your English is not so good, either."

"I understand Canadian English better than anyone in the village, though," he said, and maybe it was true because through hand gestures and broken English, he had in fact befriended the soldiers. He had brought them naan bread, and they had been overjoyed to be able to eat this with the rations of which they had become sick. The soldiers, who changed shifts every few hours, had also used a small pocket Pashto book to help them communicate. A friendship of sorts had been born, and the Canadians had given the boy candies and even cigarettes and a lighter in exchange for naan and pomegranates.

"So they will kill all of the Taliban?" the smaller boy asked with hope in his voice.

"Every last one of them," the larger boy answered with confidence.

The Taliban pushed into the northern side of the village the following week. They had moved in the night and brought with them weapons to supplement the ones that they had already buried in the village. They mixed themselves in with the locals and even slept in their homes. No one would dare to tell the ANA (Afghan National Army) or the Canadians what was taking place, but it became clear that they knew as well that the enemy was nearby. The Canadian soldiers that had left returned.

The tension was clearly thick in the air, and one by one people made excuses why they had to leave. There were trips to the city that no one returned from, sick family to be cared for, brothers' crops that needed tending, business matters, holy pilgrimages, trips to see wives' families and sudden job opportunities that required the whole family to attend. The people fled, and without their urban camouflage, the insurgents became more and more exposed.

When the older boy's younger brother told their father that he was not coming, the father had been furious. The grey-clad youth had told his sibling to tell the patriarch that he had left with their neighbours, the smaller boy's family, and the sibling had believed this and passed on the message. His father was in a rage and hit the younger son several times for being the bearer of bad tidings but, in the end he was forced to accept that his oldest son was safe elsewhere. The family then left.

The boy, who considered himself a friend of the Canadian soldiers, had hidden and stayed behind. He wanted to see these friends again and continue the relationship of trade that he had started. He could continue to bring them pomegranates, but he was not sure how he would get any naan now that his mother was gone. Before it had been easy to take a piece here and a piece there and even occasionally say it was for one of the men working in the field. Now it would be a challenge.

He would be safe. He would hide when he needed to from the fighting and from the insurgents. He just had to avoid them at all costs, or they would hurt or kill him. He also knew though that his Canadian friends would protect him from the Taliban as well.

* * *

When the hunter had come for him, the boy was truly terrified. There was nowhere for him to run, and there was nowhere for him to hide. But then suddenly the burnt man had appeared with dual swords and had struck his enemy down.

The burnt man had then led him to a single Canadian soldier who seemed oblivious of his presence. He was told that he was not to leave this being again until certain events occurred. That, he was assured, would not be very long. It had been dark, and he had been inside of a building when he had been killed, and so he did not recognize the soldier he was to stay with. It was him that had fired the shots which had killed him in the first place.

The burnt man had then shown him how to hide himself from other beings both living and dead, and a wave of powerful energy was passed to him to perform such a task. The being had then left him with a wolf he called Lupa.

The boy had watched the soldier and came to realize what had happened even as the wolf tried to comfort him. It became clear to him that this strange and foreign man, who was nothing like he imagined he would be, was haunted by his actions. Sometimes at night he would try to calm him, but in his state of *invisibility*, to all but the wolf, he was not very good at it. The thing that struck him as the strangest of all was that in many ways the soldier was not very much older or wiser than he had been himself despite having clearly lived for many more years.

Strangely, the burnt man returned, or seemed to be born, when the soldier himself had been killed. He began to look more like the first burnt man as he acquired the cloak and eventually carried both swords at once. The boy had trusted the original burnt man's directions completely and continued to follow them. When the soldier was killed, and for a time after, the young spirit had remained hidden until the events that he was told would happen had come to pass.

16

Ayumu rushed Darkmind from the side. In this way he was almost able to finish the battle before it had even begun. At the last moment, however, with his sword raised over Darkmind's exposed head, he saw the boy nestled there beside him and forced his momentum into a dive roll past the vulnerable warrior instead.

It was the same code of honour that had led him to believe that he had to kill Darkmind in the first place that ended up saving him as well. Ayumu would not harm a child; the boy had no hand in the events that had transpired and brought this judgement against Darkmind.

That brief moment of surprise had come and gone. It had been an opportunity that he now had to acknowledge had passed. Darkmind had been sitting on the ground with his back to the wall, completely unready for battle. Now he could not be taken unaware.

In life, almost all of Hachimantaro's ilk had been honourable regarding when and how battles had proceeded. The afterlife offered no such luxuries, though. This was a land where assassination and lightning-quick ambushes were necessary to survive. The original ninja spirits that had been accepted into their fold had taught them collectively how to survive. Many of the less traditional styles of fighting and ways had been adapted from the clans and were used with a great deal of success.

Ayumu came out of his roll just as Darkmind unsheathed the smaller sword, Black Dragon, from his knees. The position was not ideal for attack but was a strong position for defence. The boy was pushed back and to the side.

Ayumu stood still, silently giving Darkmind permission to stand. The ambush had been unsuccessful; he now chose to let his opponent meet him on equal ground.

Ayumu knew that this fight might be difficult, but it was a gamble. On the first hand Darkmind had not become very familiar with the weapons he now carried and had not remembered all of his training from previous lives. This gave Ayumu a clear advantage, even though Darkmind had apparently been Hachimantaro's equal at one time.

Darkmind, however, had lots of energy in these caves to draw upon, a whole life's worth, if he chose. Ayumu gambled that with every amount of energy the soldier took, he would also be taking the energy and memories directly from a source that had not trained in the use of swords. He would in fact be burying his own capabilities beneath a sheet of power.

The two beings started to step sideways, circling each other with one foot softly over the other like twin panthers. Almost in unison, both took out their second swords. No words were shared between them. They both knew why they were here and what needed to happen.

With an unspoken ascent, the beings closed space, and there was an explosion of sparks and a loud crack. The two men each faced one another once more, but from exchanged places that had a mere second before been occupied by the other.

The large sword did not feel heavy to Darkmind at all in this realm, and there was enough space not to hinder the weapon too much. It gave him a far greater reach with his right hand but disabled any sort of underhanded swipe. His left hand could take this swing if necessary, but it would be easier for his opponent to predict if the under slash always came from his left.

With a flurry of motion they clashed in the middle. The swipes were quick enough that they were nearly impossible for Alec to see. The two beings met in a flurry and stood a few feet apart from one another. They seemed to be doing some sort of synchronized dance with weapons. Suddenly they disengaged simultaneously and returned to their circling stand-off.

Darkmind's right hand dripped with blood and had clearly been wounded. However, his grip remained firm and gave no indication of lessening.

They came together once more in a clash of steel and fire as their great swords met in battle with minds of their own. These weapons also had pride and honour and refused to let down their masters. It became clear that there was more at stake than the lives of two spirits—it was the paths of four swords as well.

When they disengaged once more, Darkmind had a slash across his face and was blind in one eye. Ayumu had still not been injured.

Ayumu's rolled-up sleeves showed the heavily tattooed arms of a modern man from an era when the practitioners of Bushido were more likely to belong to the Yakuza gangs than to be from any other class in Japan. He circled carefully, fully aware that he was the superior fighter here, but he was not so egotistical to believe that the battle had yet been won.

Lupa growled and padded back and forth fiercely. She wanted to go to Darkmind, to become one with him and make him stronger, but she was committed to watching over Balzola. Balzola held firm. She knew that she was not strong enough to fight the samurai one-on-one, but with Lupa the odds were more even. Though Lupa was aware of the battle taking place nearby, Balzola was not. If she had known, she would have attacked the lone samurai at once.

Katsuo likewise sat firm. He knew that the battle fared well for Ayumu but was also hard-pressed not to act. He knew, however, that the plan was for him to make sure that the others did not join the battle so that they could be more easily dispatched after Darkmind had been destroyed.

His mind was kept busy as he watched the recurring images of the battle in the cave—Darkmind's mortal battle being played out before them over and over again—and wondered once more if they were making the right decision. Perhaps when Hachimantaro was told about the battle at the end of the cave in the tree, they would find another way to steer the course of events that he now witnessed before him. They would not need the dead soldier to intervene at all. There had to be other ways to enter the battle.

But that would have to wait until later. The course of action right now would be followed as they had concurred. Darkmind simply had to be destroyed.

Lucius banged himself bloody against the unyielding barrier. In life he had always been quick to make friends, and he was loyal to those he felt deserving, until the end. He was aware of the battle that took place just barely out of his line of sight. The fight was between his distant grandson and an unknown enemy that in his mind could come to harm the boy Alec as well.

Centuries of stillness had done nothing to curb his battle sense and his willingness to fight. He tried over and over to break free but to no avail. His soldiers, loyal to the end, smashed into the wall as well. Nothing that they did seemed to help them whatsoever.

The feelings they shared of helplessness did not diminish the attempts that they continued to make to break out.

***

The two warriors circled once more. Ayumu had a couple of minor gashes now, but it was clearly Darkmind that was being picked apart piece by piece. Wounds crisscrossed his body, and his cloak was torn in many places. He breathed heavily and tried to surmise a way out of the situation that would give him a greater advantage.

The two warriors clashed once more, and Darkmind saw for a moment that Ayumu had dropped his right arm and arched his back, contrary to any natural fighting movement that Darkmind would have expected. He stepped in and slashed at the exposed man's throat, opening a wide gash that squirted blood. Ayumu stepped back and flung his arm outwards dramatically.

Alec was sent catapulting and landed heavily after bouncing off of the wall. Darkmind's K-bar knife was in his hand, and on it was blood. He had somehow taken the knife from him, had moved invisibly, and had stabbed his opponent in the back. Ayumu had then backhanded the small lad and sent him flying.

The weapon had not inflicted any real damage but had stung and had taken him by surprise. It had been a mistake for Ayumu to count out the boy, and now he was forced to use some of his energy to heal the neck wound and stop the flow of blood.

Darkmind did not let him recover. He moved in viciously, and the two warriors met with such a fury that it was impossible to watch. He was irate that the samurai had struck the child whether he had deserved it or not. It was a rage that he could barely control.

Both of them scored hits in a battle that was now too fast to contain a reasonable defensive portion at all.

*   *   *

In another place, in the land of the living, two young men dressed in black made their way on foot from the bus station. It didn't matter to them that the night was nearly spent; they had a friend that was in need. One of them wore sunglasses even though the sun was long gone. The fatter one didn't bother; he just chewed on his moustache that draped over a long, shaggy beard. Both of them had hair to their shoulders that was slicked back from their pale faces.

They were known in certain circles as *warlocks*. They were experts in dealing with the dark spirits that sometimes liked to harass or scare people. They had been doing this sort of thing since they were only twelve.

They had been quite successful as well. Socially their circle was small, but they could attract a certain type of person for sexual rituals that gave them much of their strength. They had powerful guides who had helped them attract spirits that could assist them for a price. Over time, they had learned to see these beings and even to communicate directly with the dark ones.

The life had not come without a price. Small animals had been killed, at first, but the sacrifices were getting larger all of the time. They had also been directly responsible for two drug overdoses, so far, that passed as a sort of offering to appease the spirits. Their hunger for power was growing, though they had studied enough to know that the beings they dealt with had no concept of the price one of them might pay in this physical realm for out-and-out murder.

When Shelly the bank teller had called them, they had been delighted. They didn't know her that well, because she had moved in different circles growing up, but she had been at a few of the same parties and was well aware of their reputation. She had contacted them in near hysterics. She had told them that she believed that her ex-boyfriend, who had just been killed overseas, was possessing her house. A discussion ensued. She was willing to be sexually sodomized during a ritual in exchange for an exorcism.

The directions to her place had been easy enough. They walked across the grass and entered the unlocked front door. They had told her that they would do this; it was an important part of the ritual that they would perform. They had to show the spirits that they had claim to the home.

They found her sitting naked as instructed in the living room. They chanted as they removed all of the furniture and stacked it in the wooden floored kitchen. The two warlocks removed their small backpacks and took out various instruments such as a wand, a dagger, a brazier, a golden goblet, a large crystal gem and what appeared to be a goat's skull. They then drew a circle in chalk on the short ply carpet and lit several candles around it.

The two men undressed and poured oil over Shelly and themselves. They then had a three-person orgy while the girl sobbed.

It was important for them to gain sexual energy through excitement, but it was *very* important that neither of the males release their seed. They had to be in a frenzied state of sexuality when the ritual was performed. It was also important that all three of them have sex with one another so that the circle was not broken.

It was a ritual that they had developed on their own by incorporating a lot of research and then tweaking it as suggested by their guides. They were skilled now, though, and could adapt it to as many or as few people as needed. After the ritual was complete, they could satisfy themselves sexually in celebration, but not before. This portion of the ritual was for building up and drawing in energy; it was not for dispelling it.

They started to chant. They had told Shelly beforehand to hum along as best as she could. One of them called in the spirits of various directions with the dagger while the other drew elaborate chalk designs on the carpet within the circle.

The humming eventually started to dispel her fear, and she began to feel different, to feel something strong that brought with it a sense of peace, which she knew would exact a price. She saw dark things out of the corners of her eyes, and the flames of the candles rose even as the curtain fluttered.

She knew that whatever being had come, it would deal with the spirit that had crossed her. She promised herself that after this she would never feel powerless again. She would learn what she could from the two warlocks, and she would make Nate pay for how he had treated her as well.

* * *

Darkmind and Ayumu continued to fight. The air became distorted and smoky around them and was filled with shadows. The ground became more rigid somehow, and the color bled out from around them like watercolour paints dissipating into the depths of the sea.

On one hand they knew what was happening, but on another they were too engaged in their dance of death to acknowledge that a new danger approached.

The gears shifted ruggedly and awkwardly, and the machines of the spirit world choked out and coughed as they laboured to build the fighters a new stage upon which to play. They were dragged between realms, but only their external world seemed to notice. They did not lose step or hesitate in the fight to which they had committed. They were simply transfixed from one spot to another but were too occupied to notice or even to care.

Darkmind and Ayumu had barely even registered that the scenery around them had changed as they locked in their entanglement of blades and rage. It was the swords then that first warned their masters that danger came in a new form.

Both of the warriors spun simultaneously. It had almost been too late for them to acknowledge the new threat. Suddenly they were both aware that they were no longer in the tunnel.

Small, smoky spirits hurled themselves at them in a frenzy and were picked off quickly by the warriors. All around them were the small, reddish insect-like humanoids with wings that seemed intent on devouring them. These entities seemed to be parts of larger beings that were visually nothing more than walls of opaque darkness. This whirling fog seemed to choke the air out of them and crush their chests. It radiated a contagious fear and demanded that they submit or be destroyed.

This was not the complete picture, though, for there was an offering of sorts as well that was akin to bribery on the table before him. Darkmind was reminded in a way of the promises of the golden light. He would be given safety and protection and, most enticing of all, great power. All that he had to do was submit to the beings that seemed to hold them captive.

There was more than one being, dominant though was the main entity that wrapped around both of them and drained the power from their limbs. He was a mad rain of acid glass that fell across them, choking and destroying without apology or regard. In fact there was a sense of joy from the mightier spirit, which laughed at their futile struggle against destruction.

A searing pain shot across him every time that he heard the name that he had once been called from the lips of the warlocks. The memory of it would fade as soon as it was uttered, and he would forget once more, but the name would be called out again, and it was like a barbed spear through his guts.

Why Ayumu was there was anyone's guess. He had been so committed to killing Darkmind, perhaps he had on some level chosen himself to accompany him. The other possibility was that their energies had become so entangled that it had been impossible for the one being to be called without the other also being summoned. Whatever the reason, though, it was clear that the two fighters now shared the same fate.

The two warriors were aware that there were several other powerful entities that stood back silently and watched. They were barely cognizant, though, that they were back in the physical realm. There was no indication around them that they had not slipped into some sort of new, dark and deadly hell.

Ayumu could no longer sense Katsuo and still had no connection with any of his other clan from within the circle. The only kindred spirit nearby was the one he had been intent on killing.

The two human spirits, who had just been engaged in a fight to the death and were completely unaware of what was going on, started to circle now with swords drawn back to back. Whatever had been their disagreement moments before, it was now immediately plain that they were about to be destroyed or enslaved together.

There was a hissing sound, and within that sound was the command to kneel. Neither man submitted, and so pain shot through them once more, and they both began to scream and flail madly with their weapons.

The candles shot up and the room started to shake. Dishes in the cupboards shook and rattled, and the wood in the floors started to creak. A great storm seemed to be taking place outside as tree branches clawed at the outside of the dwelling.

The warlocks were sweating and struggled to remain composed. It was important that the spirits not be aware of their fear or anxiety, but in fact they were astounded at the power of the presence that they had called.

They had not known the soldier personally in life but had known of him. In life he had been about as regular a guy as there was. He had lacked a lot of confidence and had not seemed very spiritual at all. He had never had *presence* whatsoever. The only power he seemed to have was from his martial arts studies and the mediocre amount of breathing exercises and meditation that came from that. They had viewed him, and his spirit, as weak and inconsequential.

They were still confident, however, for they knew the power of their guides. It was true that it was rare to come across a spirit that had enough strength to accomplish poltergeist acts in death, but it was not entirely uncommon either. Such a recently deceased individual was usually enraged and spent most of his or her energy quickly, gaining back just enough to continue only if there was enough fear being harvested from those that they haunted.

The soldier would be quickly destroyed or subdued, of that they were certain, but they were aware that there was a second being as well. They concluded simultaneously, without words, that the second being had to be a powerful guide of some sort. This was interesting but of no real concern because their circles of protection had never been breached.

Strangely, it was Shelly that saw the situation more clearly. Most people would have become afraid, but a sense of purpose and calm came over her. She now saw a new world of power and opportunity never before revealed. She saw a landscape that she had only been vaguely aware of before, and the possibilities seemed endless. She saw how pathetic the two warlocks were and knew that she could easily learn all that she could from them and quickly surpass their skills.

She saw the image of her boyfriend, charred and beaten, and recognized him even with the burnt face and the swords in his hands. She also saw the tattooed Japanese warrior and realized that he was also another bodiless spirit. She saw the power and the rage in the two beings and was intrigued that they seemed to be so easy to bind and control in death.

She chanted his name. She heard the echo from her lips and saw him convulse in pain and jerk around like a marionette. She started to laugh.

Darkmind heard the laugh and knew that it was her. He cursed her even as he swung out helplessly with his sword once more. He was having a far harder time than Ayumu keeping his feet until the energy shifted its focus away from him.

The cloud of darkness seemed to roll into several beings that attacked the samurai at once, intent on annihilating him so they could focus on the dead Canadian. He was quickly being destroyed from the rips and gashes appearing throughout his being. Darkmind pulled himself together and threw himself into the fray. His swords seemed so intent on fighting themselves that he felt pulled into the battle and almost more of a bystander than a participant. The long sword from the valkyrie drank deeply of the beings, and energy flew into him at once.

The beings paused their onslaught in response to the attack. With the moments of slack, Ayumu lashed out himself and seemed to recover somewhat. He was now clearly much weaker than Darkmind, but he was far from finished. Then fire erupted around him and burnt him, and he screamed in pain even as he lashed out madly. The harder he fought, the more pain was inflicted upon him. The more pain that was inflicted upon, him the more freedom Darkmind had, and the more he flailed around, slashing and cutting anything that he could.

Both warlocks were sweating profusely and called for the other guides that were watching to now become involved. The two men were too stubborn to be afraid and knew that they would eventually prevail. They had never dealt with such difficult spirits before, but the warriors were locked in the circle and had no way of lashing out further than they already had. The warlocks chanted words of power and commands that Darkmind kneel or be destroyed and that if he did not, his guide would be destroyed as well.

They had no way of knowing, as their guides did not know, that there was a third spirit there as well.

Alec was very afraid, but he was aware that he was invisible to the dark beings around him. He knew he had to help Darkmind somehow, because he was bound to him, and even the samurai that had seemed to have become their counterpart in the engagement. He crept to the edge of the circle and was surprised that he could step outside of it.

He walked to the outer rim of the circle and recognized the woman who had been slapped on the bed. He also saw the two greasy men, one fat and one bone thin, that chanted and danced around nakedly. He had the

K-bar knife he had taken from Darkmind, and he circled stealthily around the back of the fat man. Not knowing what would happen, he thrust the knife with all of his strength.

The fat warlock arched his spine as the samurai had when he had been stabbed in the back. He was in a place of high attunement to the spirit world, and so it felt to him like he had actually been physically knifed. He screamed in pain and fell onto his side, convulsing white foam mixed with blood from his mouth.

The scrawny warlock lost his concentration and looked over at his friend, confused as to what had just taken place. His concentration was broken, and fear shot through his body.

Alec rushed at him as well and started to stab him repeatedly in the stomach. The second warlock screamed in pain.

Shelly saw the little brown boy who was no longer invisible and was calmly intrigued. She saw the dark beings look at the warlocks with disgust, leaving as they lost their power to be present.

The two warriors were unaware at first that Alec had helped them and redoubled their efforts. The dark ones began to scream in rage, and in pain as they retreated back to the spirit world from whence they came.

One of the cloud entities, a piece of the great dark being, shoved a barbed spear through the skinny warlock in disgust. Shelly saw his life energy leave his body and be consumed. She smiled and felt a quiver of ecstasy wash over her. The entity then shoved his spear into the brown boy and tried to rip it out.

Darkmind had leapt upon its back in the nick of time and slit its throat from behind with Dark Dragon. A sulphurous smell from the neck wound filled the room as the boy fell to the ground, severely wounded. Darkness gushed from the being and flew into the air. Darkmind visibly became stronger even before he stepped forward and harvested the high spirit of the dead warlock. There was a vacuum sensation as the last of the dark ones fled.

The room became quiet and empty except for the three spirits, the comatose fat man, and the woman. Darkmind looked down at her with murderous intensity as Ayumu writhed on the ground and Alec lay still with his tiny hand still wrapped around the knife.

There was a long moment as the previous lovers stared at one another.

He was hateful and wanted to destroy her once and for all for summoning him and for calling out his name. She was joyous and unafraid.

Darkmind needed to retreat from this place with his allies so they could lick their wounds and try to discern what had just transpired. He wanted to kill her, but he felt a sense of urgency to flee and protect the boy from further harm. He sensed that the arrival of any hunters would be the end of them, and he didn't know if the dark beings they had just faced had left for good or were simply regrouping.

He knew that this woman would be a problem again by the way she looked at him. Even in death it unnerved him. He could also hear her thoughts.

She knew his real name and that he had become a powerful spirit.

He sheathed his weapons, including the K-bar knife, while barely taking his eyes off of her. He picked up the boy and threw him over one shoulder. He then turned away from her and tried to help Ayumu to his feet as the Japanese spirit sheathed his own weapons. The three then began to leave as quickly as they could.

Shelly sat naked and alone in her living room. She was not yet rational enough to be concerned that there was one dead and one comatose man needing medical attention in her home. Even if she was, she was too excited with the prospects of her future to worry much about that now.

She saw a new path before her that could potentially, she believed, make her one of the most rich and powerful women in the world. She did not know how or when it would happen, but she had always known that this was what she would become someday. She had just never realized before now in what shape and form that future would come to her.

17

It was easiest for him to take in his surroundings by viewing his environment in the physical realm. Despite the attack having been on a spiritual level, this was where they had been summoned from by living human enemies. Darkmind surveyed the scene as he was leaving.

The two pasty-skinned, naked warlocks lay haphazardly on the carpet. The skinny one was an empty shell, and his open foam-caked mouth and wide eyes reached for the ceiling. Various candles littered the otherwise spartan floor. A twisted mess of furniture was haphazardly set up alongside the living room and in the kitchen, where everything had been moved except for her entertainment system and a ceiling-to-floor lamp that had once belonged to him.

He fumbled for a second over the concept of the chalk circle. It was those patterns, he believed, that had some sort of reach into his world. Strangely, he now had no trouble crossing these wards and exiting Shelly's apartment now that the séance was over. The energy that Darkmind had harvested from the warlock's fleeing high spirit and the creatures he had destroyed had given him enough strength to carry the boy and also to assist the ailing Ayumu. He could not know if the circles had lost their power when the dark ones had left, or if he was now too strong to be bound by them.

He moved past the doorway with great relief and moved across the front lawn.

"Why are you helping me?" the samurai rasped, barely able to move his legs.

Darkmind didn't answer. He was afraid. He was unsure of what had happened or why they had been brought here to his old apartment. He suspected that there had been some sort of an exorcism that had taken place, but he didn't understand the powers that they had faced or why they were now free to leave.

He moved as quickly as he could towards a nearby park. He thought about summoning a second Lupa to make an escape and was sure that he had enough energy to do so, but he did not want to possibly leave the boy behind in this world, and his sense of honour forbade him from abandoning the samurai that had most recently been his ally.

He helped the former Yakuza down to the grass before laying out the boy.

"How do I fix him?" he asked Ayumu. He realized that the boy had not been harvested or destroyed; his image still existed even if it seemed void of life.

"You can give him some of your energy," the samurai stated weakly. "Do what you might do if you were both living still. That will be the ritual."

Darkmind looked suspiciously at the samurai.

"You have my word. I owe you my life and will not attack you again if you are weakened by this process," he said from his prone position, in a raspy whisper.

"I would have trusted you before, but you ambushed me and almost hurt the child!"

"I apologize for that. I did not know about the boy. If we decide to fight again, we will discuss the terms first."

"I would have expected that courtesy in the first place. I thought that Hachimantaro would have offered me that, at least, before he sent you to kill me. Where's Balzola?"

"The jester is fine. Katsuo is watching her and will not likely attack her at the moment."

"Likely?" Darkmind's voice rose.

"He was monitoring my energy. I do not feel him right now, and I am not sure if he can still feel me. He may suspect that you killed me in battle or that we destroyed one another. That second possibility is not likely. If the wolf stayed with the jester, her presence proves you live still. He may wait, or he may press the attack."

Darkmind started to rub Alec's limbs and kissed his forehead as he willed some of his energy into the child.

"What makes you think I won't finish you now and take what energy you have left?" he asked Ayumu as he rubbed the child.

"I think you would have done that already, and I think you know that I can still help you."

The boy started to stir just as Darkmind became aware that another presence had formed nearby and was approaching them. He stood and started to unsheathe his sword as he looked towards the deeper darkness that had formed in the already blackened night like a rolling wave of pitch black smoke.

He steadied himself as he felt the presence carried great strength. He did not want a battle just now. There was no way for them to all run in their current state.

"Darkmind!" a familiar female voice called in a whisper as previous unseen clouds of smoke started to take form. The first thing that he saw of her was the green eyes, which seemed to be moving towards him, floating without a body, in the darkness.

"Bali!" he said, relieved. She would be the wealth of information that he needed to help heal the boy. Perhaps she would also have an answer concerning Lucius as well. He was excited that she was alive and more so that she had sought him out. There were so many questions he had for her, and he has so consumed with joy on one level that he had a hard time suppressing his smile despite the seriousness of the situation.

She took form, as beautiful as ever. A dark green cloak was wrapped around her, seeming to protect her from the elements and perhaps disguising her as well. Somehow her cleavage was still exposed, a statement of her sexual energy and nature.

She ignored the duo and walked over to Alec and knelt down. She did not seem surprised to see the boy, and he wondered if she had been aware of his presence in the first place during their initial meeting.

"He will be all right," she said softly. "He will need some time and some more energy given in small doses." She stood up and looked into Darkmind's face, noticing his missing eye for the first time. She put her hand on his face, and he felt a gentle warmth emanating from her.

Ayumu coughed and tried to stand on his own.

"Kill him," she stated, obviously referring to Ayumu.

"I won't," he replied.

"He will call others; you are not safe here."

"What others?" Darkmind asked as he looked at the struggling man.

"I will not or I would've already. I have cloaked my signal, or they would be here now. This should be proof to you enough, Bali-talahandra, as you know how much energy it takes me to remain invisible to my peers and how much weaker it makes me."

She looked at him through slit eyes, and there was a godlike rage that hid barely veiled behind them.

"Hachimantaro tried to kill me again. I should kill you if he will not." She gestured towards Darkmind and to the barely standing Ayumu.

"He tried to kill you!" Darkmind roared.

"He said I betrayed him by bringing you. He thinks it was the reigniting of an old disagreement we had. The arrogant fool thinks it was a trap to upset the balance."

"I'm sorry, Bali. This is my fault. I will make amends with him and tell him that you had nothing to do with it."

"That is not such a good idea right now," Ayumu interjected. "When he is like this, he is not so easy to calm."

"Why are you suddenly being so helpful?" Darkmind asked with venom in his voice.

"Listen, Darkmind, I will fight you if I have to. Katsuo and I decided you had to be put down on our own when we followed you to your life stream. We had no contact with Hachimantaro and had to make a decision after you used the sword he gave you to kill a mortal. We suspected he would be outraged as well. We were right about his rage and likely decision, if he did attack Bali."

"But?"

"I think that you have honour to a degree, or you would have killed me and the mortal woman."

"Maybe I would have if Alec had not been hurt." Darkmind already regretted not killing Shelly, but Ayumu could not have known this.

Ayumu looked at him long and hard. "Either way, I am indebted to you and will help you make certain things right."

The leaves in the park seemed to capture flecks of moon light and reflect them back into the night. There was almost no illumination otherwise, except for a small sliver of the lunar body, and even the spirits had trouble seeing very far.

Darkmind looked over at Bali, who still had her hand on his face. He felt his eye open and was aware that he could see from it again. She looked back at him, and they shared a long moment of understanding as they both contemplated the best course of action.

She removed her hand and kissed him on the cheek as a mother or a tender hearted old mistress might have. He looked back at Ayumu, who, even though he was close by, was cloaked in shadows.

"I need to find a way to clear Bali's name at least. You can leave if you want; I will not hold you to any debt. I will not kill you in your weakened state, either."

"I will repay my debt, for that is my way. There is something that we can do together that will placate Hachimantaro while making other things right."

Darkmind turned once more towards the succubus. "I've already gotten you into enough trouble. Maybe you should go somewhere safe until this is over?"

"This is a very complicated thing, Darkmind. If I stay with you, I can support you and help you become stronger. I have been taking a very big risk for some time now by not having real protection against other beings. Perhaps you can be that protection, and we can make a permanent alliance?"

"I don't understand. How can I protect you against an army of samurai?"

"Can you at least keep your scheming out of earshot?" Ayumu pleaded. "I still serve him and will not stand here and listen to your conniving plotting, woman! I said I think this can be fixed!"

"It can be fixed, little man," Bali said dryly as she suddenly moved closer towards him. "Like he said, you can leave if you want to, but if you stay, make no mistake that I do not trust you or any of the others who share your codes of 'honour!'

"I came in good faith and had no idea that Darkmind would break any of the treaties. Then I waited after he disappeared and you went after him. When he killed the boy Nate, who I think deserved it by the way, your master and friends chased me, trying to wound me and kill me, or maybe just imprison me, which is probably the same thing. They were intent on harming me! There was no benefit of the doubt whatsoever!

"But you know what, toy soldier? I don't care. Maybe some mortals don't deserve to be protected from the spirits anymore. Maybe the treaties are just garbage rules that protect the dark ones from days of reckoning and only leave the light ones hungry! If Darkmind decides to unleash hell upon them, I will stand by his side because your master has not left me with any other choice! If Darkmind falls in this pursuit, then it is only a matter of time before I am killed as well!"

"The two of you had a truce for over a century!" Ayumu said, getting angry despite his weak state.

"It was not a truce—it was slavery! I gave him his tax and made him more powerful! I stayed out of sight so that he did not have to look upon me with that gaze of disgust! I existed, feeling that it was his mercy and kindness that allowed me to! But I was just a dirty whore to him that he has never even thanked! Do you have any idea, young spirit, how much power I have given him?" She faced him squarely now, and Darkmind felt the cool strength of her radiating and was concerned that she might strike the weakened Ayumu. He was curious, though, to hear this conversation and was well aware that he was being given a history lesson that he had previously been denied.

Ayumu's face was twisting in rage, though, and Darkmind knew that the situation could explode if he did not intervene. "Stop! Both of you!" he roared.

They stared at one another, both of their faces ugly with rage, but neither one spoke.

"I will protect you as best I can, Bali, even if we have to go into hiding. I will also try to make what I can right with Hachimantaro, though. If you think I can fix this to some degree, Ayumu, I will try, for I think I owe you an apology. If you can be this upset and still not summon your kin, then I know you are a man of your word."

This seemed to have a great effect on Ayumu, and he calmed immediately at the peripheral acknowledgement of his honour. He nodded his head as he succumbed once more to his weakness and started to lose his footing. Darkmind reacted and caught him as he almost pitched over.

"I like you, Darkmind," Bali said. "I cannot predict you and you fascinate me. Do with your new gift what you will."

"Gift?" he asked, confused as he set Ayumu sitting upon the grass and stood upright to face her.

Bali smiled as she stepped towards him and kissed him on the lips. Those soft, succulent lips felt moist and electric, sending shivers of sexual ecstasy through his whole being. Energy that he could have never imagined poured into him, and he understood that with this gift he was no longer a force to be trifled with. He awakened and remembered many things and was no longer a fumbling being just trying to survive.

He longed to hold the burka-clad woman from the mosque, within his cold embrace.

Inside he heard his own laughter. The series of events had catapulted him along a path that had been chosen lifetimes ago. There would be a reckoning first, and then there would be war.

Darkmind had healed them both. The samurai known as Ayumu had then helped him move Alec as they made the journey back towards the tree that held his life stream. He did not want to risk the group separating once more, and so he summoned two massive images of Lupa in which to carry them. The samurai rode with Alec in front of him. The boy had still not spoken since the battle. Bali did not take her raven form but instead sat behind Darkmind and wrapped her hands around his waist upon the second wolf. She rested her head upon his back.

He felt her like he had never felt any other being in his life as her energy poured through him. They were connected, and he felt a sense of ecstasy and rapture. He could barely contain his sense of joy, and he was confused how Hachimantaro could spite such a precious gift.

They had been lovers once, she had said.

He felt her joy and relief that she had submitted to him, and he understood that what she said had not been entirely true. She was a lover of sorts but also a mother. There was an oneness between them that was so beautiful it felt like a symphony of electric love, but these sensations were also akin to being born and feeding upon the breast of the creator.

Her knowledge became his, as did her secrets.

She had been visited regularly by one of Hachimantaro's servants for eras. Darkmind saw this now. He or she would collect the energy, the tax, and they would then bring it back to Hachimantaro so that he would never have to look upon her face again. In time he had forgiven her for betraying him, but he had been too arrogant, at least in her mind, to shift the arrangement. She was a sensual being, and so there was little joy for her in the way that she delivered her power to him through others.

The original slight to Hachimantaro seemed insignificant to Darkmind as well, compared to what he had anticipated. She had been attracted to a new spirit that she had crossed paths with and had given him energy and helped him when he was new to the realm of death. Hachimantaro had reacted with jealousy and destroyed the spirit.

"Where is your loyalty? Where is your honour?" he had asked her.

Darkmind understood the sleight somewhat. Hachimantaro had lived in a different time with different codes and had seen Bali-talahandra as a wife of sorts. She had never been mortal and so had understood only that she had hurt him. For that she was sorry. She had stayed relatively loyal to him, even during the subsequent arrangement and despite her dissatisfaction.

There were still small amounts of charitable acts to outsiders that Bali would do that he was unaware of. Like her visits to Balzola, where she would try to ease the jester's pain in any way that she could. They were always small enough acts that the energy would not be missed when it was collected. Maybe Hachimantaro had known but had thought that the acts were too insignificant to worry about.

It was this streak of charity that had led Bali to bring Darkmind before him in the first place. This was also an attempt of hers, a grasped opportunity, to end the stalemate and bring peace between them once and for all.

You tried to kill him once? he asked in his mind.

This was true, he saw now, but was unintentional and was tied to the original incident. She had given out the energy to the young spirit right before there was a great attempt on the head samurai's existence. Hachimantaro had called for energy from her in his hour of need, but there was none left for her to give. The fight had been brutal, and Hachimantaro's army had almost been massacred. In the aftermath he had originally tried to kill her in return, but he had settled on the spirit who had taken the energy instead. He realized, as he had Bali helpless in his grasp, that he still desired her energy, and so he had spared her.

She was valuable but also dangerous, and Hachimantaro vowed never to be monogamous in such a way again. He kept her at arm's length but found other succubae to serve him. She always gave him lots of power, though, so he never discarded her, but he never fully trusted her again, either. He had always believed that the original betrayal had been more deliberate than she had admitted and part of a larger plot.

Darkmind saw that she had been naive but had been loyal in her own way. Through Bali's eyes he also saw what Hachimantaro must have seen. The new spirit had in fact been part of a plot against him. She knew this herself now and had beaten herself up for a very long time. Guilt had allowed the powerful being to submit to such an undesirable arrangement for so long.

I will never betray you on purpose. Remember how I helped you when the day comes…

He let his feelings reassure her. He let her know that she was free to give her energy to others if she chose but asked that she always kept enough so that she could protect herself and so that he could protect her.

What are you? he wondered.

She had never lived as he had, but was created, like many of the gods, by the beliefs and prayers of mortals. This interested him. If a person created their own fictional god tomorrow, the god would exist as long as at least one other person believed in them. The more people that believed in that god, the more powerful they would become, until that god was self-sufficient enough to alter this power themselves. The god or goddes, could then become more or less powerful by spending too much or learning to gather more power. If gods were harvested or destroyed, they would be born again by thought and emotion. If a hundred people believed in that one created being, it would be that much stronger. That being, the god, could actually then influence things or answer prayers. There were dark beings that existed just as easily, and he understood the entities now that had been present at the exorcism.

I am lust.

She was conceived in Babylon, before that even, by priestesses who gave themselves to men as payment from the goddess for holy deeds. That was before women had become dirtied and sullied in the ages to come, before prostitution spilled from the temples and became common and unholy.

Scores of angels such as Bali-talahandra had been born then. Others had been born in other societies as well, and many of them existed still. They fought great wars as the new waves of similar spirits came to exist and destroyed the old. There was nothing sacred or holy about many of the new ones; they preyed on the weak willed and ravaged the souls of mortals with guilt and corruption.

The old ones, the succubae, took mostly female form, and the newer ones took mostly male forms. Both could feed upon the living in dreams, thoughts or sometimes even in the flesh, but they despised one another.

An act between a hooker and a john could be sacred and holy, because tenderness and love could be shared even in a moment where money changed hands. On the contrary, a union between a man and wife could be a vile and dirty thing even beneath the flags of a holy marriage.

The new ones, usually the male incubus, served dark masters and left their victims feeling used and powerless. Sex was not holy but was composed of guilt-ridden acts that never were kind, even if they seemed so at the start. Drug-addicted prostitutes feeding habits spawned from sexual abuse, one night stands between people who did not even care for one another, quickies in the broom closet between coworkers committing adultery, and a world ravaged by porn.

The beings would often fight over the same mortal. Darkmind remembered the masturbating minotaur and the woman crying for help. He saw through Bali's memories the night he had met her and saw how she had destroyed a similar beast who had fed off the junkie on the bed. He saw that even though the brothel had been her kingdom, she had to fight constantly even to survive there, and she had to allow, and even ignore to a certain extent, the dark ones that came to feed.

Humans were still basically animals, though. There was sex everywhere, and the beings could only be in so many places at once. Monogamously married people were usually left alone, and many, many other acts were never even attended. The beings hovered like sharks around schools of fish in certain places, though. They liked night clubs and sex trade workers, raves, cities of sin and following the trails of narcotics. The dark ones, who were many more in number, also clung to porn and deviant individuals whom they encouraged and fed.

It was all such a revelation to Darkmind, who could have never conceived of the complexities of the world of sex in the spirit world. He saw that Bali's metaphor of all women being whores had not been meant to be as negative as he had originally conceived. There was a concept of a woman goddess that was a sacred prostitute that would have twisted his mortal mind in knots if he had been aware of it during his life. It was strange that the beings such as Bali held in such high esteem virginity, chastity and motherhood. There was extreme power given to mortal women who walked these paths.

In this world before him, he saw that men were most often the pawns and the weak willed. Men were more biologically prone to need to spread their seed, as Shelly's high spirit had also pointed out, and they could often easily be manipulated by the sacred and the vile. His mind swam as he saw clearly now which sex was in fact the greater one.

His mind shifted back to Hachimantaro. He saw that the man was honourable but uncompromising to a fault, and despite having felt that he had shed his ego, his ego-free existence could sometimes make him weaker still because it was his very identity. His new ego was that he had none. He had achieved a Zen-like state in life and in death, yet he was too proud of it for it to not have become a thing of and in itself.

Why do you serve men, then, and why not women spirits?

The answer was immediate. He only *saw* himself as male, and these spirits would serve either male or female as any of the created beings would. Some of the beings, like the old gods, did not give their power to anyone and ruled in their own way much as Hachimantaro had learned to live himself. Many spirits chose to align themselves with other beings for strength and protection.

Bali saw herself as better able to help another being and to be more of a consort concubine of sorts than an independent goddess. She wanted to belong to a tribe and craved direct love and affection that an immortal would rarely be able to give. Those such as Darkmind, who had once been alive, were the closest thing to a mortal lover that any of the old beings could ever hope for. The created beings often sought the embrace of mortals.

The dark ones tended to radiate towards stronger, dark created beings. The light ones were rare who had strength; they would seek union with demons and angels.

Hachimantaro had slighted Bali over and over again as a result of his pride. Darkmind, however, would love her as best as he could, knowing full well that she would care for and love Balzola as well.

He understood more clearly now what had happened between Bali and Hachimantaro, and he knew that they would probably never be the allies that he had once hoped for. Darkmind knew he would need to protect Bali from the samurai in the days to come.

Darkmind felt his new power course through him from Bali. He was also fully aware that Hachimantaro had much more energy tithed to him by many more beings than just Bali. He had surrounded himself with beings that gave him power.

As strong as Darkmind felt now, he knew that he would not be able to survive in a fight against the old master. That revelation alone helped him realize how insignificant he still was in this landscape of old gods and mighty hunters. He was no longer a force to be ignored or attacked heedlessly by many of the beings that had done so thus far.

But he was no god either.

18

Oprah was on TV, an old episode, and her guests clapped as she introduced some soft-spoken, articulate author of a half dozen books. The sound carried throughout the common area as subdued patients watched apathetically or simply stared and drooled.

Old, dusty couches and plastic chairs offered places to sit in the common room. On short coffee tables were stacked roughly treated magazines of such uninteresting content as quilting and parenting that it was a wonder to him that they were not still in mint condition.

Neon lights seemed to hum above his head and testified to him that he was in a physical world of the mundane and sterile. He could imagine no spirit nearby in such an atmosphere—or even that spirits might exist at all.

Shadow did not remember when he had become aware once more, but he sat quietly taking in his new surroundings. He didn't feel particularly crazy, but he knew that he was in the hospital wing for a reason. He felt that what he remembered had actually happened, but the voices in his head argued over whether or not it had all been a drug-induced hallucination as the nurses had suggested.

He was numb, and with that numbness was a peace and a laziness that enshrouded his mind. There was something dead in him, though. He could hear the voices of logic within his brain, but they were creatively silent. He knew if he picked up a pen or pencil in this moment that no words would come to him. His artistic self was dead, or at the very least in a coma.

He felt like he could float if he chose to, but he did not want to risk trying. He hovered on a spiritual awakening that gave him confidence despite his awareness that others would claim it was only the prescription that now carried him. He knew he could float.

He wondered if he had slept with Indigo. He had the memory that they had been in love once, but he could not trust it.

A large, teenage boy cried in the corner of the room, and Shadow continued to look over at him, wondering what his problem was. He wondered if he was a cutter who made himself bleed, or whether he had some sort of attempted suicide under his belt. Attempted suicide seemed to be the reason that most of the patients had been stuck in these overcrowded quarters in the first place—that and eating disorders. Drug addiction was probably up there as well, he supposed.

He was surprised when the dark haired boy lifted his head and looked directly at him.

He was not taken aback so much by the look of fear and pain on the teenager's face as the fact that he was obviously a Down syndrome patient. It took him a longer moment to register this because the boy was also of Asian decent and had very unique facial features. At least, they were unique to Shadow, because he had never seen an Asian with Down syndrome before.

The boy stopped crying a little as he noted that his fellow patient was studying him. They looked at one another for a long moment as he continued to sob.

"They try to kill burnt man!" Shaun whispered harshly as flecks of drool erupted from his mouth. His eyes stared fiercely out of the corner of their sockets as if peering desperately for anyone who could be eavesdropping. Despite the room having a few other patients present, the words were obviously for him alone.

Shadow sat up straight on the couch in surprise and started to rise to his feet as the boy continued to speak through his madness.

"The clown too! Everyone try to kill the clown!"

This time when Darkmind approached the tree, there were no dancers and no violinist. The bonfire continued to burn, however, while the dark forest still seemed filled with secrets beneath the flickering light.

He tried to ascertain where the people had gone, but his mind drew a blank. It was obvious to him that whatever powers he had on the outside were of limited use to him here.

Alec walked close beside him but had still not spoken and carried a serious look upon his face. Ayumu walked behind the duo, and Bali followed behind him. He could feel that she was watching the samurai closely for any indication of betrayal.

They passed by the canine guardian, but he seemed to hardly care because this path belonged to Darkmind, and it was apparent that he was allowed to bring guests inside. They moved down the corridors and past the many images of his life as they moved further into the cave. Because it was her first visit, Bali alone seemed to show any interest in the images, though she remained quiet and kept any musings to herself.

He felt Bali become very excited as they neared the site of the battle where he and Ayumu had been pulled from. "Darkmind?" she spoke aloud.

He stopped and turned towards her. He did not answer verbally but looked at her and waited for what she had to say.

"These soldiers can be freed."

"How?" He was going to ask her when they reached Lucius, but she had brought up the subject first. "We tried everything, and they seemed to be trapped."

He remembered Alec telling him that maybe the pretty lady would know what to do.

"It is a simple thing, actually." She smiled as she looked at Ayumu, who seemed to be growing more uncomfortable by the moment.

"Do you have a problem with this?" Darkmind addressed the samurai.

"I will keep my word, but with the odds so tipped in your favour, I question both my own and Katsuo's safety, and whether or not I have erred in my judgement by agreeing to help you."

"I promise you that as long as Balzola is untouched, you are safe. Also, once more I remind you that you are free to go your own way if you choose."

The samurai was clearly unnerved as he looked in the direction of the trapped Roman soldiers, of which he had only become aware during the fight. He had heard the banging and felt the rage from this direction when they had fought. He did not know until now, however, that it was trapped Roman soldiers who had been making the ruckus.

Darkmind walked down the side corridor with Alec and Bali. Ayumu walked behind them, somewhat hesitant.

When Darkmind stepped into the room, Lucius manifested immediately and greeted him with a smile and a hug.

"I thought you were in trouble, my friend, but we could not come to you."

"That never needs to happen again," Bali said with a purr.

Lucius looked at the beautiful new arrival and took a long moment to study her.

"Who is this?" he asked as he struggled to decide if he was attracted to the entity or saw her as a demon and something to be feared and shunned. She was obviously not toying with him as she had played with Darkmind on their first visit.

Darkmind said, "A friend, Lucius. Her name is Bali, and this other one is named Ayumu."

Bali smiled and Ayumu bowed deeply. Lucius held his hand up to his chest and nodded his head in greeting.

"Why is she looking at me like that?" he asked.

"We all have separate problems that can be solved by helping one another," Bali began with a smile. "Darkmind needs friends, and I know how we can free you and your men."

"How is that?" Lucius asked, trying to remain composed in the face of excitement.

There were loud whisperings in the shadows as his soldiers buzzed with anticipation to one another.

"You and your soldiers need to swear allegiance to Darkmind. You will be able to follow him anywhere that he goes and do anything that he asks you to."

"Slavery, perhaps?" Lucius asked sceptically.

"No, my friend," Darkmind answered, also growing excited as he began to comprehend the proposal. "I promise I will never ask you to do anything that opposes your code of honour. We will find a way to either release you, or I could order you to do what you want to do anyways. I guess in the end you only have my word, but I know that you are aware that I would not harm you intentionally."

Lucius stared at him for a long moment, nodding his head as he contemplated the offer in front of him.

"I have to admit, Darkmind," Ayumu stated, "this will make the task I propose—to make amends with Hachimantaro—more likely to succeed with a few more men ... But he may not be happy that you have bodyguards if he decides to attack you."

Darkmind smiled. "We will just have to deal with that when the time comes, I suppose."

"What task is this?" Lucius asked. The darkness around them seemed to rustle as some of the other Roman spirits grew restless at the proposition still hanging over them.

"There is a battle at the end of his life." Ayumu gestured towards Darkmind. "There is great evil unleashed upon many mortals, and it seems to be a great violation of the long-standing truce between various factions. Because it involves Darkmind, I believe it will be easiest for him to fix it with a little help, as opposed to huge outside armies massing for a battle that could set off Armageddon. Hachimantaro would have wanted to make this slight right again, anyways; it is exactly the type of battle that we are always fighting, and I believe this action will go far in making amends with him."

"A battle?" Lucius asked, excited.

"It would seem we could use a couple of extra men." Darkmind smirked. Even Alec's eyes seemed to sparkle with mischievousness at the samurai's expense. Bali grinned from ear to ear.

"I couldn't abandon you if you needed a couple of men for a battle!" Lucius held out his hand and Darkmind took it. The two men laughed and embraced as kinsmen and brothers.

Lucius then pulled away and fell to one knee. He removed his helmet, and with one hand placed upon the ground while the other arm continued to hold the helmet, he bowed his head. Several more Roman soldiers materialized and stepped from the shadows, repeating the gesture of loyalty and submission.

Ayumu's eyes went wide. "How many of you are there?" he asked in disbelief.

They were a sight to behold. Darkmind walked at the front of the column, his eyes filled with purpose and with power. At one side of him walked the beautiful succubus with her cape flowing behind her. She wore garments that could have passed for a bikini top and a mini skirt beneath the dark green cape. Her image was completed with long gloves and hooker boots.

To his other side walked the committed yet uncertain samurai with his facial piercings. He was armoured except for his head and lower arms. His sleeves were rolled up, revealing scarred and heavily tattooed flesh.

At the head of the Roman column was Lucius, who had put Alec up on one of his shoulders. Behind him walking in pairs came hundreds of his countrymen eager for battle of any kind, full of energy that they had never been able to spend. They were warriors like Darkmind who had chosen not to spend any morsel of power on cosmetics. They walked with battered armour and bleeding wounds and were a ghastly sight to behold. They had died proudly together and so were large and muscled more than they would have been in life because that was they way in which they had viewed themselves. At the head of the column, behind Lucius, were those that carried the hunter's spears gleaming darkly and lusting for the drink of life.

Darkmind, still electrified by the gift from Bali, did not feel burdened with the responsibility of suddenly leading so many spirits towards an uncertain future. He had never led men in life, but he felt as if he was born into this new existence to do just that. He felt a sense of purpose that he had never realized when he was alive. He could only marvel at the series of coincidences that had led him up to this moment. He understood by sharing Bali's memories that such a thing, such an amassment of power and troops, had not happened to a recently deceased for a very long time. He felt her excitement and commitment.

However, there were no such things as coincidence, he remembered.

The Romans had been quickly briefed by Ayumu of the potential risks, and he let them know that some of them could, and probably would, be lost forever. When the men laughed at the prospect of dying in battle, Ayumu smiled, seeming to realize that these warriors before him had many traits similar to the samurai with which he was used to working. Lucius had slapped him hard on the shoulder, and he had started to laugh as well, surrendering somewhat to the unorthodox situation. He knew that if it had been him, he would have preferred death to eternal imprisonment as well.

Darkmind drifted into Ayumu's mind. The samurai still felt uneasy; he wondered if he was being true to Hachimantaro's wishes. He was eager for a good fight but also was aware that Darkmind was quickly becoming extremely powerful, especially for such a new being, and was also still unpredictable. If Hachimantaro needed to destroy him, it would be a harder task than originally anticipated. The much more powerful man would have to spend a lot more of his resources to accomplish this goal, and this would most likely also include the loss of soldiers.

Ayumu, in his own way, was becoming as intrigued as Bali by the path that was unfolding before Darkmind. He had begun to like the dead Canadian soldier and the Romans, and this further complicated matters. He did not feel good about the possibility of having to fight any of them. Not out of concern for his own wellbeing, but because he was beginning to feel a kinship with them and could not resist the contagious feelings of a brotherhood that had developed amongst the appreciative Darkmind and the gleefully excited Romans, who had suddenly found themselves free.

Katsuo had been expecting them; he had become aware that Ayumu was approaching with Darkmind and some others. Their empathetic communication was limited here in these tunnels, but he had sensed from Ayumu that an understanding had been agreed upon between them and Darkmind and that they would be arriving shortly.

Lupa had calmed considerably and rested at Balzola's feet. The jester had in turn discerned that the major threat was over but had remained on her feet and vigilant anyways, for she still did not understand fully why the samurai had become so hostile in the first place.

Neither Balzola nor Katsuo were prepared for the entourage that entered the cavern. Katsuo's eyes went wide as the soldiers filed in until they could no longer enter the room. He looked back and forth between his friend and the roughshod warriors in disbelief.

Darkmind and Bali moved towards Balzola quickly. He picked her up and embraced her fiercely, sharing a passionate kiss. Bali then kissed her on the lips as well, passing to her energy and an understanding of the situation and arrangement between them. Balzola unleashed a bloody-toothed grin as she gripped Darkmind once more.

Darkmind decided to keep the lone image of Lupa present for the battle planning. He was aware that her council came from a deeper part of him that was not necessarily as easy to call forth without external dialogue. It was a symbolic gesture that was loved by the superstitious Romans and lifted their spirits to even greater heights.

* * *

Darkmind sat with the two samurai, Bali, Balzola, Lupa, Lucius and six of the highest ranking Romans, watching the scene of his final battle over and over. Alec sat quietly nearby and simply took in what was being said.

Ayumu and Katsuo were instrumental in explaining to the inexperienced warriors why the scene before them was problematic and needed to be rectified. Being warriors, they could also easily explain tactics that the group could use in the battle to come that the Romans would not have even conceived of with only their mortal combat experience. Bali was equally troubled by the scene repeating before her. Despite her power, however, her understanding of battle was limited to melees between her and other similar entities.

The immediate problem with the battle was that none of the deaths were timely. Every one of the Canadian soldiers that had been killed had been taken before his time. If Darkmind's crime against the man Nate had been grievous, then this was preposterous.

The mortal men, the insurgents that were used in the battle against the Canadians, had been heavily supplemented with ethereal hunters intent on taking the living. Many of the mortals were also practitioners of dark arts and had led naive men into battle with promises of acceptance by the great light.

There were more hunters and more powerful hunters than should have ever been present at such a battle as well. Usually in such a fight, there would be a few hunters to gather the untimely—but not scores of them.

There was also the issue of the slain valkyrie. She was a righteous harvester coming to collect what was rightfully hers. Even though the killing had seemed accidental, it was worrisome that the hunter would have been so bold in the first place as to swing his scythe so close to her. These beings generally avoided one another out of respect for the truce that they now shared.

Spirit guides were also generally out of bounds, but the supplementing spirits had killed all of them as well—even some of the surviving soldier's protector spirits. This sometimes happened as energies fought over the fates of their wards alongside the living, but again not to this extent. It became clear that the plan was to destroy any spiritual witnesses to the carnage.

If the chaos had a rhyme or reason, it was that every soldier was to be killed with every spirit alongside them. All traces of the men were to be wiped off the face of the earth, and their complete disappearance would go down in the annals of history as one of those unsolved mysteries that sometimes occur in war, where there was no trace left. Even the vehicles were to be removed from the land of the living.

Darkmind was very confused. The battle was not how he remembered it at all. There was some sort of a time loop that he became aware of that didn't fit. He saw no Romans upon the field but had remembered seeing Romans when he had died. The memory did not seem insignificant that the Romans on the road had greeted him as if they knew him. He knew that this must have something to do with what they were about to do.

Furthermore, the death of the valkyrie seemed uncertain, and the event kept changing. Sometimes he saw his spirit picking up the sword, but more often than not the sword disappeared as the angelic being did. He tried to follow his spirit in the madness of the chaotic battle but usually could not see where he went.

He also did not think that so many Canadians had been killed. In fact, the scene looked like a complete massacre with no survivors. There was no air support and no artillery raking the hills as he remembered. There was simply a series of IED explosions followed by an ambush of unprecedented proportions. The radios did not seem to work, nor had the IED blocking devices. When the vehicles had hit the bombs, most of the doors had been blown off by the explosions, leaving the wounded men vulnerable to machine gun fire and leaping out to avoid fiery deaths as the fire-preventing equipment failed them inside the vehicles.

He was extremely troubled and understood why Ayumu and Katsuo had been as well. If the attack had remained unwitnessed by them, it would have succeeded. It still could, technically. There were certain rules in place that had held for the most part between major spirit factions for centuries, even before the more strict treaties of this new era. These were clearly being violated here for one reason or another, and a vast amount of energy was being harvested by an enemy on the sly without other factions knowing about it.

Ayumu and Katsuo had wanted Hachimantaro to know about the violation so that he could make a decision. If Hachimantaro decided to openly attack the violator, though, the situation would probably quickly spiral out of control as his allies joined him. More than likely, the initial battle's true nature would never be viewed by the violator's allies. Instead they, the righteous ones, would join in a battle whose avoidance was the very reason the agreements and treaties had been set up in the first place! Full-out war would undoubtedly spill over into the mortal realm, upsetting the balance and destroying most, if not all, of the living.

Darkmind had a claim here, even if he brought with him an army of sorts. He had made no agreement and had no alliances to any side. Most important of all, he was a victim of the battle and had a direct right to fight. If the dark forces chose to call for help against him and his ragtag forces, they would be revealing that they had been the ones that had broken the truce in the first place. This was something that they obviously did not want.

Darkmind took all of this in. He scanned the faces of his new allies and contemplated the likelihood of success. The end result of the battle would be determined by all of them, but it was the Romans who would have to take up the bulk of the fighting. They seemed eager for it.

The Romans were clearly in awe of how modern battle had evolved since they had lived, but they kept their questions to a minimum in an attempt at professionalism and obedience. When they did ask questions, they were enthralled and sounded almost childlike. It fascinated them that there were horseless chariots that shot great arcs of exploding fire and that men fought at great distances with sticks that likewise threw fiery death. Blades were seldom used except on the rare occasion to finish a wounded man by the ambushers. It was good that there were older spirits present for the planning as well.

Bali was helpful in pointing out how to deal with the entities that were created like her and had never lived. The hunters could be met like other fighting men on the field, but these others entities were more devious and avoided the risks of battle. She pointed out dark streaks that had disabled equipment and caused confusion. She was able to choose a point strategically where she could take a small force to prevent the complete disabling of communications in the mortal realm.

After much debate it was further decided that Balzola and Lupa would flee upon hitting the ground and go back to Angel in New York. Balzola was lucid because she had borrowed much of Angel's spirit. If she was harmed, Angel could be left in a vegetable state or perhaps even killed. If any of the dark energies became aware that a living person's spirit was fighting, they could also send beings to destroy Angel in an attempt to get the higher hand. The risk was too great for both of these reasons. Balzola argued this point with nods and gestures, but with even Bali coaxing her, she had to submit that this was the best course of action; she could not be part of the battle. If Lupa went with her as well, she could call for help if she needed, through the wolf to Darkmind.

A small group of Romans would bring Alec to the mosque as quickly as possible for protection. Darkmind nodded as he remembered once more the Romans on the road.

The Romans would send in shock troops all along the line of vehicles to protect the living men, hiding themselves energetically until the last moment, similar to what Alec had done. Bali showed all of them how to do this, and it was the first time that Darkmind saw how this was accomplished as well. Other small groups, some with the hunter's spears, would hit the enemy from behind in many different areas to create confusion and destroy as many of them as possible before they realized what was happening.

It was Lupa and Bali that argued that the valkyrie could not be protected, or Darkmind would never have retrieved the sword in the first place. It was strange to Darkmind that Lupa was suggesting something that at first glance seemed dishonourable, but her reasoning was sound. The whole battle could erase itself if he was not the carrier of the sword in the first place, and the counterattack would have never occurred at all. It was mind twisting, but Bali was adamant on this point as well. It was a difficult thing for all of the warriors present to accept, but they all eventually did so reluctantly: the valkyrie must be left to her fate.

The two samurai were especially long in deciding whether or not they should let Hachimantaro know what was going on or let him feel their location. It was decided that if their house could avoid the conflict, the potential for it spiralling out of control was much more limited. Hachimantaro might send others to investigate their presence if he became aware of them, and they might in turn become too involved before Ayumu and Katsuo could explain what was happening.

Ayumu argued to Katsuo that by being honour bound to Darkmind, who had saved his life by not abandoning him in his weakened state, he was entitled to fight alongside the Romans in the battle. He then told Katsuo that he should leave at the same time as Balzola and Lupa because he was not honour bound to fight and might be seen as an outsider. Katsuo scoffed at this and began to argue, much to the entertainment of the Romans. Katsuo's argument was that he was fighting because he was honour bound to protect Ayumu. It was a particularly humorous exchange between the two men, and Ayumu had to concede that Katsuo would not go anywhere; although he told him that he knew the real reason he was staying was so that he wouldn't be left out of a fight. When the argument was over, the laughter amongst the Romans was so hard that the two samurai were forced to try to hide their own smiles. Ayumu and Katsuo knew that the laughter was not mean spirited, that there was a warrior kinship that was shared between the Romans, the samurai and the lone Canadian soldier, in which dark humour that laughed in the face of death was paramount.

The joke was completely lost on Balzola, who had no memories of her warrior lives. Bali got the joke but, never having been mortal, did not understand how the potential for an end of everything could be funny in any way. She was attuned enough to Darkmind to know that it was not nervousness but something profound that only a mortal warrior on the eve of battle could ever know.

The plan was that the two samurai would prematurely detonate as many bombs as possible before the fighting started, because they were far more capable at manipulating physical items. They would then manifest to the living enemy that were being misled and try to convince them to flee. As they performed these tasks, they would be forced to harvest energy along the way, making their mission potentially the most precarious.

Darkmind would leave an aspect of himself with Lucius, as an advisor and general to the Romans, with 10 hand-chosen bodyguards in a position to oversee the battle. His main body, or entity form, would be fighting in the thick, trying to protect his newly deceased spirit. If he were to fall in this fight, his limited aspect that remained overwatching with Lucius would still survive, although in a much weaker state.

You realize what needs to happen, my love? Bali asked without words.

Darkmind pursed his burnt lips together and nodded his head solemnly. If his mortal aspect did not die, then he would never have been born to this new life. If he was not born to this new life, then none of this would have happened, and the loop of inconsistencies would continue indefinitely and perhaps lead to the ultimate massacre anyways.

His mortal self needed to die—even if it was by his own hand.

* * *

They spent a lot of time rehearsing. The scene played out before them over and over, and so they were not being rushed in any way, shape or form. They broke into groups and took the time to go over different scenarios and likely enemy responses. When possible the Romans formed partnerships with soldiers that they had worked beside in life. When this was not possible, they created new bonds of familiarity.

They knew theoretically that they could fail and return to this same portal, to try the attack again, but even losing a few men would leave them in a much weaker position than the first attempt. The Roman philosophy of combat was to have an acceptable number of casualties in battle, as was the philosophy of the dead samurai. Darkmind was used to the Canadian way of trying to achieve zero casualties, so he tried to interject this into their plans as much as possible. In the type of combat in which they were about to participate, however, this was unlikely.

Ayumu and Katsuo explained to the others present how to be connected to one another through empathy and sense. It was decided that it would take too much energy to learn how to do this properly for everyone, though, so Lucius and the six Roman leaders alone learned how to do this at a very basic level.

The front line of the rear attackers were to bowl over their enemy in a phalanx, with the second row thrusting overhead with their own javelins, pila or hunter's spears. The third and fourth rows would be part of the formation integrity while a fifth row would finish off the wounded and watch for flanking or rear attacks.

Including Lucius there were 643 Roman spirits. Each of the leaders were made generals of 99 men. Lucius was in charge of them all and directly in charge of the remaining 42. The 10 bodyguards would be with him directly, and Bali would be with another 10. The remaining 22 would deliver the boy Alec to the mosque and report back to Lucius to be reassigned as reinforcements in whatever area seemed to need them the most. Lucius was also responsible for trying to gather clues as to what force could possibly be behind the attack. He would watch everything and then debrief Bali and the samurai afterwards in a hope that the older and more experienced spirits might be able to discern who their enemy really was.

Two of the generals would use their men to protect the living

Canadians. The other four generals would use their men in their area of responsibility, which was in each of the directions north, south, east and west, and 45 degrees to each side of that bearing, making a complete circle. There were not enough men to cover everywhere, and so each general was free to use his men as he saw fit and to hit where he thought would be the most effective within the zones. The most important thing would be to use the element of surprise coupled with the violence of action.

They had observed that the main human attackers came from two different directions, but the spirit attackers came in waves towards the Canadians from all directions, forming a part of a large circle of death that closed around them all. The spirit infantry were rat-faced entities that seemed to be under their own leadership while the hunters swept freely across the field. Most dangerous of all, though, seemed to be the organized, towering, red-eyed creatures that swept in and destroyed the pockets of spirit resistance.

Darkmind watched all of the planning and nodded to himself with a sense of confidence. He felt that their plan would not fail and that a full and strategic victory would be granted them.

The plan was flawed from the beginning. He had forgotten that when he had initially died, he had witnessed an aerial battle as well.

19

Ayumu and Katsuo ran along the road ahead of the carriers. As they passed each of the hidden explosive devices, they swept down with their swords and set them off. The chain of explosions caused the Canadian carriers to stop dead in their tracks and position themselves to protect the arcs around them.

"Call sign Bravo! IED! IED! IED!" the crew commander in the leading light armoured vehicle, or LAV, called over the radio.

"Get into position and cover your arcs!" yelled the platoon commander from a separate vehicle before the radio failed. It was an unnecessary command because the LAV commanders in each of the vehicles were already moving into a defensive posture.

The Bravo crew commander ducked into the hatch slightly for cover as bullets started to ricochet off of the sides of the carrier. "Bravo! Ambush at grid 27 ... Fuck!" He started to hit the radio and bang on the side of his headset. "Comms are down!" he yelled to the section inside the carrier, confident that the dismounts would be able to hear him over the racket. He hoped that the driver could hear him as well.

His gunner beside him started to fire high-explosive rounds at the enemy positions, not waiting to be told, knowing that he had a right to do this under their rules of combat to protect himself and his section.

The crew commander risked getting up high enough to fire the mounted C9 machine gun, and he started to strafe the same enemy positions. He took a round to the side of his neck and fell into the hatch, bleeding while trying to hold the wound with his gloved hand.

The back of the carrier opened.

It was madness and contradicted all of their standard operating procedures.

The dismounts thought that the driver must have dropped the ramp, and the driver thought the dismounts must have done it, yelling at them for their stupidity even though he knew he could not be heard from the front of the vehicle. "What the fuck are you doing!" the driver screamed.

All of the LAVs were firing now, but the dismounts in Bravo were in a vulnerable position with their back door open. A stray round could bounce around inside and potentially wound several of them. The Sergeant didn't have a choice. "Dismount right!" he screamed as the adrenaline-pumped and heavily-breathing group poured out of the carrier and took cover at the side of the road between the LAVs before they began to return fire.

"Bravo, what the fuck are you doing!" screamed the platoon commander from his hatch. He was furious and could not understand why they would be so reckless as to get out of the carrier.

Call sign Charlie still had comms and did not understand why the platoon commander or the other cars were not responding.

"Fucking crypto dropped, piece of shit!" The crew commander thought aloud into the radio, thinking that no one could hear him but assuming his radio alone had failed.

"HQ. Call sign Charlie, send Sitrep now!" the radio blared as the officer in charge at headquarters got on the radio and demanded the situation report, no doubt having grabbed the headset from the radio operator on duty at some desk.

His own gunner was firing rounds into the opposite direction, like Bravo's car. The crew commander got onto the radio and sat in the hatch while he tried to get a bearing.

"Charlie! HQ, we have IED contact, with Bravo probably hit! There are no comms with other vehicles! Dismounts are on the ground! Multiple contacts! Requesting guns and air support! Grid to follow."

"HQ. Go."

"Charlie. Grid is 27 ... Fuck!" He could hear that his own radio had gone dead.

Bullets cracked over the heads of the dismounts. The grenadiers fired M203 bomb after M203 bomb into the enemy positions. The C9 machine guns fired as best as they could from the low ground. It seemed like they were in a movie; the muzzle flashes could be seen from scores of rifles by unseen shooters. Occasionally a silhouette would pop up as a man would move from position to position.

"Got him!" one of the riflemen in the small group yelled, the second in command on the ground.

"Save your fucking celebration, Corporal. We need to kill more than one of these fuckers!"

A wave of fear and hopelessness came over them as it seemed that a dark cloud descended. There was a buzzing in their ears that they mistook for hearing damage from their weapons being fired without earplugs. One of the young men was hit in the leg by a round and started to curse but continued to fire. One of the others started to pray as he fought.

A heavily tattooed gunner with Norse tattoos covering most of his body started to call to his own pagan gods. In his mind he was standing tall and firing his weapon from the hip, but he was too disciplined to do this in reality even though he felt a wave of energy and rage come into him. Instead he screamed a barbaric war cry. He was already changing ammo boxes, which meant he had already fired 200 rounds.

"Mag change!" one of the guys yelled.

"Reload," another yelled as well so that everyone knew that he was out of the fight for a few second. He would have to be more disciplined with his remaining rounds and would probably still need to make a dash at some point, or send someone else to the carrier for more ammo.

This was around the time that they realized that one of them had been killed.

Initially Bali had been able to keep the spirits away from the radio in Charlie's car, but waves of spirits focused their full attack on them. The lines of protection offered by the Romans buckled and bent at the car, and the 10 men with her were being torn apart. She had manifested for herself twin short swords and spun and danced, but she was being hit repeatedly. She was a powerful being, and her age alone made her capable of combat, but she was not used to multiple attackers and felt the drain of one hit after another.

She reached out time and time again to eliminate the small spirits responsible for destroying the radio only to find that they had been replaced by hunters and other more sinister beings. She seemed to quickly realize that their cause was hopeless, but she could not even stop moving long enough to consider fleeing. The press of attack was relentless.

In fact, the radio would have fallen immediately if the samurai had not abandoned their mission long enough to help her. If they had not done so, the Canadian headquarters would have never even known that the LAV carriers were under attack.

The samurai came from a different time—or at least their philosophy did—where death was not a negative and the search for a glorious end was paramount. The more disciplined Romans or the Canadian would probably never have abandoned a mission for emotion and would have kept focus until their task was done. Instead Ayumu and Katsuo saw that Bali and her band were in trouble, and they ran straight into the melee. It was the one factor that let the Charlie commander get off even the partial message.

Ayumu, Katsuo and Bali fought bravely. Bali had been in the conflict longer and fell with the last of her band of soldiers. Katsuo cut a deadly path even as he took blow after blow. Ayumu raged at the hopelessness of the situation as he shredded any of the enemy around him that he could.

In the end, however, all three of them fell, and the radio fell with them.

The officer in charge called for air support from HQ explaining the situation to higher command. He had a map trace of the position of travel and the last location report, or LOCSTAT, and so he could surmise the area that the LAVs would likely be in within a kilometre or so. The road that they had been on would be easy to follow from the air.

The American helicopters were already en route and would be on location in less than ten minutes. They could then possibly give a better grid of the site to higher command.

The company officer hoped that it wouldn't be too late.

Darkmind felt her fall. He felt the trace amount of energy come to him and become a part of him, and then he felt her no more. He knew that she was gone. There was nothing left. He could not feel her or sense her. All that he had of her was the energy that she had gifted him.

He cried out in rage and in grief. The symbiotic relationship that they had so briefly had was more profound of an experience to him than anything that he had ever known. He waded back and forth in front of the dismounts, trying to destroy as many of the enemy as possible. The Roman line was holding firm near him.

Then they came from the air. He cursed himself for not having remembered everything that he had seen when he had died and had initially viewed the scene. Dozens of gargoyle-like, hideous, warted beings swept down from the sky, shredding the Romans to pieces and tossing them unceremoniously into the crowd of enemy that consumed them.

"Protect him!" he screamed to the Romans, indicating his own spirit, as he reluctantly broke off to finish the samurai's mission. As he looked over he saw that his mortal self had been killed. For obvious reasons he needed his own spirit to survive the onslaught.

His new spirit was speaking, thinking that he was alive. He was speaking as if he was talking to his fellow soldiers, but he was alone. He spoke of his mom and of his love not for his girlfriend but for the woman that he had let slip away, Angel. He complained that he felt cold. Darkmind saw as his new spirit was pulled towards the great light. This seemed odd now to Darkmind because his death had seemed untimely to him when viewing it before, but he saw now that maybe it was not.

"No!" he screamed at himself as he rushed off towards the mortal enemy fighters in an attempt to persuade them to retreat. "Fight it!"

He looked up and saw silver, eagle-like creatures attacking the dark flyers. There was no way for him to know that they were the spirits that were attached to the incoming helicopters. In a way they were similar to Bali in that they were created by tradition and energy, but they were built for war, and that was what they were here to do. The helicopters had still not arrived, but they heralded the appearance of a coming power that transcended realms.

The creatures were putting the fight to the dark flyers but not damaging them terribly. The Romans were given reprieve, however, from the deadly aerial assault and were able to focus on the ground attack once more.

Darkmind had not waded very far into the battle before he realized that his mission was hopeless. With every kill he gained, he grew stronger, and he was now mighty enough to wade away from the protection of the main force, but he was fighting masses that scored countless hits upon him, draining him of vital energy. He was being pushed backwards as soon as he set out.

There was a shrieking wail that he recognized at once. He rushed without thinking towards the scythe-wielding hunter that bore down upon his newborn spirit. There was a clash of weapons and an explosion of sparks. Then he was being tossed through the air as the ravenous creature flung him aside, intent on his initial prey.

The outer attacking forces had hardly fared any better. They were butchering huge groups of the attackers, but reinforcements had taken them from behind, forcing them into tactically useless circles of protection. They fought as one, preparing to either prevail together or to die together.

Lucius' position had been recognized and was being attacked as well. He could barely warn the generals below of incoming threats before he was forced to fight to protect himself or one of his overwhelmed bodyguards in a maddening, chaotic melee over and over again. He hoped that help would come soon, but he suspected that the soldiers who had carried Alec to safety were probably still some distance away.

Bravo's machine gunner fell limp and breathed no more.

He was an untimely death, but he had been praying to a god who had heeded his words. Nine valkyrie were sent forth from Valhalla to gather the soul of the valiant son.

At one time Odin had been as mighty as any of the old gods, but man had forgotten him except for small pockets of pagan war junkies and heavy metal music listeners. Though weaker than he once was, it meant that when one called to him, he was more likely to hear the plea and answer their prayers. It was in his nature to do so.

He was a created being, though, and could not change his ways even if he had wanted to. He respected valour and courage and honour above all things, and so he would only come to those who possessed these qualities themselves. Centuries of war on the other side had left the halls of Odin sparsely populated, and newcomers were rare.

By design his kingdom was hard for other spirits to get to, and harder to wage war against, and so he had survived while many other pantheon of beings had not.

The Canadian soldier, the machine gunner, would be a welcomed son into the halls of the mighty. He was a true warrior in an age that often lacked even basic courage. Truth be told, he would have been accepted into the great hall in any century. He was one of those men who would have carried a spear or a gun regardless of which era he had been born into. That was what Odin liked, that was what Odin wanted. Not the denizens of cowards that professed to worship him but lacked humility at a young age or spoke with a bladed tongue.

Odin loved the idea of man more than he actually loved them. It fascinated him how fearless and brave one could be in contrast to all of the other mortals that surrounded them. He was very selective, but when he found one he that liked, it was almost as if Odin was the worshipper, and the warrior, who would probably be given little aid from him anyways, was the god.

The machine gunner had once been gifted twin brothers from an ancient, icy age as protector spirits to help him on his journey. This was a gift of drunken joy that was in response to the art freshly scarred upon the mortal's skin. The brothers had been given then, indirectly, because images of the wolves and ravens of Odin painted his body along with old, uncompromising runes of war.

Odin was sure that the great light would reject the low spirit and maybe even the high spirit of the machine gunner because he saw that this death was untimely. The valkyrie rode to collect him. Odin was not happy, though, because he wanted this man to live a long life and fight many battles. He was especially unhappy that he had not foreseen the demise of the two spirit protectors beside him as well.

When the two spirit protectors fell unanticipated beside the living, lonesome son that Odin anticipated welcoming into his kingdom, it was an outrage that knew no bounds.

Odin sat at the edge of his seat and watched with a new vision the battle that played out before him. He saw the Romans and the burnt soldier with eyes that burned with respect; being omnipotent enough to see the whole battle and the reasons for it. When the valkyrie was cut down trying to reclaim the soul from the hunter, he stood in his chair in barely contained rage and was ready to join the battle himself.

He saw the violation that this enemy had brought to the land of men, but with the god of trickery at his side, he also saw the mischief involved and the futility of becoming a part of the conflict that would break his truce, further weaken his house perhaps to the point of extinction and drag into the battle all of the sides that needed to remain uninvolved.

All he could do was bear witness to the carnage and report to the other houses what had happened so that the violator, who had yet to reveal him or herself, could be punished. There was nothing he could do except to stand there and watch and feel as his blood boiled.

Or was there?

He saw the situation more clearly as the one who was now known as Darkmind wielded a sword that had been forged in his kingdom. He understood the loop and that this decision of his had been made before he had even been aware that he even had a decision to make.

He recognized the soldier as a son.

When the valkyrie fell in the field of battle, he concentrated his energy so that her sword would remain behind. As he knew would happen, the younger spirit picked the sword up off the ground and killed the reaper before him.

The nine valkyrie had been attacked directly when one of them had been killed. That meant that they had a legitimate claim to be part of the battle. He did not want to sacrifice them, but he had a certain nature that lacked self-preservation at times. He ached to make this unknown enemy pay.

"Assist them!" He uttered the command mentally. The remaining eight mounted winged warrior women understood what they needed to do. They spiralled into the battle to assist the silver eagles in the air and to wreck havoc upon the enemy ground forces as best they could.

The helicopters strafed the hillsides and spiralled in and out to fire rockets into the attackers. Dark creatures flew at the machines, attempting to down them alongside the insurgents' rocket propelled grenades, but these were met by the women of the air and the silver, eagle-like entities.

The pilots were shocked to see the size of the ground force attacking the Canadians because they had only ever been briefed about this large of insurgent groups in the more remote provinces of the country. They called in artillery as they pulled back before each run and teetered on the realm of being in the wrong airspace when the hits came. They would then call for the large guns to pause before swooping back over the sites again. Realistically, it was against standard operating procedures to have artillery strikes this close to air elements, but there were levels of command that were bending rules at almost every level, out of fear of losing the column of LAVs. That would be a political disaster that higher levels of command could not afford.

From the air it looked pretty bad. The earth around the first LAV, Bravo, was smouldering, and there were dismounts on the ground that they could only imagine were in rough shape. The pilots also knew that communications were down, but they took heart in seeing that all of the carriers seemed to still be firing their weapons.

Darkmind decided that his best course of action would be to follow his own spirit and try to protect him as he made the long run towards the mosque. He had felt guilty taking most of the reapers' energy from his younger self, but he had thought that it was the wisest thing for him to do. His newer spirit did not know how to fight yet.

"The mosque!" he yelled. "Run for the mosque!"

Darkmind saw his spirit trying to awkwardly run with the sword. He rushed into a group of the red-eyed demons that were trying to overtake the younger him. They tumbled to the ground together as he rolled, trying to gain his feet.

One of the beings hit him heavily with a large war hammer, and he felt the energy drain. He whirled around quickly and took off the being's head, drinking the energy back into his own body. A second one scored a hit upon him with a spear, and he answered with a downward stroke from the Japanese sword, Black Dragon. His blades screamed for blood in a mindless lust, and he gave it to them as he saw the great hunter, the charioteer, rush with his dogs towards his younger self.

His rage was unleashed, and he scored hit after hit even though the aggressive flurry left him open to take as many blows in return. He pushed himself past the pain, aware that he had once more lost an eye. He bulled through the remaining two adversaries, knocking them over backwards while refusing to stop moving. His momentum only allowed him to take enough time to kill one of them. The second one rose to his feet and prepared to give chase just as the Romans returning from the mosque passed him.

The Romans pulled the large being down and stabbed him in a flurry repeatedly until he was completely gone. Darkmind was appreciative of the aid, but he had no time to stop and thank them. He saw that they too were eager to get into the battle as they rushed towards Lucius' position on the hill.

He started to catch up to the charioteer when he saw the heavily muscled arm raise itself and let fly the spear meant to kill his newly deceased self. A dog sprang towards this other him as well while several of the other canines closed the gap.

He was too far away to do anything.

He willed his energy outwards to shield the new spirit and imagined a wall of protection between him and his enemies. He had no idea if this would work. He felt relief, however, as he saw how the spear and the dog bounced off of the shield, and he was confident that his will had prevailed. The great hunter did not seem to recognize that it was a force behind him that had prevented his attack. After cursing the mosque sentries, he seemed to be settling in to wait for his target to reappear.

Darkmind saw that this was in fact the general of the hunters on the field of battle. He knew that the leader had properly discerned that his younger spirit was the primary threat upon the field and had targeted the one with the sword, who had killed one of his own soldiers, the reaper. It seemed too focused to realize that there were two of him existing within the same moment This confusion would now be Darkmind's greatest tool.

He took out two dogs that had turned to face him as he approached in a dead run. The antlered beasts pulling the chariot turned to face the rushing madman as he came in a rage. He ducked beneath the spear that flew at him and shoulder-butted over the chariot even as the spear reappeared in the charioteer's hand.

The chariot flipped over, and the hellish deer screamed as they became entangled in the barbwire and rolled around upon the ground. Two more dogs flew at him, and he cut them down with great arcs as the charioteer rolled to his feet. He stepped in quickly as the impossibly fast spear glanced off of his shoulder and flew into the night. His two swords came down swiftly side by side but were blocked by the shaft of the weapon that had already returned.

"Fool!" the hunter spewed at him as worms flew from his face through the helmet.

Darkmind did not bother to answer him except with a kick to the chest that sent the larger humanoid back on his feet. He saw no option but to spur the attack onward at full velocity.

He ducked as a dog flew past him who had leapt for his throat, and he reached out with Dark Dragon to destroy another. The spear swept across him, and the newly gained energy left him as fast as it had come. He heard as several more dogs rushed towards him from all sides.

He felt his arms grow weary, and he started to question whether or not he had made the right decision in attacking the great hunter alone.

The mortal enemies started to retreat under the heavy bombardment. They had been in a state of rapture during the attack, but even their irrational minds started to weaken as their casualties mounted. Preparing to die to destroy the column of LAVs was one thing, but the helicopters rained death upon them, as did the artillery bombardment. Their position and the ambush itself had been compromised, and there was no hope for success, only the promise of death. They scattered into the night.

There were those that had decided that this was the night that they would meet Allah, and so these few stayed behind to finish what they had started. Their sporadic fire would allow their brothers to flee and return another day to fight the holy war, the great jihad.

The helicopters made runs at these few insurgents and protected the LAVs from further attack while the retreating men melted into the night. The LAV gunners started to fire C6 machine gun rounds at individual targets instead of using the high-explosive canon rounds.

The dismounted Sergeant on the ground assessed that he had two dead soldiers and one badly wounded. He quickly learned that his crew commander had also been wounded and had been shot in the neck. He got the wounded soldier on the ground to apply a tourniquet as the remaining soldiers continued to watch their arcs.

He tried to use his personal short-range radio to contact the other LAVs, but the device seemed to have dead batteries. He climbed into his

LAV and told the gunner through the back to shut down the radio and then turn it back on. When it powered back up, it looked as if it might work again. He tried once more.

"Bravo! HQ sitrep!"

"HQ! Go!"

He quickly recovered from the response and started to speak immediately. "Bravo. I have two pri alpha and two VSAs. Nine liner to follow!" It was not up to him to decide if the two men were in fact VSA—dead, or vital sign absent—but he was not in a position to go through all of the formalities and needed to get a medivac helicopter on the way. The priority Alpha category was reserved for those who needed immediate medical attention. The men were obviously dead, and he was now far more concerned with the two men who could die. The nine liner would send all of the pertinent information including mechanism of injury and their current grid so that help could be sent as soon as possible.

When he was finished he sat for a moment in disbelief at what had transpired. It had been a calamity of errors that had not seemed possible. He pulled himself together after the brief pause and ran back outside after telling his gunner to man the radio.

"I'll be back!" he said to his dismounts as he ran to find out the status of the other LAVs and find the warrant and platoon commander. He needed to let them know the status of his section and that medical help was on the way. He would also need to update the nine liner if there were casualties in the other vehicles as well.

He braced himself for the worst.

The remaining enemy spirits that had not been hacked away likewise dissolved into the night. The Romans kept their unit integrity and did not pursue them very far. The valkyrie, on the other hand, swept into the darkness and ranged far and wide in search of fleeing survivors. The spirits that were not strong enough or wise enough to slip into the spirit world fed the warrior women. The winged women had only lost the one soldier, but her loss was great, and it would take a lot of energy for their patron to recreate one in her stead, for there would always be nine, and so they took the opportunity to gather some of this energy for him.

The Romans, as they would have in life, fell over in exhaustion from the relentless battle. They had lost a lot of men but would count the losses afterwards, when the battle was deemed over by the generals, by Lucius directly.

They pitched over, and many of them vomited upon the ground. Their armour was more dented than ever, and wounds covered every one of them. They leaned upon one another, and some fell straight on their backs, breathing heavily but otherwise looking as if they were dead. They would rise and reform if there was a counterattack, but until then they would try to recover from the battle as best they could.

Lucius, up on the hill, rested heavily on one knee and leaned upon his spear. The returning soldiers had saved him from certain death, reinforcing him and the remaining two bodyguards upon the hill in the nick of time. The shade that Darkmind had left behind of himself was gone, presumably destroyed, and he had seen the samurai and Bali fall early in the battle. He could only hope that Darkmind still lived somewhere, but his concern for him grew as he surveyed the field of battle.

"Where are you, my friend?" he asked to no one in particular.

"Sir," the leader of the reinforcements said, "I think I know where he is."

The spear sent shivers through him as it pierced his thigh. He turned his leg in a painful gamble, trying to wrench the weapon from his foe's grasp as he swung the valkyrie's sword across its chest.

The being did in fact let go, but the result was not what he had hoped for as a dog leapt and clung to his arm. Just as the great sword fell from his hand, the spear reappeared in the hunters grasp. He stabbed the dog through the throat with Dark Dragon and stumbled backwards in pain and weakness. He took little satisfaction in hearing that the stags were still struggling to untangle themselves from the ground.

He hobbled weakly, waiting for the next wave of dogs, but he realized that he had killed them all. It was just him and the hunter now, but the charioteer looked relatively fresh and as strong as ever.

The hunter was cautious in delivering his death blow, for he had grown wary of his opponent. This turned out to be a stroke of luck for Darkmind as the hunter circled him cautiously.

The charioteer viewed him with eyes that could have almost been respect, had he been capable of such an emotion. Here was a man—a recently deceased man, no less—that had managed to kill so many of his dogs, so many of his hunters; had somehow thwarted the massacre and had fought him so hard that he had thought more than once that he might be killed. All of this had been accomplished by one man, and in this lone fight on this road, this man had been alone. It was unheard of, and he was unaware of such a man in recent times. The fact that he carried the valkyrie's sword had made him a worthy adversary, but the strength in which he had wielded it had shocked him. He promised himself to have a more healthy caution when dealing with armed earthbound in the future.

He raised his arm and held the spear far back as he prepared to give the death blow, stepping towards Darkmind as his body twisted to unleash his full force. Darkmind braced himself for the strike and prepared to raise Dark Dragon in defence, knowing that even if he was successful, it would just be a matter of time.

At first he did not understand what had happened as a shaft of light broke through the hunter's chest. His eyes quickly discerned a great silver spear that had seemed to suddenly sprout from the creature's insides, sending waves of maggots flying into the air. He did not wait to count his blessings but instead swung with all of his force, decapitating the helmeted head from the shoulders. He then thrust downward through the being's chest and felt new energy pour into him and refresh him with its essence.

The silver spear seemed to disappear as the being melted into nothingness, and Darkmind took a step back to look around him for his saviour. He heard the flapping of great wings and look up into the air.

At first he only saw the one. She was beautiful to behold. She was a winged armoured woman upon a mighty winged steed, and she shone in silvery light. She flew in circles over his head. As he watched her, he saw that she was joined by others.

He looked at the silvery sword that lay on the ground several feet from him. He wondered if they had come at last to retrieve this great sword. He would not stop them because in truth it had never belonged to him.

They spun around him in the air with movements that seemed to be made from the dreams of composers. They were graceful and elegant, and yet they radiated a feminine power that was brilliant to behold. It was obvious that they were studying him, but he did not feel threatened by them in any way.

One of them started to make circles around him very close to the ground, and as she made several passes over the chariot steeds, she destroyed them. Like their master they melted with the chariot into the ground.

"You are brave, mortal," she said in a musical voice.

He could not find the words to respond.

"Perhaps we will fight alongside one another again."

With that she pulled her steed up into the air, and the valkyrie slowly disappeared.

He walked over to the sword. He was confused but guessed that he had proven himself worthy to wield the weapon, or else they would have taken it back or it would have disappeared altogether. He picked up the mighty blade and looked at it long and hard before he put it back into its sheath.

"Perhaps I can do a favour for you someday," he said into the silence of the desert night.

His words were not unheard.

Darkmind met up with Lucius on the hill and surveyed the scene of the battle. He was filled with regret. Bali was gone, as were Ayumu and Katsuo. Lucius had gotten the number of dead and now reported to him that there were 247 Romans left, including him. Four of the generals had been killed.

Grief hit Darkmind for all of those that had fallen on his behalf. He knew that they had probably saved forty of the Canadian soldiers and had helped to take the fight to an enemy that did not deserve to live, but it was hard not to feel the weight of these deaths on his shoulders. A living general could perhaps reason that the fallen would now exist in a better place, but he did not have that luxury. For those that had fallen this day, including the one Canadian who had been destroyed by the hunter, they simply no longer existed.

The score of Romans that had been carried to the hilltop unmoving were counted as the living. Like Alec had been before, they could be given enough energy to be saved in time.

"I wish I had known what Ayumu had planned for me to do now, as far as making amends with Hachimantaro," he said to Lucius. He had only known this part of the plan that involved trying to make the battle right, but he also knew that Ayumu had planned to state a case for him before the grand samurai.

"You can ask him in time," Lucius replied.

Darkmind looked over at him, and his eyes went a little wide with incomprehension.

"He is lying over there like the others." Lucius gestured towards the rows of seemingly dead Romans.

Lucius looked over and saw the hope in Darkmind's eyes.

"I am sorry, my friend." He put his hand on the burnt soldier's shoulder. "The beautiful Bali is not there. And the other one, Katsuo, has not been found either. They are both gone."

Darkmind looked back over the scene of the battle and nodded his head grimly in acceptance.

"It doesn't make a lot of sense to me," the tattooed Sergeant said to the officer and warrant that stood beside him as he lifted the ground sheet that had covered the corpses. The full moon offered them enough light to see the two fallen men. "I didn't hear an explosion at all, but he must have been lying right on top of an IED to get that messed up." They looked at the soldier that was mangled and appeared to have been burnt to a crisp. "I could have sworn that he had been shot, and I certainly didn't see any fire."

The officer nodded his head. "There are a lot of things about tonight that don't seem to make a lot of sense," he said, feeling the weight of having lost two men from his platoon for the first time in his career. He wanted to say more, but the words wouldn't come to him.

The three men were silent as they heard the sound of the approaching medical helicopter over the circling war birds that had saved them. The Sergeant let the groundsheet fall back over the two men that had seemed so full of life such a short time ago.

20

His plan had failed. It had been perfectly orchestrated, but it had been undone by chance and by the actions of a puny man who was not even strong enough to remember his own name.

He was as powerful as any on the other side, but he had to tread carefully, or else his alliances could unravel and his enemies could unite to bring him down. It was only a minor concern that he had lost so many assets, as he had many more, but it was the potential of what this could cost him in the long run that bothered him greatly.

He was as old as they came, and so it was easy for him to devise a plan that could protect him from further fallout. He could not use one of his own to do the job, and neither could he ask the assistance of anyone else that could be compromised or tied back to him.

He had very old alliances, though, and an idea came to him that he thought could mutually benefit both him and an old friend. No, friend was not the right term; they simply had similar objectives and no concern for how those objectives were achieved. They would never be friends, but they had enough in common, and perhaps now a similar goal, to be allies.

It did not take him long to find the worm, for it had lain dormant in the same cave for centuries.

He smiled to himself, for the worm was a parasite like no other. It could lay dormant in its host for as long as it chose and then suddenly take control and commit the most heinous of acts. It could distort the host's perception of reality and even change his or her memory. It was the perfect plan.

It took little convincing, for they were both beings that thrived on chaos. The worm grew excited when the old god explained to him the plan for total destruction of the mortal realm and the domination of the spirit one. It thrived on trickery and deceit and was not one to be impressed with uncomplicated matters and direct approach. The rewards it was offered were secondary to the game that it could now be a part of and play.

So the worm was released once more into the world and sought out the one who was only known as Darkmind so that his oldest "friend" could cover his tracks and protect his future.

It was not hard to find the spirits, as there were two, but he saw that he already existed in the stronger one's mind, and so he swam towards the weaker one.

They had healed enough so that they could move as a group. It had taken several days, and Darkmind began to experience all of the pains of death once more in his weakened state. The hunter had given him a lot of power, but he had used most of it to heal the Romans and Ayumu.

The stronger Romans had given him power as well to perform the task over and over again until the injured were all able to move. None of the energy could be spared at this point for anything cosmetic, and so they looked even rougher than they had before.

They had watched as the living soldiers, Canadians and Americans, had cleaned up the mess, performed investigations, searched for unexploded IEDs and eventually left the site altogether. When the time finally came for them to move, the land appeared as peaceful as it must have once looked to the nearby villagers in the days before.

Darkmind decided that to prevent separation, they would travel overland to the church in which he had found Balzola. He did not know how long this would take, but he remembered that overland travel seemed to be a lot faster than it would have taken in a physical form. He suspected there was a problem crossing great bodies of water, but he did not understand that yet. This innate knowledge left North America out of the question as far as a destination that they could all retreat to.

The church was familiar to him and had not seemed to have any major power figure present as an occupant. It would be easy enough for any beings to track them from here to that church, but they should be relatively safe inside the building once they had arrived. From the church they could travel more safely and invisibly from location to location. He also wanted to see if Bali's guards could potentially be recruited from the brothel nearby.

He did not know if they would want this or not, but he figured that he owed it to her to at least ask them.

Then they could rebuild their strength and decide what they wanted to do. His intentions were to find out who had been responsible for the attack and to seek revenge. He also planned on releasing the Romans from their pledge, or at least make them free to come and go as they pleased. He wanted to make amends with Hachimantaro as well.

For now he would leave Alec in the safety of the mosque. Lupa had told Balzola of the results of the battle and that he would come to her when it was safe for him to do so. Until then he asked that her higher spirit help Angel to live a relatively normal life while Balzola the jester and Lupa stayed close by. Lupa informed him that Balzola was deeply saddened by the loss of Bali and was heartbroken she couldn't come to him. As before, she resisted at first but eventually complied with his wishes.

They began the long trek, with him at the head and the Romans marching in pairs once more. Some of the soldiers acted as scouts, but the path before them was relatively uneventful. Oftentimes they would see armies massing as they approached, but they gave them wide berths to let them know that they were just passing through and not coming to attack any of the existing armies that occupied certain lands or ruins. Occasionally a curious messenger would come to ask them what they were doing, and they would tell the truth about most things, including the battle.

They would always lie about their strength, though, and say that this was just a token force, trying to discern if any of the unknown enemy would reveal themselves by attacking such a diminished-looking fighting group. This gave the impression that they had more resources at call if they needed, to thwart any ambitious harvesters of energy from considering attacking the force.

A few times they were even invited by various bands to rest and visit, but they explained that time was of the essence. As they moved this way, the path that would have taken men months to traverse took them only a few days.

The Romans were happy too as they entered their old homeland of Italy, but they were shocked by the changes, so foreign as to make it almost unrecognizable. Lucius in particular seemed saddened as he recognized the land that had once been his father's. A highway now stretched upon it, and it was apparent that no one had tilled that soil for a very long time. He looked hopefully at the lost, wandering souls that they passed, but he did not recognize any of them.

When they finally came to the church, it was apparent that the resident spirits were not happy. As powerful as some of them were, they could not dare to oppose the spirit army that boldly entered the building. In a show of respect, though, Darkmind led the battered remnants of the legion into the hidden catacombs, where they would make their home. The darkness was depressing, but it was necessary for the time being so that none of their energy could be drained, as had happened a few times along the way by those of the living that could see them.

In a few days he felt he would be strong enough to finally go and meet Hachimantaro and ask that he be at least partially forgiven for his actions. He would go with Ayumu as his witness and would try to give the sword, Black Dragon, back as a token of good will. He would also bring Lucius so that the three of them, with what they had seen, could possibly give Hachimantaro clues as to who may have been behind the attack.

Darkmind walked through the graveyard alone. The time to meet Hachimantaro had come, but still he lingered. He had been given energy once more from a nation that mourned his loss. Much of his power he used to heal the Romans even further, but he kept enough so that he could defend himself or flee.

He tried to keep Lucius as strong as himself, so that he could do the same if there was a sudden need for self-preservation. The future was uncertain, and it would be wise to keep his friends happy.

Ayumu had recovered well. He acted as a living wounded man would have behaved. He limped, he seemed to have trouble breathing and conversation was sometimes strained. Nevertheless, he insisted on teaching them how to harvest energy from living plants and from the celestial bodies themselves. He warned against taking energy from water and fire, the sun, because these sources were so powerful and pure that they erased memories and could make a lucid spirit become zombie-minded quite quickly.

Darkmind was contemplative in the garden that was the graveyard, and his thoughts were heavy. He was becoming more and more aware of the complexities of this new realm and of the dangers. Everything fed; all beings served higher beings; everything came to an end.

He heard the crickets sing, thought of Bali once more and was heavy with loss. The philosophical succubus had existed for thousands of years, and now she was gone and it was his fault. He thought to himself that she had been his one chance at true happiness. Balzola could not stay lucid without harming Angel, and when Angel passed away her high spirit would move on to be reborn eventually, if she had lived a good life and died at the proper time. The most he could hope for was to possess the spirit of Angel in a state devoid of lucidity as another companion.

It was clear that sooner or later, some being would come to him and demand that he serve them. The alternative was to try to survive much like Hachimantaro had in a cat and mouse game of hiding and striking at various targets; even then he suspected that Hachimantaro must serve someone higher. It was clear that the samurai had been trying to recruit him, but he had also mistreated Bali. He did not hate the spirit, but neither would he serve him.

This new world was complex to him, and he thought of the many spirits that existed. These spirits brought religion, war, lust, love, visions, power, sickness and music to man. They then took energy through emotions, dreams, sickness and death. The possibilities were endless. On top of all of this, they fought and destroyed one another, created powerful alliances and treaties and were born themselves as new spirits all of the time.

There were apparently beings who had used man to harness the powers of the earth, sun and water, and even to create new sources like nuclear power. Many of the spirits were so hungry that they wanted to consume all of the energy of the Earth in her entirety. They had man destroying the land and sea animals, making the skies and lakes barren, and they would continue until there was only one another left to feed upon. Eventually, given a long enough time line, there would be only one greedy spirit, or a coalition of a handful of spirits, that would probably take their mass amounts of stolen energy and create a new world, starting the whole cycle over again once more. The whole thing was both disheartening and baffling.

Ayumu had said that the great light was one of the old spirits, the original ones, and it had a more naturopathic approach to using human spirits. The high spirits were put on the mortal realm with a type of baby spirit to mentor and bring up. In theory, the high spirit would come back to the light in the end. The successful ones would bring with them a low spirit as well. The overall result was that the great spirit became more and more powerful as long as this process was fruitful. As more and more low spirits were lost, and some high ones too, there would eventually come a time when this arrangement was unprofitable to even the great light. At that point, the whole thing would probably be shut down, and humans would either cease to be born or would begin life without a spirit.

He remembered how differently he had imagined life was when he had been alive. Life had been so simple and mundane; the Earth was not being destroyed, and man was not living out his final days.

Darkmind respected Hachimantaro and his token campaign of righting the wrongs in this new world when and where he could. He did not think in the end the samurai would make a difference, though. The complexities were enormous. What could one group of fighters do in a realm where combat was not even the tool used most of the time to create change and collect the bounties of power in all its myriad forms?

He looked over at the few spirits that were milling around the graveyard drunkenly and realised how futile the afterlife was. He had always been told that when he died, he would go to a better place. As he felt his body fight rot as it sat on ice in a freezer somewhere in Canada, he knew that the realm of pain and suffering was just starting to open to him.

He also knew that he had stayed in this realm to right many wrongs. He knew that the more he remembered, the more it would all make sense. He tried to keep his dark thoughts from climbing into his conscious mind. There would be time for that later. He could not reveal his hand quite yet, even to himself.

Ayumu led the way. Darkmind and Lucius walked side by side through the garden towards the meeting that had been arranged with Hachimantaro. As a gesture of good faith, they had come to the same Japanese garden once more.

They had passed the same beautiful cherry blossom trees and man-made streams that held colourful koi fish. He was struck again by the beauty, which his memory had failed to recreate even partially for him. The sense of peace was profound, and he had closed his eyes for a moment and took a deep breath in of the fragrant night as he listened to the songbirds and the wind chimes that sang for him.

Ayumu sat beside Lucius and Darkmind as if he were a guest as well. The warm wind seemed to alleviate the cold only slightly for him, but Darkmind had learned to ignore the pain somewhat and consciously chose not to focus on it.

Hachimantaro sat silently across from them. His face did not betray any emotion. The same soldiers were behind him as had been before, except that there were vacancies where Ayumu and Katsuo had sat. A beautiful woman brought them tea once more, and even Lucius grinningly accepted a cup.

"Ayumu has told me of all that has passed since we last met," Hachimantaro began. "I do not understand your vision that forced you to leave prematurely the first time you were here, but I believe you were tricked somehow. Acting in my behalf, Ayumu and Katsuo first tried to seek you out to help you and then decided to try to kill you when they observed your actions. For that I take full responsibility."

"I don't harbour any resentment towards them," Darkmind answered. "I might've done the same thing in their shoes."

"Do you still call yourself Darkmind?"

"It's a suitable name for one such as me."

"You have not yet spent energy on remembering your past or altering how you look to reflect your life instead of your death. That is interesting to me. Perhaps you will do so later?"

"Perhaps. I have remembered much of my life, but it seems like a strange dream for the most part."

"Aren't they all?"

Darkmind nodded.

"Bali is gone?" the samurai finally asked.

"She is."

Hachimantaro looked like he was truly sad and stared into space.

"She did not understand how I felt. I think she was incapable of love."

"You loved her?" Darkmind asked with a hint of venom in his voice. He was also confused that the samurai would turn the table on Bali and say that she was incapable of love, which he did not feel was true.

"This surprises you. In this land weakness is death. I could not allow myself to ever be in such a weakened state of vulnerability again. I did not want her to die, but neither did I want her close enough to me to be in such a state of pain again. I knew that she could not understand my position and that she never would. I was too weak to let her that close to me again."

"Were you really so hurt as to cast her aside like a piece of garbage?" Darkmind said the words without meaning to say them. He did not want to throw salt into the wounds of his host, but he couldn't ignore the sadness that he had felt that Bali had suffered.

"I was Darkmind, I was. She was special, you know."

"Yes, she was."

"You do not understand. I mean no offense, but you are too young. She was special. She was different than almost any other spirit that I have come across, deceased or created."

Darkmind nodded his head as Lucius slurped his tea.

"Have you ever heard of an explorer by the name of Jacques Cousteau?"

"I don't think so."

"He was a diver and a conservationalist; he was also her favourite author. I do not know where the spirit of this man is now, but he was one of the first mortals to really see the rapid destruction of the Earth by hungry spirits intent on consuming everything through their mortal minions. He was a very interesting man. Before him, her favourite writer was a man named Jack London, who wrote mostly fiction; she liked John Steinbeck as well. She would quote these men. Before them there were others, countless others. She liked Plato and the books by Solomon, and then parts of the Bible. She loved the poet now known as Rumi, and she liked to talk about which passages of Lao Tzu's were true and which were bastardizations of the truth."

"Do spirits read?" Darkmind asked, confused.

"No, not usually. This is my point. She was a created being, and yet she was fascinated with the human heart to the point that she would find ways to steal books or scrolls and read them. She saw that when one put his or her heart to paper, the heart would became transparent. She would try to take books that would go unnoticed and return them later. She was hungry for knowledge that revealed to her this human heart. One could say that she was a student of the human heart, of love, of emotion and of social connection. When her energy was passed up to me, I would sit with it for a while and feel what she had felt and learn what she had learned. I gained knowledge through her.

"She wanted to make a difference because she had come to love humans in her own way. She wanted more than anything to find a spirit that could bring her to a place where this would be possible."

"I do not understand; why didn't you take her back, then?"

"She wanted a spirit that would do this for her, teach her to love like a human, but it was not me. Do you understand? In her energy I did not fill this role. She had decided on some level after our falling out that I was not that spirit. Maybe she would lie to herself and believe she wanted to be with me, but she did not. Every time her energy was passed up to me, I searched it for some trace that she could love me the way that I loved her. Whether she believed it or not, it would have only been a matter of time before she joined with someone other than me. Even if that day did not bring my demise, it would have hurt me all over again."

"I understand," Darkmind stated genuinely. He was surprised that the samurai had revealed so much to him, though.

Hachimantaro seemed to read his mind.

"As samurai, in life, we do not talk about emotion. In death we lose the luxury of always being stoic in the company of friends. I have never explained myself to those you see around me today, but they know me and the words were not necessary. I share with you these things today so that you know that I grieve with you at her loss. You did not know her for very long, or perhaps very well, but I too remember feeling her full energy the first time, and I know the pain that you must be in. At least I got to keep her in a sense, though in a much more limited way."

"She died fighting in a battle that I believe you would've encouraged yourself."

"You are right. Now that you understand that I was going to ask you to join me, perhaps I can convince you now? There is safety in numbers, and I think we both want similar things: to fight those acts of injustice where we might be able to make a difference, however small."

"I must humbly ask that you allow me to continue on my own way," Darkmind said as he bowed. "I do not feel that it is the right thing for me to commit to, before I understand many of the mysteries that surround me."

Hachimantaro smiled. "You have not changed so much, old friend. Once we would fight each other as often as we would be side by side. I think you will be amused when those memories come back to you someday."

"I think you're right," he responded, and there was a glint in his eye that was quite subtle but that may have suggested to Hachimantaro that perhaps some of those memories already had.

"A very long time ago, you chose to enter the life cycle again, and you were the one and only person that I am aware of that has ever found a way. Since then, you have never sat across from me until now. It makes me wonder, though, if some of us are destined to be lucid spirits, and some of us have a path before us that is guided by an even more mysterious force than those we are aware of around us."

"I do not remember that much, so I can't say."

"It is okay. I do not know the answer, either."

"I came to return the sword and try to understand the riddle of who was behind the attack," Darkmind said, shifting from a topic that seemed to be growing cold.

"The sword has always belonged to you. Dark Dragon was yours once and is now yours again."

"Somehow I knew you'd say that." Darkmind was humbled. "Thank you, Hachimantaro."

The older samurai bowed deeply. "Now, tell me about the battle," he said.

Hachimantaro was impressed with Lucius' description of the fight and in how the Romans conducted themselves in combat. He was intrigued by the events that led up to Darkmind's gaining of the collector's sword and the words of those valkyrie at the end of the battle. He was bothered by Darkmind's lack of memory when it had come to the flying enemy and was puzzled over this to great lengths, asking many questions. In the end, however, Hachimantaro could only hazard a guess that the attacker must have been one of the generals of the one that they called "The Prince of Darkness."

Such a large gathering of hunters could not have been used by a lesser being. The one they called Lucifer could not easily be accused of such an attack. If cornered, he would claim his general acted alone and might even say it would be impossible to discover which particular general was even responsible. Even if they *could* prove which general was responsible, they would have to believe in good faith that Lucifer would deal with the infraction in his own way, if at all. If it was discovered that he didn't know, or worse yet that the general had been acting on his orders in the first place, then who would bring justice to those responsible? The answer was no one. There was no one group that had the power that would risk all-out war.

Hachimantaro suggested Darkmind forget about the battle. Darkmind suspected that he wouldn't.

Before they left, Hachimantaro told them that he would be nearby if they needed him, but he also gave them some ultimatums. They would not harm any more living mortals, and they would not attack any other group unless they were attacked first. He was told that if they did, they would be put to the sword by the samurais.

The words of Hachimantaro erased all of the goodwill that had been built between the men.

Ayumu then asked that they wait for him outside of the gate.

As they stood in the tall grass near the top of the steps, Darkmind waited silently and did not initially share his thoughts as he studied the night. Lucius stood beside him in comfortable silence, and neither of them spoke.

"I am not sure I like this man," Lucius said at last.

"Me either," Darkmind answered. He did, though—and that was the problem. There were simply certain things about the samurai that he couldn't accept. He did not look forward to what he knew in his heart he needed to do.

The two spirits stood in silence for a long time. They had both thought that when Ayumu came to them, it would be to bid them farewell. They were surprised when Ayumu said he was coming with them.

"I owe you my life," he said to Darkmind.

The burnt soldier nodded and was glad that the more experienced spirit would be joining them. He couldn't help but wonder, though, if it was Hachimantaro's way of keeping an eye on them. He knew that on some level that was exactly what it was. Regardless, he would welcome the company of the man he had come to see as a friend.

He could still factor him into the events that were about to take place. In his mind's eye, Darkmind began to shuffle the cards that he was about to throw on the table.

The time had come.

21

"So, how are you doing?" Indigo asked from across the table. She was wearing a T-shirt that Shadow had lent her a couple of weeks before they had even hooked up, along with tight black jeans. She looked beautiful to him, with her dark makeup that completely circled her eyes. The blue in them looked mysterious and predatory at the same time.

"I'm doing better. I feel better. Just embarrassed, that's all," he responded.

"There's nothing you should be embarrassed about. It could happen to anyone!" she said motherly.

He dropped his gaze. He really was embarrassed, and he felt guilty too. He wished that he hadn't told Jinx the whole story the day before. Now he would have to convince him and Zarah that it was an aftereffect of his original hallucination. It would be better if all of them thought that he had taken something that he shouldn't have, that he just had a bad drug-induced trip, as opposed to the truth. At least they had really shown him that they were his friends. Jinx and Zarah had visited the day before, and Thorm had come every day, like Indigo. It had only been a few days, but it had seemed much longer.

"Why does he keep staring?" Indigo whispered to Shadow as she looked at his roommate.

It unnerved him. Ever since he had felt compelled to try to comfort the Down Syndrome Asian kid by hugging him, there had been a shift. Now the young man just sat and stared at him with a look akin to hate. He sat now in an armchair in the corner and watched the couple, unblinking.

"Just ignore him. I'm sure he's got his own problems, too."

There was a long silence. It bordered and hovered on the edge of becoming uncomfortable, but it never got there. "I didn't want be the first to bring this up . . ." she started.

"I know ... me either."

"I like what we have, or whatever it was that happened between us last weekend."

"I do too."

"I don't want it to go away because of what happened. I saw a side of you that I always wished that I could see. I always thought that maybe someday something would happen between us, and it finally did."

"I'm so sorry, Indigo."

"Don't apologize! I want to be your girlfriend. I want to read your poems and fall asleep in your arms. I don't want things to go back to the way they were before—or worse yet, to let things become awkward."

"Me too." His voice cracked and he cleared his throat. "I've wanted to be with you for so long, and it just makes me angry that when it finally happened, I screwed it up like this." For a moment he almost convinced himself that what had happened *had* in fact been a drug-induced, psychotic episode instead of something much more sinister.

"Tomorrow, when you come home, if it's okay with you, I want to come over and make you dinner. Then maybe we can snuggle up and watch a movie?"

"I would like that, a lot," he said.

She rested her arms on the table and lifted from her chair as she brought her face towards him. Even through the numbing drugs that he had been prescribed, he felt his heart quicken. He met her warm and gentle lips and tasted in her the promise of a normal life.

He knew, however, even as new images and experiences from the being Darkmind continued to flow into his mind, that his life would never be normal again.

Thorm had picked him up from the hospital and walked him home. Shadow had thanked him repeatedly but had explained to him that he needed to be alone. He set his keys down on his kitchen counter and took a bottle of orange juice from the fridge. He unscrewed the cap before drinking from the bottle greedily.

He set it down on the counter beside his keys and the juice lid and leaned heavily against the surface.

"I was wondering when you'd show up," he stated calmly, not turning around to face the spirit that was standing, perhaps unseen, in his kitchen.

"I hadn't intended to, but I thought of you, wondering how you were doing, and I heard you calling."

"The kid in the hospital would have seen you if you had come there. That's why when I tried to reach you, I asked you to meet me here."

"I know."

"What's that about? The kid, I mean."

"His mind is blocked to me, but some people can see spirits. I kept an eye on you in the hospital as best as I could, from a distance, and I noticed him too. I found out he's gone. He left shortly after you did, less than an hour ago."

"Did someone come and get him?"

"No. He just walked out."

"Is that normal?" He was tempted to turn around and face Darkmind but decided against it.

"I don't think so."

"Do we have to worry about him?"

"I think if he was going to do something, he would have done it to you there."

"So what now?"

"I owe you an apology, Shadow. It was my selfishness that has brought us here. I do not know how to undo what I have done. I have no idea how to fix this."

"I don't want you to," Shadow responded, to the surprise of Darkmind.

"My world must be strange and terrifying for a living person to witness."

"In a sense it is, but I feel enlightened as well. I have seen things that most will never even conceive exists. I know it will be a tough road, but I also see it as a gift."

"You surprise me."

"Do I really? Perhaps it was no chance that you chose me. I have been interested in your world for as long as I can remember. You are just as interested in mine now that you have passed onto the other side."

"You're proposing an alliance of sorts, aren't you?"

"Yes, I am." Shadow spoke slowly but with a surprising amount of confidence.

"You scratch my back, and I scratch yours?"

"Something like that."

"What is it that you want? Money? Power?"

"I want to write your story."

"You what?" Darkmind had not been prepared for that, and Shadow could feel his discomfort immediately.

"Hear me out. I want to write your story. I understand what you understand. I will write it as a type of Gothic horror, in which it will be sold as nothing more than a tale. I think people will know on some level that it is real, though, and their energy will feed you. I think this is the type of story that I have always wanted to write. In the process, maybe we can immortalize you to some degree."

There was a long pause as Darkmind processed what the kid was telling him. The idea started to grow in him like wildfire. "Go on."

"From time to time maybe I will ask you for a favour, but what I want most is for you to help me to become like you when the time comes for me to pass on to your world."

"There are flaws in your dream, Shadow. I do like what you propose, but you know there are going to be some hard fights in the days to come. I want to kill whoever is responsible for taking Bali away from me. From where I'm standing, it doesn't look like the odds are in my favour. I might not last until next week, let alone however long it is before you are going to pass to the other side. Wouldn't it be better if you joined the great light? If your lower spirit was not lucid, you could also end up being a burden to me and yourself, when you could just as easily continue as you have been, hopping from life to life. This is no way to exist, and I'm sorry if I glamorized it in any way."

"There are many ways that I can help you," Shadow responded, seeming to avoid the argument against recruiting him at the time of his death. "I have an idea that you might want to hear about before you dismiss me completely. Besides, it looks like we are stuck with each other for now. I have a feeling that your enemies are now my enemies."

Darkmind was not so sure that he could disagree.

* * *

"Lucius would like to see you," the Roman soldier said to Darkmind.

The Romans had been practicing battle formations every day since they had returned from the Middle East. They moved back and forth in the cemetery at night and kept themselves as busy as they would have in life. It offered Darkmind long periods of peace to meditate and gather his strength. The drill also seemed to give the Romans back a lot of their power and kept the energetic Lucius occupied for long periods of time.

The Romans to a man had refused his offer to set them free. They acknowledged that they were free to come and go as they pleased but they were intent on serving him. He believed that it was just as likely that they needed a sense of purpose as it was that they felt indebted to him. Ayumu would spend the majority of his time exploring the area and taking an inventory of the spirits around them. He was also an invaluable source of information. Events, alliances and luck had all favoured Darkmind heavily, it would seem.

Or was it luck? He remembered things now. He had come here for revenge before revenge was even needed. He felt it through his whole being, and he would kill whoever and whatever stood in his path. It existed before Bali had died and even before he had died himself. His mind tried to put the pieces back together. He had given up Angel on purpose; he had been born and had died when he did on purpose. He needed to finish remembering. This had been a plan centuries in the making. Soon it would be time.

First he would build his army. Then he would go to her and set her free.

When Ayumu and Darkmind went to the building that Bali used to occupy, they found that the two soldiers were nowhere to be found and that the place was overrun with unclean, lustful spirits.

Ayumu had continued on to search for entities that might be interested in joining them. So far he had turned up nothing, but it was the reason that he was gone a lot, this particular day being no exception.

Darkmind looked up at the Roman who had come to summon him. He had been waiting to be called to the cemetery. Lucius had warned him that there was something that he had wanted to share with him, something that had obviously excited the general.

Darkmind was more than happy to show his support, and his depression lifted more and more every day with the success that Shadow was having with his own meditations and projects. He had left an image of Lupa with the young man as an extra source of protection, in case something went awry and he couldn't respond quickly enough to prevent disaster.

Darkmind rose from his seated position that he had adapted from the meditating samurai and followed the Roman through the catacombs. The pair walked through the church and outside, beneath a shining half moon and into the sounds of night creatures within a gentle breeze. He couldn't see them at first. He realized that he needed to shift his perception somewhat to the spirit of the place before there were buildings. At one time the place had been a farmer's field. The field provided a lot more room for the troops to manoeuvre, and that was where they stopped.

What Darkmind saw shocked him.

Lucius came and stood beside him with a wide eyed grin. "So what do you think?"

Darkmind was dumbfounded.

"I would have told you sooner," Lucius continued, "but it took us a while to figure it out and to make it work. We are still not entirely sure that it is anything more than a mirage, but I have a feeling that it is very much as real as it needs to be."

"I don't understand!" Darkmind said in gleeful disbelief. For the first time since he had met Lucius, he sounded like a child. Bright banners displaying a being half goat and half fish on flags fluttered in the wind.

"When we break formation and wrap up for the day, they slowly disappear. They are not lucid by any means, but they perform their duties and hold the line to a man. We found at first that we needed to mix in with them and take over officer positions; it would seem that us *lucid* ghosts act like a kind of mortar for the others."

"Unbelievable."

"What I think is that there are enough of us that we can summon the very spirit of our cohort that existed within our legion, that perhaps we *are* the cohort. It is interesting, though, because some of the men were from other cohorts as well. However, this was my cohort, our cohort, and we have even recognized some of the faces of the spirits that were destroyed in the desert battle—and others we have not seen for hundreds of years."

"So what do you think?" Lucius looked at him grinning.

"Impressive," he said, still in disbelief. "How many are there?"

"Including us? There are 800 men when the cohort is summoned. It's not the whole legion *yet*, but we're working on it. Beats 247, though, doesn't it?"

22

The samurai walked fearlessly with his small companion through the darkness. He did not even bother unsheathing his sword. He was a powerful being, and even if a larger force dared to attack him, he could summon friends quickly. Dark shapes followed him curiously but did not dare to approach very closely.

Darwin put a handful of sticks onto the fire. He could sense his protector spirits growing uneasy, and he knew that a guest was approaching. He took a long drought of his heavily sweetened tea and sat back in his chair.

It was a ritual he had often practiced after moving out here. Almost every night after his children were asleep, he would build a fire outside and sit and meditate as his grandfather had. He would listen to the cackling of the coyotes and stare up at the northern lights in the sky. He would often talk to the spirits or just let his mind capture images, which he would try to decipher from the fire itself or from the environment around him.

For the last several months, he had been coming out here less and less as he became engrossed in the mundane tasks of a man with too little time.

He was only a man, though, and being a man, he only understood the spirit world to a limited degree. When the being stepped out of the darkness in front of him and took a place at the fire, he was startled. He was wise enough to make an attempt at hiding his fear, but he knew that he had failed. He asked the spirits quickly for protection and returned the stare of the unlikely warrior.

"So you have acquired the paper from the woman once more, haven't you?" the entity asked in flawless English.

Darwin stared at the Asian man and studied him for a long moment. He wore traditional samurai armour but had no helmet upon his head. He could see at least two primary weapons, swords, which rested easily upon the warrior's body. Most interesting of all was the facial piercings of the man and the neck tattoo of a dragon. No picture of a samurai he had ever seen matched that of the image that had manifested in front of him.

"I have," he answered. He knew that if the spirit knew this already, it would make no sense to try to lie.

"You were friends once?" The dark eyes reflected the orange from the fire.

"We were very close at one time," Darwin confirmed.

The samurai nodded his head and stared at the flame for a very long time. It was long enough that Darwin wondered if he would speak again and even questioned if the image before him was perhaps really that of a living man and not a spirit at all. "He is my friend now. If it were up to me, I would kill you."

The threat was said with a calm voice, but somehow this made the situation border on the terrifying. Darwin would have run if he could have, but he was frozen in place and did not speak. Instead he waited for the guest to continue the conversation. He could not have known that Ayumu would have been reluctant to kill any living being, let alone a human.

Ayumu did consider killing the man, though. He knew that Darkmind would not, and he questioned his new master's wisdom in taking the course before him now.

"You told him that you tried to free the one who sits beside you as well. This too was a lie. Just like recovering the piece of paper makes you believe you will enslave Darkmind, you want control over as many spirits as you can."

"Darkmind?" He remembered using the name the night he had eaten peyote.

"That is his name now, and you are better off if you do not forget that."

"Okay," Darwin answered, sensing that this was no random visit and that his life was about to be altered forever.

"You have some fairly capable spirits around you, but you know this, don't you?"

"Yes."

"They protect your old friend as well as you. Without them the doorways you open would have consumed you, and the spirit you call Steve would have been feasted upon."

Darwin nodded his head. He had never considered that Steve could have been in danger by being around him.

"How did you convince her to give you the paper?" Ayumu asked.

"She has not been well since he was killed. She came home for the funeral, but she was like a drugged person. She could barely talk, and when she did her words were sluggish and weak. She loved him very much."

Ayumu nodded his head and stared deeply at the young medicine man. He waited for Darwin to continue.

"I told her that he had visited me and that if she gave me the paper, I could try to set him free to a better place."

This was when Lupa had informed them, or Darkmind at least, of what was happening. Balzola had been unsure of how to proceed, already confused herself by sharing the high spirit with the living woman. Darkmind had still not visited them since the battle, but upon hearing the news he had told Lupa to allow the exchange.

"You are lucky, red skin, that Darkmind still values you, or your remains would be but particles blowing in the wind."

Darwin was confused. His friend had been a simple enough man in life, and yet before him sat as powerful a being as he had ever met who seemed to serve his old friend, the fallen soldier.

"You will be given one chance to live with honour," Ayumu continued. "You will keep the paper, but if you ever try to manipulate Darkmind in any way, you and everyone you hold dear will be tortured in ways that no living soul has ever experienced. I will head that effort myself, and I will not be alone. I will bring with me an army of spirits and beings the likes of which you have never even imagined. You will remain unscathed, but everyone you hold dear will be possessed by unclean spirits. They will perform heinous acts, and your name will be known throughout the nation as synonymous to the very idea of accursed. Do you understand me, Darwin?" Ayumu seemed to hiss his name with venom. Darwin could feel that his protector spirits were as afraid as he was, if not more so.

"I do."

"Good. This is good because as fate would have it, or karma if you will, you now serve Darkmind."

Darwin resisted the idea in his mind with growing terror and did not respond.

"This is not up for debate. If you try to perform any type of exorcism, all of your spirits around you will be destroyed, and Steve will be taken away. Do you understand?"

Darwin nodded his head.

"Say it!" the samurai yelled. Somewhere in the distance, a dog started to cry and whine.

"I will!" Darwin answered with fear in his words.

"Good."

"What am I supposed to do?" Darwin, asked trying to steady his voice.

"Nothing much for now. I am leaving in your care the spirit of a child. If you treat him well and make sure he is protected you will be given certain things in return."

"I am sure I can do that."

"Good."

"What types of things?" Darwin asked with a curiosity braided with greed.

"Power."

Darwin smiled at first but quickly suppressed the response as he saw how the young samurai looked at him.

"You mortals are all alike," Ayumu responded. "You think that this world will continue to exist indefinitely, and that within your short lifespan you can do something that will matter. Even the most famous of us leave almost nothing by which to remember them but a few stories and compost for a less and less fertile earth. Is your mortal soul worth a few winnings at the casino, so you can buy a bigger boat and spend more time out on the lake? Is the health of your wife and kids enough for you to feel content knowing that within a hundred years the world you know will be so poisoned that cancer will be the norm instead of the exception?"

Darwin hung his head in shame being chastised by the spirit who spoke so calmly yet with a cold, hard venom that sank down to his bones.

"A war comes, red skin, that you mortals can only dream of in legend. Your holy books and prophets cry to you that the end approaches, yet you dream that all is well. You will be given power, my friend, more power than you can ever have even conceived, but it will be so that you can fight when the time comes. Your spirits tremble beside you because they know that what I speak of is true. They know that you will fight, holy man, and they will fight as well."

The samurai stood up and seemed to brush himself off in a very human act as Darwin glanced indirectly up at him. Ayumu looked up at the stars and then down at the diminishing light of the fire.

"The boy's name is Alec. Treat him as you would treat one of your own."

The spirit then seemed to fade from sight in front of him, never having made eye contact with him since standing up. In a few moments he could not be seen at all, and the coyotes in the distance seemed to grow wild.

Darwin looked at the fire in stunned silence. He felt a sense of shame that he never would have believed possible. He put his head in his hands and started to cry.

Darkmind had sent Ayumu to Darwin with the spirit of Alec. The boy was much stronger and was able to speak but still seemed very detached and emotionless. He wished that he could take the boy with him and make him feel safe, but what he was about to do held with it the possibility of annihilation.

Lucius was waiting to be summoned, and Ayumu had been kept in the dark, which meant that sending him had served a dual purpose. He would make no attempt, however, to block his actions from the scrying eyes of Hachimantaro when the moment came.

He still chose to see the mullah of the mosque as an old man. He saw now, however, that the old man was in fact a created being, the spirit of the mosque itself that had been born from generations of worshippers. He was a good spirit, and Darkmind felt bad for what he was about to do.

"I am taking Laila with me."

"She is safe here! Why would you do this?" The old man seemed distressed. The two large bearded guards, who no longer seemed as menacing yet were still formidable, stood nearby.

"Because she has asked to come with me."

"You have never even spoken!"

"You know as well as I do that words alone are not used here. She called to me before, but I was too young to hear. Only when I fought outside your gate did I hear her calling me."

"She is safe here!"

"You have said this already. I'm sorry. I am grateful for everything that you have done for me, especially when I needed your help, but this is something that I need to do," Darkmind said calmly.

"I know what she wants. You cannot, you shouldn't ... Please, she has been in my care, and I would be heartbroken if any harm came to her," the old man pleaded with tears brimming in his eyes.

"I know what she asks for bothers you, but I will give it to her, and I will protect her as best as I can."

"You are mad!"

"Perhaps I am."

"Is there anything I can do to talk you out of this? There is a truce you plan to violate, and your actions are more dire than you could ever even imagine!"

"You give me so little credit, old one. Once upon a time, not so very long ago, you came very near to calling me a liar when you said that I must have a plan, and I said that I do not remember anything. Do you remember that?"

"Of course I do," the old man answered. His hands were raised in front of him, with his palms exposed in a gesture of humility as he tried to plead with the dead soldier.

"Perhaps I remember now."

The old man looked at the spirit with a sense of dread.

"The sword?"

"A part of me now, and mine to keep."

"That hunter you killed?"

"Only one of the first."

"I will be dragged into this too, dark spirit! All the beings that roam these lands know that Laila lives here and is under my protection!"

"They will know that she left here with me. If they don't, you will tell them."

The old man put his head down as his hands gently returned to his sides. His beard started to tremble as he began to sob. He was created to be compassionate, and a more compassionate being he could not have been. The two sentinels stared at Darkmind with looks that bordered on murderous.

Laila had entered the room, her body covered from head to toe in a burka, and she gently but wordlessly placed a hand upon the old man's shoulder.

Darkmind waited a long moment before nodding to her that it was time to go. He then turned around and headed for the door to the mosque. He physically opened it so that the woman could follow him outside. She left the old man, who had fallen to his knees in tears without saying a word.

The two dark spirits walked into a night that whispered to the wind that a new era had come.

A darkness thick as hate had come then to the land. The silence fell like death from angelic mountaintops raking across the flesh of the very Earth. The moon watched in pitying horror the breaking of the seal.

There had been others of course who had acted similarly. Blind fools mostly, or those too new to understand the need for the treaties in the first place. No one, however, had acted with such a deliberant hand in over half a century.

When it had become clear to all of them, back then, that mankind was too wise to have his energies harvested without subtlety, a new era had begun. The wise ones had all agreed that the great wars at the height of power had almost destroyed mankind and the Earth. The crusades, the black plague, the witch trials, kings and queens bathing in blood and great holy warriors like the Nazi and kamikazes—these raped the physical while unholy battles plundered the spiritual. Shape-shifters were more common then, as were mighty beings that roamed the dark places in search for blood. Gods answered the prayers of the devout and were trampled beneath the hooves of hungrier and older fangs. The old ones agreed that a truce was to take place before a point was crossed from which they could not come back. Coalitions either agreed wholeheartedly or were destroyed by the collective.

All still played in small ways in the dark, though it was subtle. Blatant manifestations were rarer than virgins in a whorehouse, for the purpose of harvesting energy. Better to work through dreams or emotions ... or better yet, wait for the host to die.

The truce was being broken.

Darkmind did not care for their rules. He had seen clearly through his own eyes that someone or something was making an end play of their own. The battle that he had been killed in could have been the beginning of the end of all there was. It could have been the beginning of the eras of the Great Wars once more.

Maybe it *was* the beginning of the chaotic times again. He had in fact been born in that very battle and now shed all obligations that he might have otherwise felt to help maintain the peace. He had not been born to promote peace.

There was also an ancient, foreign voice inside of him that told him that it was his destiny to find his own way. It was a voice that did not fear the dark ones or the beings of light. It only wanted chaos in all of its forms and a thousand sparks to start a thousand fires upon the fear filled Earth.

He held the cloak tight to him as the sensation of feasting maggots crept across his face. He gritted his teeth through intense pain, choosing not to invest a shred of energy towards easing it. His footsteps crunched loudly in the silence of the desert night. Her steps were padded with the grace of a jungle cat.

On some level she told him where to go, and so he knew where to move into the weeping night. She carried herself silently and gracefully behind him. Theirs was an unholy pact between two minds that met in the place of nightmares.

He stopped suddenly. This was the place. This was the very spot that she had been raped and murdered. He felt a strong grip on his arm and looked down and saw that her fingers clutched him in anticipation. He could almost feel her piercing gaze through the burka.

He lifted both arms into the air and called into the night. He stood with his feet shoulder width apart and clutched at the sky. All around him the dust rose out of the broken ground and swirled. He harnessed all of the energy he had saved for this moment.

The wind wailed and hallowed as moisture was pulled from her. The rocks themselves screamed as matter was called forth from their pores. Jackals in the night vomited into the wind and fell in epileptic fits, foaming blood and hate. Carrion birds fell dead from their perching places, and insects were carried struggling into the wind.

The ground puffed and shook and became a soup of dancing matter. Creatures of the night sent wild calls out to inhuman masters that the end was near and that the truce was being broken. His cloak spread impossibly around him like black tongues of fire.

The first part of her corpse emerged from the shallow grave in only a few short moments. He was already spent but could not afford to pause. The crushed skull lifted itself and dragged its greasy hair across the electric soil. The teeth of the jaw seemed to smile as the head became more and more full.

She lifted herself from the shallow, unmarked grave that her body had been tossed into unceremoniously with her broken skull and her torn breasts. She felt the flesh be born again in all of its putrid and foul stages of decay. She felt everything as life entered her body more and more, as her spirit stepped into the form and became one with it.

Darkmind collapsed from the exhaustion, but he was prepared for this. Lupa sprang from the shadows and breathed into his mouth. He rose to one knee and then back to his feet as she faded out completely. He had enough energy to finish the task, no more or no less.

Laila understood: this was as far as he could take her towards being whole once more. She would have to complete the next stage herself. She was a ghoulish figure that looked like a rag-wearing corpse of a voluptuous young woman who was dead and left to suffer the elements for a month or more ... if that corpse had not been feasted upon by carrion creatures and starving insects.

Laila looked down upon her hands and seemed to study them through golden eyes floating in a sea of red and yellow slime. She stared at them for a long moment before looking up with a smile at the patiently waiting dead soldier.

In life she had been gentle and humble and had worn her burka with honour and with pride. Even in death her God had forsaken her, though. She stood now with the most hideous of unhidden faces, with breasts that were rotted and exposed and seemed to scream in rage toward a dumb and deaf god that she had a new master now.

He may have had no name, but he was now her god nonetheless.

He veiled their movements from unwanted eyes as she moved slowly and with a sense of purpose, stumbling through the night. She was drawn in the direction of the largest pieces of her missing energy. She moved forward and he walked protectively behind her, unseen in the physical world.

Jerkily she picked her way over the rocks and eventually over the lip of one of the old and short mountains that sprang from the flat desert like a spine between the infertile farmland and the great southern desert that began across the river, if one could call it such, less than 10 miles away.

Almost no one lived out here except for the nomadic Bedouin. It was on this side of the mountain that there were a few scattered caves in which the insurgent fighters could make a camp.

This cave was deep enough that they could afford a small fire of camel dung that they had carried with them. Normally they would have just wrapped themselves in the dark, but morale was low. The path they walked along was hard and fraught with hunger and great risk. Death had seemed to come for them every night that they were out in recent days.

There were some of those present that had an uncanny ability to survive and radiated great power—and great darkness and hate. These men had fought against the Canadians and Americans and survived, even managing to kill some of them. They had looted and raped and killed, and they had grown strong and respected over the years.

Rat-faced spirits hung along the back of the cave and laughed amongst themselves at the harvest that perpetually fed them. It did not matter to them if one of the "holy" warriors fell or if it was a supporter of the new government of Afghanistan. The situation was perfect: a violent world that never seemed to end meant that they would continue to grow powerful until they were godlike in their own way.

There was little conversation between the dozen or so men that shared the cave together. The fighters who had stayed here this night would gain some much-needed rest and a break from the never-ending night operations. They shared naan bread amongst themselves and sparingly drank small amounts of water and bitter chai tea.

They all sensed her at once and all stopped what they were doing and stared. Not one of them could comprehend what it was that stood in front of them. An unveiled naked woman that looked sexual and grotesque at the same time pawed at their common sense.

There was fear, though. With fear came gunfire.

Darkmind waded into the room and started to hack away at any of the spirits that did not flee immediately. He understood now how timid these protector spirits could be and why so many mortals did not seem to have them when he was near. He wielded a great sword and radiated power and death. In that he delivered.

Laila shrieked an unholy wail as bullets from old Russian rifles and newer AK-47s pounded into her body and bounced around the cave. She reached a closer man and tore his head out from him, with a chunk of spine attached. Blood washed over her, and the neck geysered life onto the floor as the torso slumped over and the hands dropped the weapon.

She chose her targets carefully, the most innocent first except for the child, letting the most guilty of them suffer the greatest and the longest. Their fear fed her and made her stronger by the second. She let some of the energy make her whole once more. By the time she killed the last of them, she wanted them to recognize her.

She punched into the ribcage of one man and crushed his beating heart into her smiling face and across her breasts. She then threw it unceremoniously upon the ground. One man tried to run for the cave entrance, but she caught him with a great leap in midair and dragged him to the earth with her teeth unhinged around his neck. His eyes were wide with terror, and he begged her to let him go. She ripped out his throat with one bite.

The bullets stopped flying; there were no more to shoot. The last few men pulled out rusty knives or held their rifles as awkward clubs as they cowered in the darkness. They had torn off her burka once as they had laughed. They knew her face as they knew her body.

"You called me a whore once, but I was a virgin. You dragged me out here where no one would hear my screams and ravaged my body. Do you want to fuck me now?" she asked them in Pashto.

"No, sister! We were wrong for what we did! Please forgive us in the name of merciful and compassionate Allah!" one man pleaded desperately.

"Allah is a myth to you, or you would not have done this thing. He has forsaken us both, brother. Now you will see that there is no paradise for the dead, only one more shadow life that will also end for you soon." She stated this with a calm yet commanding voice that had never spoken to men before this very moment.

Then she plucked from them their limbs as a bully child pulls legs from a helpless insect. They writhed with only their torsos and heads as they quickly bled out from the sockets.

Darkmind waited until they were barely coherent on the other side before he likewise stabbed them repeatedly and in a careful, methodical matter. He did it slowly enough that they understood what was happening. They were being erased completely and forever, and it was amusing for the two beings to watch.

He let his protective guard slip intentionally so that his actions could be seen, but not hers, if anyone was watching him as he suspected they were. They would see what he was doing now.

Laila went over to the 11-year-old boy huddled and crying in the corner.

"If you leave now to tell this tale, you will live. If you do not leave now, you will die here as well."

The boy looked up in tear-filled horror but summoned the courage to rise to his feet and run. He was gone so quickly it was as if he had never been there.

Darkmind and Laila looked at each other with newfound respect. He had fed enough here to be at a healthy level of strength. She was as powerful a physical being as there was wandering anywhere upon the Earth. She no longer looked like a rotting corpse.

He had helped her be born, and so was akin to a father to her. Through their connection, he shared with her in a moment how to remain hidden from spirits, how to call him, how to give him energy if she chose and how to heal her wounds. He suggested that she travel only at night and in remote areas. It was already understood that she would be hunting evil men. It was why she had wanted to be born. When she was ready, someday perhaps she could shed the body and join him.

She was hungry, though. He smiled as he understood the chaos that she would bring into the desert. She would not shed this body soon.

He looked upon her naked, rag-clad body with love and adoration. Blood caked her cheeks and coagulated in her cleavage. Her arms were awash in it. Her golden eyes sparkled with both human and inhuman beauty. Her full lips appeared moist and succulent, and her graceful neck sparkled with gore. Her shapely legs had rivulets of blood racing down them, and perfect painted footprints of red marked where her graceful feet had passed. Her fang-toothed smile melted his heart as she stared deeply at him. He could feel her gratitude.

He would fear for her.

* * *

The pounding of their hooves echoed through the dusty-walled canyon. The armoured men with the fearsome devil masks coiled into the passage in a single file before quickly fanning out and drawing their weapons. The twenty samurai radiated power, death and destruction, and it would have been clear to any passerby that the hour of reckoning was at hand.

Hachimantaro almost felt a sense of pity as he looked down at where Darkmind and his handful of scraggly Romans had stopped to rest. They were a pitiful lot with their dented armour and ragged, threadbare cloaks. They had no sense of pride in the way they looked, and old wounds covered them and marred their appearance. Darkmind himself looked like a crisped piece of fat that had been forgotten upon a hard and bitter flame. His exposed teeth through an open cheek reminded the onlookers though that he had at one time been all too human.

The twenty samurai had surprised this meagre band of a dozen or so and had left them nowhere to run. The samurai's steeds would overcome Darkmind and his soldiers, even if they tried to flee into the spirit world. Nor did Darkmind's band have the numbers to oppose the samurai outright. Even if Darkmind had been hiding a reserve of strength, he could not hold his own against the superior force.

Hachimantaro had come to the bitter realization that Darkmind had to go. His compassion wanted him to spare the former samurai and simply teach him a lesson by destroying the Romans, but he had decided they all must perish. Darkmind was a menace, and his continued disrespect of the living, even after being warned, meant that he needed to be eliminated. He himself had aided the new spirit after his passing, and so Hachimantaro felt that it was his duty to exterminate the group and preserve the treaties.

The Romans rose to their feet and moved in hasty bounds to prepare for the cavalry charge. Lightning hooves raced towards them as mighty swords whispered in their master's hands in anticipation of glory. The air fell still as it paused for the explosion that was rising in the heart of justice.

There was a moment where Hachimantaro should have anticipated that something was amiss. His focus flickered, and he noticed that Darkmind was calm. The fallen soldier had unsheathed his weapons but was holding firm instead of rushing towards the horseman or trying to manoeuvre himself and his men out of the way.

Pity and pride had blinded the samurai.

A wall of Romans materialized out of nowhere, and a hail of pila, or legionnaire javelins, rained upon the horseman at almost point-blank range. The new Romans' centurion armour gleamed in the starlight, and their uniform was pressed and impeccable. No wound could be seen upon their flesh.

Horses screamed in agony as they plunged and slid upon the earth, and experienced swordsmen scrambled to find their feet even as they met a wall of iron and men and thrusting spear points.

Hachimantaro had brought his personal bodyguard into this melee, though, and each of the armoured warriors rose from wounds that would have killed them if they had been mortal. They then slashed wildly in an attempt to gain the upper hand or to fight their way free. They were more trained for one-on-one combat, even in death, and could have never even conceived such a style of fighting in the afterlife. The effort was futile.

Hachimantaro realised that he had been fooled and had completely miscalculated Darkmind. He had allowed himself to believe that the seemingly simple man had learned nothing on this new plane of existence and that he had remained simple and survived by luck alone. He had also assumed Darkmind had still not recovered most of his memories. All of these assumptions were a terrible mistake, for the samurai had learned centuries ago never to underestimate anyone. Yet here he had rushed headlong into a trap that had been carefully laid for them.

Horses and men screamed, and Hachimantaro saw the brilliance of the collective force against which they stood. Every wound that the Romans took was collective. It was how they fought. This meant that unless the whole force fell together, it was virtually invincible. It was a machine comprised of hundreds of soldiers that became one in battle.

One could say that in those final moments before he fell, Hachimantaro was in a complete state of disbelief. His army had survived countless battles because they were disciplined and fought in a world of chaos and disorder. Their discipline, however, was still the discipline of individuals, not of a collective force that became, when unified, as mighty as a god.

Hachimantaro twisted and tried to rise as the murderous, pilum spears plunged overhead and into him, and the short swords reached towards him from beneath mighty shields. He knew no more.

Epilogue

They stared at each other for a timeless moment and then stepped into one another's arms. There was a long embrace before Balzola pushed him away and punched him repeatedly in the chest with her fists as she made a snarling face and avoided his eyes.

"I'm sorry," he whispered.

She pulled him close once more and buried her head in his chest. Her makeup, though perpetually regenerating, smeared onto the front of his cloak.

"This is difficult," he began.

He believed Angel was asleep in an apartment several blocks away, and so he had gotten the manifestation of Lupa that had stayed with Balzola to summon her here, to an old graveyard near the water. Lupa had then left to return to Angel.

Balzola and Darkmind were alone at last.

He held her for a long time, dreading what came next. He was not sure he could do it, or how he would do it, but he knew that he had to. At last he pushed her to arm's length as tears rose in his eyes.

"We can never meet like this again." He spoke, and time seemed to hang and twist as he did so. He tried not to surrender to the tears because he still saw himself as a man, but a selfish part of him persisted, and his cheeks filled with moisture.

He gazed down at her, and she was staring at him wide-eyed with a look that seemed to be pleading. She hit him twice more in the chest.

"My whole life I loved you as Angel, but I was weak and afraid, and I was such a coward that I let things go too far and we lost each other. Part of me believed that somewhere, somehow, we would be together again, that old wounds would heal and egos would not be bruised."

Balzola carried the scythe on her back and seemed to have found a way to shorten the shaft because it did not look awkward on her. She slid her hands down his chest as she began to silently cry and fall to her knees. He looked at the sky and felt such pain that it was hard for him to pull himself together. He collected himself. He crouched and went to his knees as well. He then held her so tightly and for so long that he wished that he would never have to let her go.

"On some level I believed that even if all else failed, there would be a reunion between us in heaven, and we could love each other forever then, or we would be reincarnated and could be together in another life. I always knew that it was you and me, and I'm sorry if I ever led you to believe that I didn't."

He spoke into her ear and ran his charred hand over her head, removing her cap and freeing her hair. His burnt fingers moved their way into those locks, and he felt how similar that hair felt to Angel's hair many lifetimes later. He kissed her temple before continuing even as he felt her tears moistening his neck.

"If you are ever a lucid spirit, that means that somehow you failed in life or died untimely. I see that this is not your path. If you were to stay lucid, in your current form as the jester ghost, Angel would be weak and at best a mental health patient. I'm a lucid spirit, so by my understanding I will likely never live again. From every angle that I look upon, we cannot, nor will we ever be, together in any way, shape or form." He stopped as he sniffled hard. He knew that there was another option, and that was that Balzola stay with him as a non-lucid, drunk-like spirit, but the temptation would be too great for her to pull the high spirit away from Angel often, and if harm ever came to her ... Even if she didn't, it would be like having a child, and one who needed constant supervision at that.

He had avoided this moment for too long because he did not want to walk away. The best solution was that she stayed as a guide to Angel, or a protector who could borrow from the high spirit if need be. He could not see any other course of action, and from the way that Balzola sobbed in his arms, he knew that she realized this as well.

All of his life he had believed, on some level, in love. Now he realized that this was the hell that Christians spoke about. Here he burned, here he suffered, here he hurt. He could not be with her and never would be again. Love would not find a way. Love had failed.

Life had in no way been about any 10 commandments or meditative enlightenment or praying to an omnipotent god. Life was about love and love was everything. Nothing else mattered in the end, not the laws of man or the teachings of the holy books. With love came the tunnel of light at death and a oneness with the Earth in life. With love came joy and happiness and compassion and a complete disregard for selfishness or the propping up of an ego in need for recognition.

But *they* would not allow that. The darkness had made love impossible to find and feasted on the efforts of humankind in mirthful fury. The darkness fed. The darkness had declared war upon him and all of humankind.

He saw this now.

He looked upon her and saw such a miracle that it took his breath away. He saw that they were twin spirits and that they had a sort of energetic weave that was almost completely identical, dancing and twisting around one another. He held the image for a long moment in the present before finally crying aloud. He cried like a child and held her in a crushing grip, and she fell like a baby in his arms.

Finally he pushed her away and started to rise to his knees, as they had fallen to the ground completely. They rose together and met there on their knees in a fierce kiss that they hoped would last them forever if need be.

As one they rose to their feet and collected themselves as best as they could. He took her fragile chin in his hand and looked deep into her eyes, the mirrors of his soul.

"I love you, Angel," he said to the high spirit that was both her and the jester.

She mouthed the words back silently, and they kissed for a long moment once more.

She hung her head as she walked away and spilled tears down her cheeks silently.

On his face, as he walked away from her, was heart-wrenching pain ... but there was also a fierce determination.

The war had already begun. They would pay for this. Of that he was certain.

Shadow had tried to call Darkmind repeatedly. He did not know where she, *the other spirit*, was either. He did not even know the whereabouts of the image of Lupa, who had been a companion of sorts in the last few days.

He was utterly alone.

The images in his mind were faster now, and he threw a black duffle bag open upon the bed. The bag bounced atop of a newspaper that had the headline "Real Life Bonnie and Clyde: Bank Robbers Execute Six" on the front page.

To Shadow this headline had been the proof that he had needed. What he had seen was real.

He had not heard from, or been able to get a hold of, Indigo for the last couple of days, either. He was worried about her; Indigo was a predictable woman in many ways, and this absence was unlike her. She would usually message him every night if they hadn't talked throughout the day. She seemed to have fallen off the face of the Earth.

It had been at least two days since he had heard from her, but maybe it was three.

Comfortably Numb by Pink Floyd blared on the stereo and steadied his nerves. If anything, the transformation that Darkmind and Shadow had been through together had made him a more fearless and potentially reckless man. He saw things differently now.

He placed a small knapsack that was already packed onto the bed. In it he had his laptop and his writing stuff, as well as his journal and half a dozen books that he had been meaning to read or, in the case of certain metaphysical books, study. The idea that he would get a chance to finally read Jiang Wong's *Wolf Totem* or George Orwell's *Burmese Days* was a ridiculous notion, but it would have been more his personality to forget his toothbrush than to have not brought along some reading material. In fact, on most trips he returned with more books than he had set out with. This would be no shopping trip, though.

A few pairs of jeans and shirts were airborne across the room, landing haphazardly near the duffle bag. He grabbed a hunting knife from his sock drawer and this too was thrown into the bag along with socks and underwear. He zipped up the duffle bag and left the room for a moment.

He returned wearing an army green coat and looked over at the poster of Stephen King's *Roland* for a brief moment before grabbing the two bags and leaving the bedroom. He set them by the entrance near the sliding glass doors that led to the majestic view of the city.

He walked over to his book shelf and removed several books from the top row. He reached behind them and pulled out several boxes of ammunition. These he placed in his left coat pocket.

He reached once more behind the books and pulled a beat-up 9mm pistol out. He reached one more time and brought out a single magazine. He tapped this against the palm of his hand and by weight determined that it was full. He slid it into the handle of the pistol and attempted to cock the weapon.

The action resisted him, and he turned it on a side angle, forcing the mechanism back as he gritted his teeth. The weapon cocked. He turned it over in his hand, seeming to examine all of the missing flecks of black. When the pistol was almost completely horizontal, though, the opposite side of the weapon now facing upward, he placed the weapon on safe.

He lifted his coat and tucked the pistol into the back of his jeans.

He had left the bedroom window open a crack, and the wind trickled into the room and rustled the newspaper upon the bed. The pictures of the robbers, somewhat grainy because they were obviously from a CCTV camera, flickered and fell. There was a beautiful woman, blonde, so striking that she could have been a model or a Hollywood actress. The man, though, had very strange features.

In the picture he held two pistols at shoulder height, and the camera had captured his open mouthed smile as he was apparently firing the weapons. He wore sunglasses but looked to be of Asian descent, although he could have been a Latino male perhaps. He was somewhat chubby. His facial features almost looked like those of someone who had Down syndrome, but this would have seemed unlikely.

He picked up his pair of Ray Ban sunglasses from atop the bookshelf and put them into his empty coat pocket. He then threw one of the shoulder straps of the knapsack over his shoulder and picked up the duffle bag. He took a long look around the apartment before abruptly leaving it altogether.

Special Thanks

I would like to thank all my friends and family for their encouragement during this process. I have often viewed this project as being shaped by the community of support around me, especially during those darkest of moments. Without you, I not only would have stopped writing long ago, but also would not have had the strength to process the challenges that emerged in my life over the last two years. I was never alone.

Thank you to my dad, Steve, and stepmom, Sandy; Sunni and Curtis L.; Stacey and Curtis B.; Kim, Haley and Scott for all of your encouragement. Thank you also to Sean Enns, Ed Lyons, Chad Prescott, Craig Ball and Rui Lopes for always supporting my writing with more than just words. A special thank-you to Nadika Viswakula. Your clarity and vision are always appreciated more than words can say.

I would like to especially express my gratitude to my mom, Sharon, and stepdad, Wes. You helped me at a critical moment when it seemed that all would be lost. Without you this project would have never been possible.

My deepest appreciation for Elle Campbell, whose patience, understanding, love and support during this process helped me more than words can convey. You have been a blessing to me in so many ways.

Thank you to fellow 3-09 veteran and friend Cpl. Max Birkner. Our conversations about my first draft and your reading of my early notes while still in Afghanistan helped me to write a stronger story.

A special thanks to those who taught me clearer ways in which to view the world and gave me a stronger basis for my spirituality—most especially Debbie Deimert, Jaysun O'Scalleigh, Johesh Stacey Baron and Sensei Dan Rheaume.

I would like to thank Kathi Wittkamper for her guidance and for helping me to navigate through the publication process, which was often overwhelming. I enjoyed our many conversations and appreciated your support and encouragement throughout. Thank you also to Susan Retten for her clarity and suggestions as she evaluated my manuscript and helped me to shape a better story. My gratitude also goes to Kevin Jebens for his astute editing, his shaping of the final manuscript and for also teaching me how to be a better writer. I would also like to thank everyone else at iUniverse for all of their hard work and for helping me to create the final project as it is today.

A special thank-you to the men and women of 1PPCLI, Charlie Company, who served during Operation Athena (Roto 8) for bringing me home safely. Thank you also to the Royal Westminster Regiment for all of your support and training, most especially Warrant Scott Boyd, who has taught me more about being a warrior than anyone else I have ever met.

I would also like to remember Cpl. Zach McCormak and my uncle Neil Godwin, who both were taken from the world too soon through acts of unnecessary violence during the writing of this book. Your contribution cannot be put into words but only appreciated by those who share in such loss. Until we meet again. May you rest in peace.

Quotes from *Macbeth* are from William Shakespeare. Thank you for the words that continue to speak to us even generations after you initially wove them.

A special thank-you to all of the men and women who have researched the history and mythologies of humankind—most especially Joseph Campbell and James Frazer. I also give my appreciation for all of the spiritual teachers of print—foremost amongst them John and Caitlin Mathews.

May the spirits that carry me, nourish me, hold me and guide me be aware of my heartfelt gratitude. May I learn from the darkness but never succumb to it. May I walk my path with honour and make you proud. May my voice be clear. Thank you for this story.

CPSIA information can be obtained at www.ICGtesting.com
Printed in the USA
LVOW042105021011

248774LV00001B/7/P